ZUU

THE ULTIMATE FIELD TRIP

ZUU

THE ULTIMATE FIELD TRIP

THERON LANGHORNE

COVER ART BY DAO NEYUNG

CHARACTER ART BY FABIAN SARAVIA

ZUU © 2018

ISBN 978 - 1717133250

CONTENTS

Chapter 1
THE FIGHT

I guess the universe had other plans for me before I graduated from high school. It seems that working as a barista at a local coffee house while studying the arts at a community college was not my calling. It kind of sucks, too, because I love coffee and I love art. A hot caramel macciato with a 2H pencil and a sketchbook is a portrait of peace for me. If I found a career that would enmesh the two indefinitely, I wouldn't have to work a day in my life. However, the universe has a warped sense of humor. There was no way I could have seen the curve ball it threw my way.

Before its unholy pitch knocked me upside my head, I was a sosh, the "o" pronounced like "oh". I'm not sure if I spelled that right though – I don't even think it's a real word. Anyway, the word, sosh, comes from the word "social", which I find kind of odd because sosh means the complete opposite – "not social". I had to have my sister explain it to me one day because she kept calling me that. I guess I'm not that much of a social butterfly as she proves herself to be. I never paid that much attention to my public relations until she started teasing me about it. And believe me, there's nothing worse than having your little sister attend the same school as you and remind you on a daily basis that she has more friends than you. It's especially frustrating when I constantly

7

remind her that I don't care. But it's just like telling a hyperactive puppy to go read a book.

Despite her immature nonsense, I'm still content on going to the library on my lunch break sketching theme parks, dragons, and other things that only exist in my mind. I consider it my "me" time. I use it as a mind break from all the other subjects that Langhorne High School insists on stuffing my mind with. Some subjects, such as English, Spanish, and Biology are cool. I actually find them interesting and useful. But math and history are sickening. The devil's arithmetic and the battles of old, ruthless men do not tickle my pickle. However, I do get the gist of how all of this mind-altering, base-building, yet enlightening information is just a taste of what's to come in college. And how I do in high school will affect how I do in college, at my job, in life. I'm making plans to build my own theme park and be a black Walt Disney. It's been my dream since I was six years old and I'll be damned if I let something as stupid as my own laziness get in the way. But like I said, the universe has a warped sense of humor and abruptly threw me off course.

So, I got into a fight with Derek Simmons.

If you mixed the intelligence quotient of oatmeal with the brute force of a pit bull in heat, you'd get a clear picture of what I was up against. Forget about his position as halfback for the high school football team or that he's built like an SUV or that he's four inches taller than me. The only reigning factor of his description is that he's a genuine, bonafide, grade-A, honest-to-goodness jerk.

Before I met him, I had no idea that slime came in human form. If it weren't for his fit physique and startling grey eyes, he would lack any redeeming qualities. On the other hand, his existence verifies that pretty packages sometimes contain absolutely nothing.

Of course, our reason for fighting had no meaningful cause – fights usually don't. If I can remember correctly, we brushed against each other's arms as we headed towards our own classrooms. We traded a few threatening, heated words that quickly turned into flying fists. I remember seeing bright flashes of light with every hit even though we were in a well-lit hallway. I could feel my heart banging against my rib cage and I was holding my breath. After several blows were thrown and a warm, viscous liquid wet the inside of my nose, a heavy hand grabbed my shoulder and pulled me out from underneath Derek's body. My feet were still kicking like a pair of caught fish as Derek grappled with a towering proctor. I was surprised to be detained by a female proctor. If I didn't feel her firm breasts crushing against my back, I would've thought Hulk Hogan was working at our school. As they forced us down the hallways toward the principal's office, I then noticed that the crowd around us was in hysterics – cheering, laughing, shouting, egging us on, practically mirroring a pen of wild chickens. They carried on like they were watching a long-awaited boxing match. I was disgusted! But what disgusted me even more was that *I* was the one who actually started it.

Thoughts of suspension and being expelled flooded my mind. How did I get myself in this situation? I've never been in a fight before. What happens next? Do I get a slap on the wrist and get sent back to class? Or will my worst fears come true and I'll get shipped off to some hidden and remote military school where loud-mouthed drill sergeants scream in your face ordering you to crawl face down in a bog full of mud? Knowing the reputation of our stone-faced principal, the latter seemed quite probable.

Miss Cadzow is not a nice woman.

Have you ever seen those little old ladies that seem to have a frown carved into their face with deep wrinkles yet have a gentle demeanor that resembles angel food cake in springtime? That is not Miss Cadzow. Replace the angel food cake with chili pepper and stuff it inside a sixty year old leather-clad biker that runs over possums on purpose. That is Miss Cadzow. She is awesome! She alone has the power to make today's youth respect their elders. I remember watching her march through the quad between classes one day and I could've sworn students left and right were scurrying out of her way to make a clear path. One poor girl ran smack into a locker as Miss Cadzow strode past her without even blinking. It's not so much the brusqueness that I admire about her, but the authoritative decisiveness in which she runs the school - all nails and no fluff. That was the main reason why I feared for my life.

After Helga and Mungo (that's what we called the school proctors; I have no idea if that's their real names) delivered us to Miss Cadzow's office, I felt like I was going to jail. Now I knew why her office was called The Cell. Her office had two tiny windows shaped as thin slits located in the far corners of the wall that were facing Derek and I. If it weren't for the frosted glass, the room would've been sixty percent more cheerful. The sea green colored walls were lifeless and depressing. No shelves, no paintings, no plants, nor decor were included in the space in an attempt to bring this room back from the dead. Miss Cadzow was a simple woman. All she needed was her huge metal desk, a low, two-tiered bookcase packed with books and manuals, and two adjacent chairs to face her culprits. For the life of me, I still couldn't believe that I was sitting in one of those cold chairs, facing a woman I both feared and revered. I just felt that I didn't belong there.

"So what the hell happened?" Miss Cadzow barked, stark and to the point.

Unfortunately, my biorhythms must have been stuck on stupid cause I immediately blurted out, "What happened? You want to know what happened, Miss Cadzow? This addlepated numskull has the gall to start some mess with me for no reason! He's a straight-up punk!"

By the look of subdued fury in her eyes I knew she disliked that response.

"If you ever address me in that manner again, Mr. Johnson, you will be suspended without questioning. Now just recall the details so I can dispense my sentence. You got 30 seconds."

I tried a different approach. "Sorry, Miss Cadzow. I didn't mean to be disrespectful but I just lost it when Derek ran into me. He thinks he can just..."

"I didn't run into you, dude," Derek cut me off in mid-sentence. I hate for people to do that! "You threw your shoulder into me. Don't be making up stories, man."

"I'm not! That's exactly what *you* did. You threw your shoulder into me and knocked my books out of my hand."

"Why would I waste my time with geeks like you?"

"Because you got tired of putting square blocks into round holes?"

"Dude, shut up! You're just looking for attention. You're just as lame as your sister."

The moment he closed his mouth, mine fell open. My sister?!

"She was never good enough for me."

WHAT THE...?! Has this boy lost his mind? Did I really hit him *that* hard? I wanted to strangle him, jump on him, spit on him, kick him, punch him, throw him out the window of a ten-story building into oncoming traffic and then run him over with a school bus. But I was so overcome with a cool shock that I couldn't figure out what to do next - punch him in the throat or wait for my body to spontaneously combust. In the end, I exploded.

"FOR REAL?! DUDE, ARE YOU NUTS?!!" I screamed as I power-kicked his chair. Derek leapt to his feet, fists at the ready. But Miss Cadzow was faster. She was already on her feet and violently slammed her fist on her desk.

"ENOUGH!" she shouted. I had no idea a woman her age

could exert so much force. Derek and I were both stunned into silence and stared at her wide-eyed. "I will not have you making threats to another student in my office, Mr. Johnson! What's the matter with you? Your behavior is unacceptable and absolutely unexpected. I would never have thought you'd be capable of exhibiting such a violent attitude."

Actually, neither did I. My encounter with Derek brought out the worst in me. It took a screaming elderly woman to suddenly make me realize that I was acting out of character. A wave of guilt seemed to literally push me back down in my seat and reminded me that I had just broken a promise to myself: to never, ever get into a fight. As my body filled up with shame, Miss Cadzow continued on.

"You are one of the finest students in this school, Jarvis, and I would hate to let a setback like this ruin your future. You're better than this. You know that."

I could feel Miss Cadzow glaring at me as I nervously adjusted my black-frame glasses, then folded and rubbed my arms as if I was cold. Even though the weather inside The Cell was more than chilly, I still tend to do that when I feel a little less than myself.

"I expected this sort of thing from you, Mr. Simmons."

I could practically hear Derek roll his eyes.

"Aw, man, come..."

"Are you interrupting me, Mr. Simmons?"

Derek turned away, indignant.

"You must be as thick as mud if you think I'm going to let you parade around this school like you're some invincible super hero who's above the law. I know who your father is and he would be extremely ashamed to know his son is acting like this. You've been in my office one too many times. This *cannot* be good for you."

At the mention of his father, Derek's attitude quickly changed from arrogant smugness to quiet regret.

"Yes, ma'am," he said in a barely audible voice.

"Consider this your final notice. If you want to continue throwing that pigskin then this will be the last time I see you in my office. The next one you'll see will be at another school if you act up again."

"Yes, ma'am."

Miss Cadzow then turned to me, preparing to render her judgment as I continued my pitiful, shivering act.

"You're lucky that I'm in a good mood, Mr. Johnson. It's not in my nature to let two fighters leave The Cell unscathed and dry-eyed."

I was somewhat surprised that she knew what all the students called her office.

"But know this: if either one of you even look at each other funny or become entangled in a confrontation with another student, you will be shipped out with the trash. No questions asked. Juvie is always taking in new tenants. Are we clear?"

"Crystal," Derek and I said in unison. As we were

14

dismissed from The Cell, I was too angry to even look at Derek. I've never been in trouble before and now this chump had the nerve to ruin my reputation? He's not worth it. I refuse to let him get under my skin...well, again, anyway. After all that's happened, I still couldn't understand it. What did my sister ever see in this guy?

The students moved like a herd of weary cattle unsure of their destination as they passed by the glass windows of the administrative office. I watched them with an unkind eye wishing my day at school ended as theirs had – simple and uneventful. As I sat fuming in that icebox they call a lobby, I had the unholy displeasure of sitting next to my nemesis. It was bad enough that my mom had to push pause on her day to come and pick me up so the school staff could feel like they did their part to keep the peace. But the truth of the matter is that nothing was done. For once, I thought Miss Cadzow had made a mistake. One of us had to go. And seeing that I had a grade point average of 4.3, I didn't think it should be me. I had a future planned out and I did not want anybody to get in the way of it. I know it sounds devious but the choice was obvious about who had to go. Quasi-star football players were a dime a dozen.

These less than admirable thoughts were quickly put to rest when a tall shadow of a man loomed in the doorway of the lobby. He swung open one of the double doors and threw a piercing, unrelenting gaze toward Derek. I heard that Derek's dad was a cop, so I pictured him to be the plump and rotund type that sits behind a desk filling out forms, pushing pencils, and stuffing glazed twists into his mouth. But this guy totally surprised me. He looked really young, like he was in his mid-thirties or something. He must've been about 6'4", was very muscular; had dark brown hair with a grey streak on one side, a five o'clock shadow on his chiseled jaw, a strong, angular nose, and thick eyebrows that showcased those electrifying grey eyes. If I was a single, middle-aged woman, I'd probably swoon at the sight of him, but that's just not my style. I'd rather see those muscles flexing as he gave his son a good, old-fashioned whoopin'.

"YOU!" his booming voice echoed through the lobby, almost knocking me over as he shoved his finger in Derek's direction. "IN THE CAR! NOW!"

I'm not one to revel in someone's misfortune, but I couldn't stop smirking with a glimmer of content as Derek bumbled clumsily and gathered his belongings to leave. Always the mighty warrior, I was startled to see Derek tense and nervous like a little boy who threw a baseball into his neighbor's window. This man had power over this kid. Why couldn't I be like that? Strike fear into the hearts of your enemies with just five words?

With the composure of a frightened, little kitten, Derek gathered his gym bag and schoolbooks and headed for the door. However, his father left before he got to the threshold and let the door slam in his face. I heard Derek give a deep sigh as he closed his eyes in dread. Then he pushed against the door and followed his father to his car with a reluctant gait. Curious as to how this drama would play out, I crept up to the window and watched as his father yelled at him. Even as Derek climbed into his father's Chrysler, I could see a rain of spittle spewing from Mr. Simmons' mouth as he chewed him out right there on the sidewalk in front of other students. He slapped his head once and Derek absorbed the assault with a stinging expression. The whole scene looked kind of sad. Derek didn't display any of the normal bravado he usually flaunted around the school. If I didn't know him, I'd probably even feel sorry for him. But, then again…

"Boy, get your butt out here now, right now!"

Oh, God. Mom.

Her voice collided with the window of the lobby. The administrative staff in the office froze and looked up to see who was in trouble. Regardless of the protective barrier, I could still feel the power of her voice grasp at my spine and make my hair stand up (even though I had a shaved head). I feared for my life as I gathered my things from the lobby seating area and stepped outside into my mother's fury. When I emerged from the lobby, she just looked at me with a gaze similar to a rabid warthog. It's amazing how a single look can make your stomach do a series of somersaults. What's worse is that she didn't even say a word. Nothing. She was completely silent and stared angrily at me as we strode toward her black Camry, a disturbing resemblance to a sleek coffin. We both stepped into the car, speechless, with the soft thump of the car doors sealing us in, and then, silence.

Come on, mom, I thought. Just get it over with. The suspense is killing me.

My mother turned the ignition key and started the engine. Her motions seemed slow and languid, as if she was moving though water. I was too nervous to even look at her cause I didn't want to see the madness in her eyes. I didn't want to argue. I didn't feel like defending my actions. I didn't want my mom to think that I had emotional problems. I just wanted this strained moment of anxiety to be over. I mentally prepared myself for a barrage of angry questions and accusations, but the moment never arrived. My mother simply pulled away from the curb and began to head home, her lips sealed shut.

I couldn't understand what was going on. My mother was a very vocal woman. She was extremely social and never held anything back, especially when she got upset. I uneasily took a glance at her from the corner of my eye. She had on her favorite black and brown scrubs that were covered with a pattern of chocolate candies. Her hospital ID badge shimmered in the late afternoon sun as she brought her hand up to her face and moved her fingers in a familiar fashion. Immediately, I knew why my mother was so quiet this whole time. She was trying to keep herself from crying.

I hate to see my mother cry. Even as she wiped her tears away from her almond-shaped eyes, a powerful shot of discomfort hit my stomach and a warmth rose up behind my eyes. My body became a shell of a selfish person whose insides were gradually churning into a mush of something undesirable. I couldn't bear it any longer. I knew I had broken a promise to never lose my temper and I hurt myself just as much as I hurt my mother. Before I could even begin to think about stopping it, my eyes began to blur. I put my face in my right hand and leaned against the window, tears running down my flushed cheeks.

"Sorry," I practically choked on the words. I removed my glasses and wiped my eyes clean. I said it again with more sincerity and conviction. "I'm sorry."

My mom just shook her head in disbelief.

"I know you are, Jarvis," she said sadly. "But you're not him. You're nothing like him."

I knew that was coming. We had made a silent agreement to never speak about what happened to our family so many years ago. It wasn't something we talked about or thought about. It was something we wanted to forget. Today's events triggered an unpleasant memory in both of us and reminded me that my mom was so much stronger than I was. She never lost her cool. She'd get upset at times but would never get physical when things went wrong. I never did either...until today. I never thought anyone could make me as angry as Derek did today. I know I heard him say something sinister about my sister, Jade, in the hallway just before we started our fight, but I can't even remember what it was now. Although I hardly ever got along with Jade, I'm very protective of her. If anything ever happened to her, I would blame myself completely. She's my little sister and I don't want to see her get hurt. But she still had horrible taste in boys.

Yeah, you guessed it. She was dating Derek.

I probably wouldn't hate Derek so much if he had never been involved with my sister. But as fate would have it, the two bumped into each other when Jade auditioned to become a cheerleader. I mean, literally crashed into each other. Jade was practicing some lame cheer as Derek was intercepting a pass from a teammate. It takes the common sense of a goat to realize that it's virtual suicide to yell self-righteous cheers on the same field as a group of thickheaded boys running amok with a pigskin. No one's paying attention to each other and a collision was bound to happen – and it did. Not only did Derek knock Jade off her feet, he dislocated her knee. After screams that rivaled the siren of the ambulance that picked her up, Jade was taken to the nearest hospital where she was quickly discharged a few hours (and five hundred dollars) later.

Derek appeared to be very apologetic to her after that. He gave her a card, a piece of gum one other time, and then offered to buy her a soda at lunch break. After seeing them chat happily in the hallways for a month or so, I was appalled to see Derek giving her a peck on the cheek. I'm not at all phased by interracial relationships, but like I said, Derek's a punk. He may be Mr. Congeniality when he's with Jade, but as soon as she's out of sight, here come the horns and the tail. Three of my classmates had unfriendly encounters with him and I know for a fact that he took Johnny Acklin's lunch money just to show off to his arrogant teammates how the school respects him. Sick! I gave Jade the benefit of the doubt cause she's a freshman, but trying to tell her that she's made a bad choice for a boyfriend is like telling a lion not to eat meat. She does her own thing no matter what I say.

I had no idea what to say to her when she got home from school that day. My mom and I didn't say much after our journey home. I could tell she was mad, but she was sad, too. When I get upset, I get quiet. But when my mom gets sad, she makes root beer floats. And when she makes root beer floats, I get chatty. And when I get chatty, my mom starts to smile. So when Jade got home from dance practice, the mood of the house had completely changed for the better. Jade rushed into the kitchen and dumped her gym bag on the floor. She had this wild-eyed expression as she gaped at my mother and I.

"Did I miss it?" she said excitedly.

My mother arched her eyebrows.

"Miss what?"

"The beat down! Did you whip Jarvis' butt? I wanted to see it."

I thought she was joking, but then she whipped out her cell phone to take a picture.

"Girl, are you serious?"

"Yeah, mom, he started a fight with Derek. Aren't you going to do anything?"

"She did," I said as I raised my root beer float in

salute. "Cheers!"

Jade looked utterly disappointed.

"FOR REAL? Jarvis, gets into full-blown fist fight and you reward him with a malt shop delicacy?"

"Well," my mom said decidedly, "I had to do something. Want one?"

Jade rolled her eyes and sucked her teeth as she put he phone away.

"No, I want to see Jarvis get busted for beating on my ex-boyfriend."

My heart skipped a beat. I almost choked on my float.

"Ex?" *Could it be true?* "What do you mean ex? You broke up with Derek?"

"Duh! Like almost a week ago. Man, you really are a sosh. Keep up."

I ignored the remark cause I was too happy to even hear it.

"Jade, you're cured. You're no longer an idiot!"

"Watch it, Jarvis," my mom warned. I forgot she was in the room. "That's your sister, not Derek."

"But, mom, did you hear that? Jade used her brain for once and made a wise decision. She's no longer dating pigs."

"Shut up, Jar Jar!"

"Jarvis Johnson, you got out of one fight. Don't get into another," my mom said sharply.

I shut up then...for my mom's sake, of course.

"I don't want to hear anything more about fighting or

people getting beat down. There's too much anger going around and I don't need you guys bringing it inside my house."

That statement meant so much to my mother and myself. Jade was just a baby at the time. She wouldn't remember what happened. My mother sighed and looked at us.

"I want you guys to promise me something."

Jade and I gazed at our mother, pleasantly plump and good-natured, about the height of one of those fuzzy costumed characters at Disneyland. She wore her hair short and curly, which accentuated her cute demeanor along with a set of excessively round and sleepy eyes. People would always tell me I look just like her except that I have a gleam in my eye. I used to wipe my eyelids when people said that, but I later understood that it meant I had potential, I had promise. My mother would always say that we ourselves don't even know what we're fully capable of doing until we're forced to do it.

Sometimes, that can be a bad thing.

"I want you to promise me," my mother continued on, "to be a better human."

A giant question mark must have appeared over my head and my sister's cause my mom immediately chuckled and explained herself.

"I say that because humans, well, I guess I should say people, have done horrible things to each other. I mean, you guys are in high school, you've had history, you see it on TV and social media, you know what I'm talking about. People are capable of doing extremely violent things to each other, not only to strangers but to their own families."

My stomach started to tighten. I thought she was going to start talking about it.

"It's okay to get angry, but don't let that emotion control you. People who do bad things are consumed with a force and a passion so strong that they forget who they are. They forget where they come from. They're practically blinded by the rage that's inside of them. They don't stop to think about what they're doing or the consequences that come with their actions. They become something less than human. Do you guys understand what I'm saying?"

Jade and I nodded silently.

"I don't want you to ever be less than what you are. You're both at an age where you have to make some very important decisions that will affect you for the rest of your life. Getting into fights is not a good start. Don't ruin it for yourself by being a slave to your fears and weaknesses. There is a force inside you that you cannot even begin to comprehend. Look for that power inside of you and bring it out. You have that power because you are human. So, please, promise me, promise me to be a better human."

I thought my mom was about to turn on the waterworks but she was dead serious. She had us both locked in a dead stare which seemed impossible since there were two of us, but Jade and I were entranced. Somewhat ashamed and humbled, we both mumbled, "We promise."

It's not easy listening to your mom when you're recovering from being in a bad mood. High school seniors normally know everything already. But I was in a weird state that night. After fighting Derek, seeing my mom cry, revisiting an old wound, and hearing about my sister's breakup, my emotions were a jumbled mess. If she told me I was Obama's long lost son I probably would've believed it. But once she had my undivided attention, I couldn't help but listen to every word. It made sense to me. I guess being an imperfect human does have its advantages. When we're at our worst, we have a chance to reveal our best. (Sigh) I guess today was not that day.

Chapter 2
A HERO'S WELCOME

Yesterday's events were still swirling around in my mind on my way to school when my mother's voice rattled my senses. Jade was laughing and I then realized I was still in the car. The morning light failed to keep me alert and prepare me for another day of educational input at Langhorne High. I was so deep in thought that my mother had to use the ol' pony chant to get my attention. I guess I need to explain this - the pony chant is a foolproof method to get the full attention of a Johnson family member.

My mom came home one evening while Jade and I were watching a movie. It must've been a really good movie because my mom was talking non-stop and I wasn't listening to a word she was saying. I caught a couple of words here and there and assumed she was complaining about those same two orderlies at the hospital again. She then mentioned something about a horse. Horses? That kind of caught my attention since it didn't go with what she was talking about.

"What?" I said, still not listening.

"Horseplay..." she said, but the movie blotted her out.

"Horseplay what?"

"Horseplay causes..." Still didn't get it. The movie was really that good.

"Horseplay causes what?" My head was almost in the

television. Then my mom grabbed the remote and turned off the TV. She stood in front of me looking like a wild woman and shouted, "Ponies! Horseplay causes ponies! Ponies! Ponies! Ponies!"

Jade, myself, and my mother burst out laughing. It's not very often where we experience full-on, hearty laughs like that where everyone is in on the joke and it's at no one's expense. It was a moment you look back on, smile, release a light chuckle, and hope you're lucky enough to have another one like it. So from that moment on, the pony chant became a substitute for "Hey, listen to me!" but with a dash of humor and nostalgic whimsy.

Immediately, I gave my mom the attention that I tore away from Derek and his father. I felt like I woke up from an annoying trance.

"What?"

"What do you mean 'what'? I'm telling you my life story here and you're in La La land. Are you okay?"

My gaze drifted from my mom's visage to where Mr. Simmons car was, but all I saw were his taillights exiting the drop-off zone. My mom then drove up to the steps of our everyday jail yard known as high school.

"Yeah, I'm okay."

"You sure? Cause I don't think you heard a word I said. I wanted to make sure that you remember that I have class after work tonight. Think you can handle making dinner?"

"Yeah," I said half-heartedly, not because I dislike cooking, but because I'm an awful cook. I could ruin cereal. "What do you want me to make?"

"Whatever it is, Mom," Jade interjected, "I'll be sure to have a fire extinguisher and the number for poison control nearby."

I reluctantly suppressed a rebuttal because that was probably a good idea. So, I did the mature thing and just rolled my eyes.

"There's a DiGiorno in the freezer and a salad in the fridge. I should be home by 8:30 to bake some cookies."

My mom's a superwoman. She makes so many sacrifices to make it through the day. She works crazy hours as a full-time nurse, she goes to school part-time to get her masters, and somewhere in between all that madness, she manages to provide breakfast, lunch, and dinner every single day for her family, religiously. How she does it, I'll never know.

"Mom, don't worry about it," I told her reassuringly. "I can take care of the cookies, too."

My mom looked at me as if I was wearing a tutu.

"For real? Ok. Now, you know you don't just don't throw the dough in the oven. You gotta use a cookie sheet."

"What's a cookie sheet?"

"Jarvis, I..."

"I'm kidding, Mom. If I can handle a frozen pizza, I can handle scrambling up some cookie dough. Really. There's no need to worry so much about us. We'll be okay. We're grown kids."

When I said that, I thought about our incident in the past and how strong my feelings were for my mom. She truly lived a very difficult life. She was bedridden as a child for months and later sexually abused by a relative. She later married and had Jade and I. Then there was a period in our lives that we still do not even wish to talk or think about. Her second marriage was to another man who made an awesome dad. We had such good times with him going to theme parks and playing games in the backyard. However, unrest in the Middle East claimed his life and my mother hasn't felt the need to look for anyone else since. Between my dad's insurance money and my mom's income, we've been able to live a decent life in middle-class suburbia and keep a roof over our heads and food on the table. She was determined to do it all alone. She was an amazing woman and there was no way I could let her down again.

"I know you'll be okay, Jarvis," she sighed as she pulled the car up to the curb, "I just worry about you. I'm your mother. It's in the job description."

I smiled as I gathered my backpack and lunch that she packed for me. When she stopped the car, I could feel her ghostly hazel eyes scanning me.

"Besides, I love you. The two of you are all I've got."

It was true. Not many of our extended family members stayed in touch. The rest of them were dead. I was surprised when a slight sting in my chest warmed me up. I immediately wanted to hug her. So I did.

29

"Love you, too, Mom. I mean it."

Jade leaned through the front seat and gave her a big bear hug, too.

"Wait a minute, now, give me some of that," she giggled as she wrapped her arms around her neck and shoulders. My mom beamed happily and pecked her on the cheek. As Jade opened the back door and climbed out, my mom called out, "Have a good day at school, Gigi."

"Mom, stop," Jade whined.

She hated it when my mom called her that. My mom used to call her JJ when she was little, but Jade couldn't sound the vowel correctly so she would always repeat GG instead. My mom thought it was the cutest thing. So the name stuck, all the way to high school, much to Jade's dismay. When I opened the car door, I grabbed my bag and started to leave, but my mom softly laid her hand on my shoulder and gave me a look of concern. Her expression was casual, but the worry in her eyes was real. She just gave me this look that made me not want to leave. It didn't surprise me that her countenance also gave me a twinge of guilt – a foreboding emotion that had been stalking me before my day had even begun.

"And Jarvis," she said in that rich motherly voice, "be a better human. Whatever happens, be a better human...for me. Ok?"

My shoulders slumped, my stomach sunk in back towards my spine, and a chill ran over the surface of my skin. But, in reality, I hadn't moved a muscle. It was just that the responsibility of being a stronger person struck me in my gut.

"Of course, Mom," I said to her. "Anything for you."

I got out of the car and waved to her as she left to go start her adventurous day at the hospital. I turned to face Langhorne High School as if it was a towering obstacle in the way of my peace of mind. As much as I wanted to enjoy my education here, its gleaming white buildings with blue trim and manicured cypress trees leered down at me and regarded me as an insignificant speck. I may have good grades, a high grade point average, and a few academic recognitions here and there, but the truth was, I despised this place. I've struggled to fit in for four years on this God forsaken campus and my sister was assimilated and exalted within her first year. I could almost sense my skin turning green as she skirted around the entry gates greeting her friends. It wasn't fair. Why did she always have to be so carefree? After all, she was basically the cause of the fight. Or was she? I don't know.

Something struck my shoulder from behind, a strong grip from out of nowhere. I spun around expecting to see the crooked smile of my nemesis, but instead saw the grinning face of someone I've never met before.

"Way to go, bro," the kid complimented. "That was an awesome beat down yesterday. I'm gonna put that on YouTube."

Frankly, the kid was lucky I didn't respond with a knee-jerk reaction and pop his lip, but I was bewildered by his statement. He walked away as I stood there speechless. Before I could say anything, another teen around my age walked by, putting his hand up for a high five.

"Alright, man, that was dope," he cheered. "That fool had it coming."

I just nodded and cracked a half-smile as he tormented my hand in one of those endless handshakes with ten different moves. Little did I know that these two individuals preceded a parade of students who enjoyed yesterday's brutal performance. Throughout the whole day, students slapped me on the back, high-fived me, shook my hand, saluted me, nodded at me, threw a thumb's up, smiled or pointed at me, clapped, cheered, and flashed gang signals at me. What in the world?! How could an invisible person like me become an overnight sensation just because I lost my cool? I felt like a celebrity, like I was the Langhorne High School Ultimate Fighter Champion.

After fourth period, I was getting irritated. I couldn't go ten feet without someone wanting to be my friend. Requests for juicy details about how the brawl got started were accompanied with invites to parties and hang-outs, friend requests on Facebook. I find it particularly disturbing how kids admire people who get into pointless fights. They praised me like I was some kind of hero. Maybe it was because Derek was a jerk to so many people and I was the first one to stand up to him. Did they not know that that little performance almost cost me my graduation? True, I'm older - a senior, but unpopular and less established as a figure of superiority. So, maybe it was a case of the underdog fighting all odds to take his place among society. But the truth was that I didn't need their acceptance. I don't need their compliments to make me feel like a better person. They didn't support me nor did they come to my aid. I didn't need anyone. And that pretty much summed up the status of my mentality. I can do anything without anyone. I whipped his butt all by myself. I did it once - I could do it again.

But then that delusion of grandeur quickly dissipated on my lunch break when I saw the moron that started it all. Perched on top of a lunch table surrounded by his football goon teammates, they resembled a herd of obnoxious yaks in the middle of the outdoor common area. They were joking and laughing unnecessarily loud. They probably found out that the world was round or something. Although I was a considerable distance away from them in a large, open yard, Derek had still managed to lay his eyes on mine. Fearlessly, I stared back at him hoping he would just ignore me and return to his idle chatter with his buddies.

Not a chance.

A burst of anticipation strangled my chest when Derek came to his feet and boldly stepped down from the lunch table. Aft first, his group didn't understand what was up. But once they followed Derek's mad dog stare into my direction, an expression of gruff disdain swept across all of their faces.

He can't be serious, I thought. Not after what Miss Cadzow said yesterday. Not after his father yelled at him and slapped him upside his head. Not after I promised my mother to never get into another fight. Come on, Derek. You can't be that stupid.

Almost immediately, he started to march straight towards me.

Wow. I guess you *can* be that stupid.

I began to go over in my mind how I held my own when I wrestled with him yesterday, except it probably wouldn't have worked at that moment. He had half the football team with him. It was then that I realized that Coach Williams must've laced their victory pizzas with Miracle Gro. Derek was thick (as well as his body) but some of his teammates were bigger than seniors. I don't want to say that I was scared, but what are you supposed to do when a herd of cattle come after you? Yeah, I wanted to run, but I am NOT a coward. I couldn't live with myself if I turned yellow. Besides, Derek was already in my face when I decided to run. So, I froze.

"It's not cool to make others look as bad as you, Jarvis." I almost passed out from his breath which reeked of tacos and Doritos.

Even though every bone in my body was shaking, my voice came out sounding surprisingly calm.

"You obviously don't need my help to do that, Derek."

"My old man was all over my ass last night cause of you. What's your problem, bro? Why'd you come after me like that?"

"Like what?"

Gradually, other students were keen to the face-off occurring and began to gather around us. Seriously? They want another show?

"You know what I'm talking about, dude. Don't play dumb!"

"You're all up in my face about nothing, Derek. What exactly is YOUR problem?"

"Jade said..." he started to say, but he stopped himself short. He just stopped.

His face transformed from youthful anger into utter confusion...or fear. It took me a few moments to then realize that he wasn't even looking at me. Then someone next to Derek cocked their head slightly to the side and began staring in the same direction. Eventually, the other kids facing me were gazing up into the sky and pointing. So, naturally, I wondered what they were all staring at that so fully stole their attention. When I slowly turned and looked into the sky, my heart almost stopped when I saw what it was.

Chapter 3

THE INVASION

About a mile in the sky closing in on the school was an astronomically huge, gleaming, metallic ring. It was the size of the whole campus as well as the surrounding neighborhood. The sides of it were smooth but were covered with hard, sharp lines and textures that indicated it was manufactured not by man, but by...I'm not going to say aliens. I don't believe in aliens! But it was obviously a flying machine of some kind, even though I didn't see any propellers, engines, turbines, or anything that could make it fly. It was floating and slowly rotating as it neared the school like a stealthy predator. From where I stood, the ship looked almost 400 feet thick and about two miles in diameter. Several satellite dishes and spires were scattered all over its topside and a loud, humming vibration began to resonate through the air. I'd never seen anything like it before. It was both fascinating and frightening at the same time.

"What the hell is that?" said Derek, which nearly made me jump out of my skin. I had completely forgotten about him. Then I noticed how the whole school was completely still. Absolutely every student, teacher, proctor, and staff personnel were in the outdoor quad staring upwards at the ominous ring-ship that dominated the skyline. It felt kind of weird cause in movies this is the part where people started running and screaming.

The thought was cut short when a loud mechanical

cranking sound echoed from the sides of the ring-ship. I squinted into the reflecting sunlight that bounced off the hull and witnessed long, cylindrical pylons spinning outwards from six different locations on the ship's sides. They spun and squealed as if they were unscrewing themselves from the ship. When they stopped rotating, the cylindrical tubes expanded and opened up like a flower and shot off the sides of the ship. They became mini-ships zooming through the air at magnificent speeds and headed straight for the school.

Now, people were running and screaming.

I was, too. People immediately panicked. If you've never been in the middle of a chaotic event, do your best to stay out of one. It's an incredibly terrifying ordeal! Try to imagine yourself being dropped in the center of a stampede of blind cows that are running in a hundred different directions at once. I hardly had a chance to find out what was happening since I was immediately knocked off my feet. My books and glasses were sent sliding down the sidewalk as people ran around and over me.

A great thud suddenly rocked the earth and people screamed at a level I didn't know was possible. Now, being as blind as a bat's grandfather, I couldn't see what everyone was freaking out about. I scrambled to find my glasses before someone else found them with a heavy foot. Finally, my hand brushed against the metal frame and I quickly put them on to see what I needed to run from. My eyes just about popped out of my head when I turned around and saw one of the mini-ships standing – yes, actually standing – in the quad area. When these mini-ships unscrewed themselves from the ring-ship and blossomed out to look like flowers, their "petals" were actually long, shiny, and metallic legs. Their smooth, reflective material was steel but it moved like skin and their "bodies" were just huge, black orbs that sported rusty and odd projections sticking out from their undercarriage. It behaved like a curious spider analyzing its new surroundings, crawling upon the sides of buildings and walls. What creeped me out even more was that one of them seemed to be staring straight at me. I could feel a flutter of fear brush against my heart. With it was a bold message...

RUN, YOU IDIOT!

I flipped over onto my feet and started running blind out of the large, open quad toward the English building. The thunderous crashes and horrific screams told me that the "octopod" was following not too far behind me. Was it actually coming after ME? Why me? There were dozens of other kids out here and this creepy machine had to come after me?! What did I do? This just wasn't my day. But I guess I shouldn't be so selfish. There were about six of these octopods from what I could recall. Not all of them were pursuing me. When I wasn't fleeing for my life or dodging debris from the crumbling school, I had a brief moment to hide and take a glance at the neighboring track field where several classes were at P.E. when the invasion had begun.

All I could see were kids scattering across the field and this giant, 25ft tall, silvery octopod from outer space was picking at them like a gushing little brat at a pet store. One blonde-headed girl broke away from the masses and headed into the weight room, a medium-sized anteroom that was attached to the side of the cavernous athletic gym. My heart did a little jump when the octopod noticed her escape and pursued her.

The octopod was merely steps behind her. It was way too big to use the door so it demolished the whole wall instead. It crawled over the wreckage and scampered inside as the poor girl continued to pierce the dusty air with her helpless screams. I also heard dumbbells and weights clang and crash against the floor. I assumed she used a 20lb weight or something as a projectile because I heard a loud BONG, an obvious screech of pain, and another feminine scream. Next thing I knew, the girl was running top speed out of the weight room rubble and into the open. Unfortunately, the octopod was not so easily defeated. It emerged from the weight room debris and began to chase the girl, but with legs that long, it was hardly a chase. What was freaky though was how it caught her. The eye of the octopod was actually some kind of a cage or capture unit. As it chased the girl, the eye opened. Then the octopod jumped into the air, flipped over, and crashed onto the running girl, catching her inside of its cage. Immediately, the octopod flew back to the ring-ship with its prize in tow.

If I were her, I'd be screaming at the top of my lungs, too. I didn't want to be abducted. I don't want to be taken away to God knows where. I never believed in aliens before, but what choice did I have now? All of those campy alien horror stories started to come back to me and none of those images were bringing me to my happy place. Was this the start of a world invasion? Were they going to use our blood as fertilizer for their new world? Were they going to suck our brains out for food? Were they going to enslave us? Were they going to experiment on us? Thanks a lot, Hollywood, for getting these ideas stuck in my head. Now that the fantasy was real, what do we do now? We plan for earthquakes and tornadoes, but alien invasions didn't quite make it on our list of priorities.

After witnessing a real, genuine alien abduction, my fear increased ten-fold. That was when my thoughts suddenly shifted to Jade's whereabouts. But then a massive, rectangular, yellow object sailed over the English building and brought me back to my problem. I was still being chased! After the yellow object hit the ground, I realized it was a school bus and a scream left my lips that even surprised me. The bus tumbled and flipped down the path that several kids and I were running on. As if by magic, none of us were hit, but the math building wasn't so lucky. The bus flew right over our heads and made a permanent bay window on the second floor.

Momentarily stunned, I had to stop for a second to see if I was still alive. My head, two arms, two legs, no blood – okay, I'm good. It was just enough time to let the pursuing octopod catch up to me. Its shadow swallowed my figure whole, but I didn't turn to look at it. I jumped out of its reach just as one of its legs struck the spot where my butt had just been. I made a mad dash for the English building, flung open the glass doors, and rushed inside. As I stood against the back wall catching my breath, I was surprised that the octopod failed to follow me. It just disappeared.

"Are they gone?"

I must have lost two years of my life from the shock that kid gave me. He was less than five feet from me and I didn't even see him when I came in. He must have been hiding in the corner somewhere. The kid was Latino, about my height, dressed in baggy cargo shorts, a black T-shirt advertising some unknown indie music band, an unbuttoned blue shirt, and covered in dust. His black hair made him look like a sandy blonde now that it was saturated with dirt and ash. There was an expression of utter fear on his face which I know I wholeheartedly reciprocated.

"No, there's one after me," I answered breathlessly. "It's still out there."

"There's one after me, too. I think it's still in the building."

My eyes fell on him in disbelief.

"You're kidding, right?"

He wasn't. The ceiling exploded above us forcing our bodies to the ground. We scrambled away from the doorway into the hallway and saw another octopod crashing its way down through the second floor to ground level.

"Techie Room!" the boy shouted. I quickly obeyed and followed him to the computer room. The Techie Room was a room within a room. The computer lab held at least 30 computers that were available for personal use. In the back of the room was a small room where the lab tech ruled over his realm, fixing the bugs, destroying viruses, and acting as savior of the digital realm. His throne room would serve as the perfect hiding place. When we ran into the deserted room, I could hear the octopod from upstairs landing on our floor. These things were fast and brutal and I was not interested in becoming the Predator's latest kill.

My new friend and I shut the door and hid underneath the lab desk that was directly below the windows that overlooked the lab. The silence that overtook the room was immediately disturbing. Even though the sound of us trying to catch our breath was unsettling, the abrupt sound change from total destruction to an astonishing silence was sickening, as if death had already found us.

"This is freakin' crazy. Can you believe this? We're in the middle of an alien invasion!"

I quickly shushed him because a sound like a washing machine filled the hallway. I could only imagine that it was the octopod, but this was a new sound. I dared to peek out through the Techie Room's window and stuck my head out into the land of computers. Beyond the windows of the computer lab was an empty hallway. The sound of screaming kids and school destruction were faint but still terrifying. I felt like a soldier in a war zone, except for the unfortunate fact that I had no weapon of my own to defend myself. The odd sound had become louder and I was startled to see what it was. The octopod had somehow collapsed into itself, shortening its legs and rolling its body down the hallway like a giant bowling ball.

"No way!" I whispered.

"What? What is it?" the boy said, but I motioned him to be quiet. The octopod was rolling by the computer lab's windows and I found myself holding my breath, but with my heart beating at five times its normal speed, it was somewhat difficult. The rolling octopod slowed down a percentage of its speed when it passed the computer lab's double doors and then it rolled out of sight. The washing machine sound diminished into nothing. A wave of relief washed over me and I sat down next to the boy.

"What did you see?" he asked.

"That...thing, it became a ball and was rolling through the hallway."

"Ok, good," he stood up. "We should keep moving."

"Are you nuts? This is the safest spot. It can't see us in here."

"I don't think they need to see. It just seems to know where we are."

I looked at him funny. These things just landed and he already knows how they think?

"What are you talking about?"

"Come on. We can't stay here."

I couldn't stop him from leaving the Techie Room. He went out into the lab cowering behind the blinking computer screens. Static fields flashed on their screens as the lights in the room flickered with erratic intensity. I wanted to go back to the Techie Room because I felt safe and secluded there, but once we got just a few steps from the lab entry, I was extremely grateful that we had left.

The servers in the room had exploded into dust. The wall burst open as the octopod crashed its way through in a violent manner, shattering the windows.

"GO! Get out of here!" I screamed. We started running past the rows of computer tables as the octopod spread out its legs and headed for us. Suddenly, my foot caught an electrical cord and brought me to my knees. As I fell, a large, spherical object shot out from the octopod's eye and snatched up the boy's body from in front of me. It shot back into its eye like a paddleball as I could hear the kid hollering out for help.

"NO!" I picked up a keyboard and threw it at the metallic beast which, of course, had no effect. The octopod then proceeded to ignore me as it loped out of the lab with the kid in its transparent belly.

"Get me out of here! Help! Help me!" he screamed.

I never felt so helpless in my life. What could I do? The monster was already in the hallway and heading out toward the entry doors before I could even catch up with it. It collapsed into a ball, rolled out through the entry doors, and then flew into the sky toward the floating ring-ship. I don't know why, but I was running after it, which was probably one of the stupidest things I've ever done.

In the smoke trail of the fleeing octopod, the legs of another octopod came into view. I wondered if it was the one that was chasing me earlier, resembling a fox waiting for its prey to come out of the cave. It crouched down into the hallway and looked straight at me causing me to have what seemed like an adolescent heart attack. I slid to a stop and did a 180, then started running for my life deeper into the English building.

This time, the octopod decided to follow me and end this game. It didn't even bother to collapse into a ball so it could fit into the hallway. As I headed toward the staircase, it merely crouched itself lower to the ground and scampered after me mimicking a massive crab tearing up the ceiling and walls in its wake. I hurdled up the stairs taking three steps at a time and made it to the second landing in record time. By the time I started my way to the third landing, the octopod began to make its ascent not by using the stairs, but by extending its legs across the void in the center of the stairwell. By just raising its body vertically it would be at my landing in no time. I had to throw something at it to slow it down.

Thanks to Fire Marshall Bill, the school was required to have a fire extinguisher on each floor. On the third landing, there was a fire extinguisher hanging against the wall at arm level. I never used one of these things before but I did know that we had to pull out some kind of pin first. So, I looked for the only pin that I could find, yanked it out, and pointed the hose at the spidery robot. I squeezed the handle and a fluffy, white solution shot out at the other end. Nothing interesting happened. It was just as effective as spraying it with tree flocking.

"Dang it!" I shouted. "I need some Raid!"

I then pitched the extinguisher down at the octopod, which easily caught it and crushed it with one of its lethal appendages. I heard a loud pop and a freakish screeching sound. Nitrogen gas was everywhere. I started running down the third floor hallway when I saw its legs retract from the stairwell causing it to stumble back down to the main floor.

My plan now was to make it to the stairwell on the opposite side of the building. Then I could slide down the banisters and make it out with my life in tact. But before I made it halfway down the hall, I was stopped short by a huge, gaping hole in front of me. The first octopod had come down from the third level and left a huge chasm that emptied out onto the main floor where the boy and I first met. I may be young, but I'm not Superman. I couldn't jump across that! I had to do something quick. I could hear the octopod making its way up the stairwell to my floor. I had to get out of there!

I scanned the doorways on my right and my left. All of them led to classrooms that were nothing but dead ends. I couldn't hide in them since the octopod would see which room I ducked into. Then I saw the letters ROOF ACCESS on one of the doors.

Okay, that'll work, I thought.

Anything's better than being cornered by an aggressive, two-story, eight-legged, relentless hunting machine. I kicked open the door thinking it was locked (it wasn't), climbed up the ladder, broke through the hatch (held together with a paper clip!), and exited onto the roof of the English building. I ran to the edge of the building and was granted a horrific view of the school campus.

It was complete chaos! Smoke rose from various areas across the campus, a fire hydrant near Home Economics was spewing water a hundred feet into air, buildings looked like crumbled crackers, the cafeteria had a bus sticking out through its roof, and a handful of people were still running around looking for a way out of this mess. But near the school drop-off zone, I saw something that made me sigh with relief: the authorities. Bright flashing lights, fire trucks, cop cars, dozens of military trucks and transports pulled into the driveway and dumped load after load of troops into Langhorne High. I think I did a little jump for joy.

"Hallelujah!" I said to myself. "It's about time."

My whole body suddenly spasmed when an ear-deafening blast erupted behind me. The roof burst open and sent an enraged octopod straight into the air. When it landed several yards in front of me, I took a step back and looked over the side of the building. Lucky for me the outdoor swimming pool was only three stories below. If I made a safe jump, I would hit the water with little or no damage to my body. I wasn't that high and I was closer to the deep end anyway. The octopod spat out its caged jaws in a failed attempt to capture me. I dodged its strike and then decided to jump.

"Not today, spiderman!" I shouted. I held my breath, stepped onto the edge of the building, said a quick prayer, and jumped. Unfortunately, in mid-jump, I caught the glimmer of shimmering metal soaring through the sky on my right. I didn't want to believe it at first, but like I said, these things were fast. A second octopod swooped out of nowhere, shot out its caged orb, and captured me in mid-air. Just like that, as if I was a piece of popcorn being tossed to a pigeon.

"NOOOOOOO!" I screamed. I just couldn't believe it.

It got me.

After ducking and dodging and running and hiding for the last ten minutes, it picked me up out of the sky as if I was just casually thrown into its greedy clutches. I failed. My stomach dropped as I saw the ground falling away and the hull of the ring-ship coming dangerously close.

"Oh, God! No! No, this isn't happening! Wake up, Jarvis. Wake up!"

The sudden cold sweat and the thumping in my chest told me that this was all too real. What scared me the most was that I was completely out of ideas. I was almost a thousand feet off the earth with no wings and no means of escape. In every sense of the word, I was stolen. No one could help me. I was alone and terrified and I had no idea what was going to happen to me. This day really sucked.

Through the otherworldly mesh of my capture unit, I could see the grooves and valleys of the metallic ring-ship that hovered above my school. I could hear helicopters and gunshots going off down below at the campus, but it was too late for me.

The cavalry had arrived, but I was already in the hands of the enemy. My hands, however, were trembling as my captor and transport slowly docked into its original port on the side of the ring-ship. Its legs slid into a set of circular openings as my cage was gradually brought forward to a gigantic ring of lights that was practically blinding me.

The heat from the light wasn't so bad until my cage was within a foot of its blazing rays. I was soaked in a white light and was forced to turn away just to save my eyesight. Then an abrupt jarring locked the octopod in its place and immediately the light shut off. The sudden silence signaled the beginning of a light mist that rained all over my head.

They're putting a seasoning on me, I thought.

Then a laser pinpointed my forehead from out of nowhere. I didn't feel anything, but I ducked anyway, hoping to keep the vital innards of all four of my brain lobes in tact. The laser beam spread outwards to the width of the cage and did a vertical scan of my body. After another laser scan spread horizontally across my body, a guttural, warped sound like an unidentifiable foreign language filled the space and a series of clicks and hisses surrounded my cage. Without warning, the floor disappeared beneath my butt and I was sent careening down into a slick, dark tube.

After being blinded by the light earlier, I felt I had been dropped into a pit of black ink. My body slid down a slick surface that ended abruptly and left me flying several feet above a hard floor. I landed on the softest part of my body, and, no, it was not my head. I knew my backside was going to be sore after that ride, but it was better than breaking a leg.

The room I was in wasn't really a room. I landed in an abnormally tall and extremely long, tubular hallway that seemed to run along the circumference of the ship. It stretched into a hazy nothingness on both sides that made it look like it went on forever. There were gargantuan pipes and wires that went along both sides of the hallway leaking gases and smoke into the dank, musty air. I felt insignificant and small in this giant space, similar to an ant lost in an alien sewer pipe. However, I wasn't alone in this horrible place.

"I guess we didn't do too good in getting away, did we?"

My buddy of escape was only a few yards to my right. There was a look of anticipation on his face but there was a calm in his voice, as if he had given up hope in trying to escape again.

"You're alive!" I responded. The fear in my voice was unmistakable.

"For now," he said.

"What do you think is going to happen to us? You think there's a way out of here?"

The boy raised his eyebrows.

"Um, have you looked out of the windows recently, my friend?"

No, I was sliding through a tube of death less than a minute ago, my friend. But I held my tongue. I noticed the thin, shallow slits of light that spanned the length of one side of the hallway. At first, I just thought it was an incredibly long light fixture, but as my "friend" pointed out, it was indeed a window. I ambled over to the expansive portal and saw billowing puffs of cotton streaming past the window. The greenish-brown and speckled surface of the earth began to give way to the curvature of earth's atmosphere. An empty sensation stung in my chest when I saw how the swirling patterns of cloud formations a thousand miles away seemed to be smiling at me whispering "Bon Voyage."

This isn't happening, I thought. I'm having a dream.

"No! I must have fallen asleep in economics again. Quick! Wake me up. Slap me!"

"Dude, relax."

"Slap me. I don't like this dream anymore."

He hesitated, but I was serious.

"Come on, do it!"

He struck my face, not hard enough though.

"No, not like that. Like this."

Then I slapped the boy with my whole hand. He recoiled then glared at me like I had lost my mind.

"Dude," he stated calmly. "What are you doing? You just slapped me."

"To wake you up. I don't want to be in your dream either."

"You're not dreaming, dickwads," said a new voice. We both spun around and saw what we thought was an alien creature, but at a closer look, she resembled a vampire. She was one of those kids that loved to wear nothing but black while making their skin look as white as baby powder. I never understood the concept. Did they want to look like they were dead? I don't think she's going to have a real problem attaining death upon this ship. Whatever her ideology was, this girl embraced the look with open arms by sporting black and white-striped leggings, a black petticoat skirt, black T-shirt, black combat boots, and a jet black bowl haircut with two long bangs that hung unusually straight in front of her pasty pale face.

"Dreams aren't this much fun," the Goth girl made an irreverent smirk.

"I would hardly call our abduction fun," I shot back at her, annoyed that she would take all that's happened as a passing joke.

"Where did you come from?" the boy asked her.

"I just arrived on the 12:45. Boarding was a little rough, you know, with the lunch table and trashcans flying everywhere. But my flight snatched me right out of my hiding place and brought me here, safe and sound."

"Wait! Ssshh. You hear that?" I could distinctly hear someone crying. I looked around our immediate area but I didn't see anyone. I listened again to hear where it was coming from. It was coming from further down the corridor so I motioned for the other two to follow me. They seemed reluctant, but I couldn't blame them. This was a very uncomfortable and strange environment. There's no telling what we might find here.

We ran further around the huge passageway and we soon came upon a feminine figure walking slowly through the light gas in the corridor. She was walking away from us, hunched over, and she looked scared out of her wits. Her crying must've been yielding some serious tears because she didn't even hear us as we approached her from behind. I could've smacked the boy next to me when he called out, "Hey!" A very unwise greeting in a place like this.

The girl jumped two feet into the air, spun around so fast she tripped and fell, and then started screaming. It was a little melodramatic but it seemed sadly genuine for this girl.

"No, no, it's okay. It's alright," I cooed. "We're not going to hurt you."

But it didn't work. She was seriously freaked out. As she crawled backwards away from us while screaming bloody murder, I realized it was the girl I saw being attacked on the field. No wonder she was terrified. I sympathized for her, but the Goth girl did not. She sighed with heavy exasperation, took a step in front of me, and shouted in the girl's face.

"SHUT UP!"

The poor girl was so surprised that she seemed to have suddenly lost her voice. The Goth girl looked pleased with herself.

"There," she said succinctly. "Now we can talk."

Actually, I had to hand it to her. It was heartless, but very effective.

"Who are you? What do you want?" the frightened girl stammered.

"Do we look like body snatchers to you?" the Goth girl

replied. "We don't have long, metallic tentacles coming out of our..."

"Hey, come on! Stop!" I interrupted. I only met this girl for less than two minutes and already her attitude was getting out of line.

"She's been through enough already. She doesn't need you talking down to her."

I heard the Goth girl give a huff while I offered my hand to the blonde girl to help her up. She looked at me skeptically. She was dressed in her cheer uniform because for some odd reason, the school required their teammates to wear a white-trimmed, crimson skirt and a white, oversized PE sweater at least once a week just to remind everyone who's representing the school. I recognized her as one of the cheerleaders from the school's football team. I remember seeing a write up about her mother from the school's newsletters. Her mom was a big time cheerleader queen or something, was the current color guard coach, and a very active member of the school PTA. And I'm sure her hefty donations to the sports and athletic department helped her to become a sort of school district celebrity. I don't remember this girl's name, but then again, I'm not an avid follower of the sports department.

"Y-you, you guys aren't...aliens?" she said scanning us individually.

"Gosh, I'm not *that* ugly, am I?"

The girl barely cracked a smile as she cautiously got to her feet. I thought it was a good idea to keep her talking.

"I've seen you before. What was your name again?" I asked.

"Cindy."

"I'm Jarvis."

The boy next to me extended his hand to her.

"Alex," he said stiffly. Cindy barely smiled, probably cause the fear inside of her kept her mind busy. I glanced at Goth girl to see what she would do and, oddly enough, I was not surprised at her reaction. She had her arms crossed and just had this apathetic leer directed toward Cindy.

"Yeah, yeah. You know who I am."

There seemed to be an odd exchange of sentiment between the two, but I couldn't make out what it was.

"What? You two know each other?"

"Yeah, well...kind of," said Cindy, still in an uneasy state. "Marlene tends to make herself known as a cheerhater."

"A cheerhater?"

"Hate is such an ugly word," Marlene responded, "I just have a high level of disgust of self-righteous chants that should be outlawed in all 49 states. Alaskan kids need to do it to keep warm, so they're ok."

It's annoying to encounter people who manifest their pointless pet peeves as a political statement. Before our conversation went any further, a wall several yards away slid open and two bodies tumbled out onto the floor. They landed in a heap near a steam vent. One of them immediately stood up and frantically looked around. My heart sank when I saw who it was.

"Jade!" I broke into a run toward her.

"Jarvis!" Jade ran toward me and wrapped herself around me, knocking the air out of my lungs. "Jarvis, what's going on? Where are we? Where are they taking us?!"

"I don't know, but are you ok? Are you alright?" I could feel her trembling in my arms.

"Yeah, yeah, I think I'm ok."

I glanced down at Jade's traveling companion and I did a double take. He stood up quite dramatically and had the look of fury in his eyes. I couldn't tell if he was angry at seeing me or angry that he was kidnapped. Whatever the case, he was obviously not happy to see me.

"Oh, great. You're here, too, huh? You following me?" he said almost sneering at me. I couldn't believe he could ask me such a stupid question.

"I'm a stowaway, you idiot," I hissed. "First class was booked up."

"Derek!"

Cindy suddenly rushed into Derek's arms and started crying.

"Cindy! They got you, too," Derek suddenly changed his tone. He sounded like a guy with a heart of gold. "It's okay, don't worry, we'll be alright."

"Cindy, you know this creep?" I asked in shock. Confused, she gaped at me.

"He's not a creep. He's a good guy."

I then remembered that they're both associated with the football camaraderie. People in football and cheerleading had an infamous clique where everybody were friends with everybody even if they didn't know each other's name. They considered it as a positive and trusting bond between teammates but it was more recognized as a system that shunned outsiders and the physically uncoordinated.

"Good guy?" I said in disbelief, but I decided not to start anything. Maybe she missed our infamous brawl yesterday. "Yeah, right."

"I don't think we should all be standing here," warned Jade. "There might be others on the ship, too. Maybe we should start looking for them? We should find a way out!"

"Well, as I pointed out earlier," Alex began, "we don't have much chance of escaping."

He approached the thin row of windows that had now become dark.

"We are airborne on a route to our destiny."

Alex didn't seem like a dramatist but his words disturbed me anyway. I came to the window to see what he was staring at and a chill rushed through my body. I could feel the hairs on my arms stand up and my mouth go numb. I heard the muffled footsteps of the other kids file out to either side of me. I heard gasps and soft sobs, but I was too petrified to acknowledge where they came from.

We stood staring at our home. A beautiful, cloud-covered, blue and white orb suspended in a sea of black ink. Huge and elusive, it beckoned us to come back. A strong, sickening tug in my gut hit me as I watched my home of eighteen years drift away from me. I could almost feel something shrivel up inside of me, as if it was dying. I wondered if anybody else felt it, too. It was an uncomfortable sting near my intestines and the rest of my body was too shocked to move. I always wanted to see the world, but not like this. Not as a prisoner of an alien spaceship.

"We're not going home anytime soon," Alex whispered sadly. "We've been abducted."

Chapter 4

WELCOME TO ZUU

The discomforting sight of seeing our home planet drift away made me hold onto Jade even tighter as I found her tightening her grip on me as well.

"Mom," I heard her say in a daze. "What's going to happen to Mom? What's going to happen to us?"

Jade and I have always been opposites but this was one of those rare moments where we were thinking the exact same thing. I started thinking about Mom, too. What would happen when she got word that the school had been invaded? How would she react when she finds out that her only two children are missing? It's a parent's worse nightmare. My mom has experienced too many tragedies in her life to endure another loss. But what could I do? What could any of us do? We were powerless.

These depressing thoughts were interrupted by a loud humming and a soft vibration that radiated through the hard floor. Earth's visage gradually stretched back like taffy into the emptiness of space then disappeared leaving a field of black and streams of light in its place.

"No!" Cindy screamed. All of us started panicking and talking at once.

"What happened?" I cried out. Jade grabbed a hold of my waist.

"What happened to earth, Jarvis? Where'd it go?"

"I don't' think anything happened to earth, you guys," Alex said trying to calm us down. "You feel the floor? That loud humming? We must've gone into warp or something."

Cindy turned whiter than Marlene.

"They're taking us to their planet," she said fearfully. "They're going to kill us. Why? What could they possibly want with...?"

Her sentence was cut short as she released a bloodcurdling scream and fell face first on the floor. Everyone jumped and saw her being dragged backwards through the mists of the corridor. Then her body was dragged upwards into the air by a small, robotic object. The device was the size of a small dog yet it managed to handle Cindy's body as if it was holding a tissue. It floated in mid-air and had the appearance of a blue, shiny, and angry giant mushroom with two spindly appendages that were locked around Cindy's ankles. Before we could respond, the rest of us were seized by our ankles and were pulled up into the air, too. They were so fast and agile that by the time you saw one, it was too late.

All six of us were flipped head over heels...or is it, heels over head? Whatever. We were upside-down, keys falling out of our pockets, phones and loose change raining down upon the floor – I even saw a condom wrapper which I swear wasn't mine!

The pickpocketing, flying robots, seemed to start communicating with each other. They beeped and blipped at each other as their human captives squirmed and screamed uselessly in their clutches. Then without warning, they took off down the corridor, zooming through the mists like a swarm of giant insects.

"Jarvis!"

I heard Jade scream from somewhere in front of me. Or was she behind me? When you're upside down and flying through an unfamiliar environment, it's hard to determine what's up, down, front, or back, especially when you're in the grip of a vile, airborne goomba.

"Jade, where are you?" I hollered out.

"Over here!"

I twisted my body toward the front of the swarm and saw Jade's nasty escort leading the pack. The robot holding her seemed to have no trouble restraining her as she writhed and kicked. No matter what move she made, her captor easily compensated for it.

Beyond Jade's body, I saw that the swarm was heading toward a towering and nightmarish aperture that seemed to be the source for all the conduits that snaked throughout the ship. It resembled an enormous yawning mouth consuming hundreds of pipes and plumes of colored steam. Our helpless bodies were flown into its depths and were enveloped by a world of bright lights, huge moving contraptions, and ear-deafening machines. My body was carelessly tossed into the air with what seemed like a lackadaisical attitude from the robot's grip. But I knew that couldn't be possible because a robot doesn't have emotions. But, silly me, I forgot. I'm on a spaceship now. The former rules do not apply.

After being thrown into the air like a wet rag, another

machine caught me by the wrists and ankles and snapped an iron collar around my neck. This machine was on a conveyor belt-like system that slowly moved through a series of weird and invasive devices that inspected our bodies. I couldn't move out of the apparatus that restrained me but I could still see a few of the other kids in front of me who were in the same position as me. I heard Cindy screaming at the top of her lungs again, her voice echoing through the assembly line. To prove my point about the flying robots having emotions, one of them flew up to her face making her scream even more. It actually glared at her and sounded a playback.

"SHUT UP!"

It was a recording of Marlene's voice. Then it looked as if it sneezed a fine mist in Cindy's face. Cindy's screams stopped abruptly and her head fell limp just as the robot flitted away. I wasn't sure what happened, but it made me extremely uncomfortable, not that being in the solid grip of a monstrous machine wasn't uncomfortable enough already.

No matter how much I struggled, I became a victim to a number of intrusive actions such as a machine that patted down every part of my body, and I do mean, EVERY PART. We went through a freakish X-ray machine that sent a plane of blue light directly through our bodies. We were submerged through a gelatinous liquid that flowed into our lungs and mouth. When we were extracted, I immediately felt sick and threw up. That must've been the purpose because everyone else did the same at exactly the same moment. It grossed me out when floating receptacles caught all of our vomit and churned it around. We then went through a hellish room that almost singed our skin, a wind blower, a freezer, and a dishwasher that still managed to leave us dry. The most painful device was formed like a distorted horseshoe that came down around our heads and burned a tiny piece of metal behind our ear lobes. I could see stars and a blinding light when the metal seared into my flesh. Even though it lasted only a fraction of a second, the pain was unbearable.

The elaborate assault on the sacredness of our bodies came to a brusque end when the steel apparatus that restrained us released us onto a steeply sloped plane. We were sent hurtling into a dark chamber that reeked of an odor that was a cross between feces and pineapple juice. The smell was grotesque! I've never smelled anything like it before. When the other kids slid into the room, it was obvious that they were equally disgusted.

"Dang, who farted?" Derek said waving his hand.

"Don't look at me," Jade said plugging her nose. "Nothing that smells that bad comes out of me."

"Wha..what ha..happened? What are they..what are they doing to us?" said Cindy, who looked lazy-eyed after that flying machine sprayed a sedative in her face. She brushed her fingers over her ear lobes where the hot piece of metal was seared into our skin.

"It feels like we've been tagged," Alex acknowledged. "You know, how they tag animals in the wild? They do that to keep track of them."

"But why would they want to keep track of us?" I asked.

"Who cares?" said Jade. "Maybe that means they'll take us back home."

As if to answer her query, the chamber we were in made a thunk and a roar and its four sides began to sink slowly down into the floor. The descending walls revealed a complex grid of bars woven in an unusual pattern that completely surrounded us. It only took a second to realize that we were in some type of otherworldly cage. But it wasn't the cage that twisted my sense of reality, it was what lay beyond it.

Hundreds, if not thousands, of other cages were spread out further into the ship. We were planted in what looked like the cargo hold of the ring-ship and there was a whole world of different aliens in every single one of the cages. Some aliens looked like giant sperm whales on skinny legs while some looked like giant birds with trunks and palm frond manes. One alien resembled a dinosaur-like tiger with a giraffe's mantle. What was also fascinating was that all the cages were different shapes and sizes and textures and materials. Each cage was made unique to what creature it detained. We even saw some eerie aquatic creatures that were held in a gigantic tank. Cages were piled up almost a hundred feet up into the air in a helter-skelter fashion where the roof of the ship hovered another 70 to 80 feet above them. The ceiling had a wide, long skylight that followed the huge circumference of the ring-ship acting as a lofty median for the cargo hold. The colossal line of crates and pens followed the roundness of the ship so there was practically no end in sight. The six of us stood in silence for almost a full minute soaking in the unbelievable view.

"It doesn't look like they'll be taking us back home," Alex mused.

"So, that's why it stinks in here," said Marlene. "We're smelling alien manure. How lovely."

Jade looked around, wide-eyed and jittery. "And to think, I didn't even believe that aliens existed."

"Kind of makes you wish you had a camera, huh?"

As soon as Marlene said that, an idea struck me. I had a camera on my cell phone! Maybe I could call home? I reached into my pocket and felt nothing but fabric and lint. Those flying toasters had emptied my pockets completely.

"Hey, does anybody have their cell phone?"

I got several blank stares that made me feel like an idiot. I could totally understand why.

"Dude, are you stupid?" said Derek. "You're not going to get service out here."

"Derek's right, Jarvis," agreed Alex. "We're nowhere near earth's satellites. There's no phone plan in existence that will give you that kind of reception."

Alex was right. It was a dumb idea. Cindy must've seen my shameful expression cause she quickly stated, "It was a good idea, though."

"Thanks."

However, I could count on Derek to bring the negativity back.

"No, it wasn't. It was a dumb idea," he said matter-of-factly. I kept my cool, but it still pissed me off.

"Yeah, I guess so. It was about as dumb as running the wrong way to make a touchdown."

Derek smacked his teeth and shot me a look. I knew that would get him.

Last season, the Langhorne Lions went up against the Gibson Griffins and suffered one of the most humiliating defeats in high school history. I despise sports so I wasn't there to witness it, but I couldn't ignore the comments and news that came after the game had ended. The Griffins were already beating the Lions by 18 to 6, but in the last 8 seconds of the game, Derek had intercepted a pass and made a touchdown for the wrong team. There was no way he could redeem himself because the buzzer went off and the game was over. It must've been a pitiful sight because I heard he did a little dance and everything. I can only imagine how invigorated he felt as the crowds cheered for him. Too bad it was the opposing team cheering for the heroic stupidity of their adversary. Over time, Derek regained his popularity thanks to the shallow rules of acceptance among jocks, but Derek was thoroughly mortified. He remained low-key and isolated for almost two weeks after the game. I wish I could've been there to see how his strict, demanding father reacted. When I thought about that, a devilish smirk would always land itself upon my face.

"Why don't you just shut your mouth?" he snapped, standing up and ready to fight.

"Derek, knock it off," Jade stepped in. "What's the point of fighting here?"

"No proctors," he said threateningly. I swear, sometimes he looked just like a pit bull.

"Whatever, dude," I responded. I was hardly in the mood for his bullheaded nonsense. This was obviously not the time.

"You guys, stop it," Cindy said weakly. She didn't seem to be a forceful girl. She was very thin and had a small frame. When she spoke, her voice was high pitched and nasally which I found odd because she was a cheerleader. I would assume her voice would be more projected but she was the complete opposite of the norm. Maybe she was one of those girls that hid in the back of the group that always gets drowned out by the rest. She seemed so frail. I thought that if I bumped into her I'd break her arm.

Derek almost had smoke escaping from his pupils. Then he turned away with a grunt and leaned against the bars of our cage.

"What is it with you two, anyway?"

Cindy's question went unanswered due to the stubbornness of its recipients. One second ago, we were ready to rumble, but now we sealed our traps shut like obstinate clams. Derek glared unkindly at me, but I just got tired of looking at him. Even if we did get into another scuffle we'd still be stuck with each other. I rolled my eyes in frustration and turned away looking back at the ship's hold of weird alien creatures. For a few moments, my thoughts burned inside my head.

What cruel twist of fate put me in this situation? Did I deserve to be stuck on this ship and be shipped off to some mysterious planet? Am I being punished by God or something? The more I thought about these questions, the more I realized I was focusing on myself. I was being selfish. I then focused my thoughts on Jade and my emotions tried to straighten themselves out. I can't call Mom. My cell phone is useless out here so I can't call 911 or anybody else that can save us. The school was virtually obliterated by the octopods. We're locked inside a cage on a spaceship that is light years from our home planet. And we're completely on our own.

We were screwed.

We sat around silent for a long while, our thoughts going crazy or too scared to think at all. I started to feel a little light-headed and my stomach felt a little queasy. I stayed still for a long time concentrating on not throwing up while the others began to chat quietly amongst themselves and talked about the different alien creatures on the ship, worried about their friends and family back home, or what these aliens would do with us once we landed. I was beginning to feel really weird. I couldn't tell if I was nauseous or just plain sick. And then something brushed across the back of my arms, neck, and back. I looked behind me and nothing was there. Weird thing was, I didn't expect to see anyone or anything. It didn't feel like an actual person behind me.

It was more like a sensation. I sensed a huge, ominous presence coming toward the ship. It's kind of odd that I could sense a planet coming toward us. It's similar to sensing a person walking into the same room without seeing them. You know they're there, you just haven't seen them yet. When I felt that odd buzzing of energy brush against the tiny hairs on my arms and neck, I looked up through the skylight of the ship and saw it: a new planet.

From what I could tell, this planet seemed huge. But we were on a ship that appeared to be coming in for a landing and I couldn't compare it to the size of earth. The colors of its surface were streaked with blues and peach colors and I could identify swirls of cloud patterns that honored hues of dark pink and mauve. If I wasn't a prisoner being dragged to its surface, I'd probably say it was a beautiful planet. But instead, a shiver of apprehension came over me.

"You guys," I said pointing up to the skylight above the caged aliens, "Do you see what I see?"

Everyone tilted their heads upwards.

"You gotta be kidding me!" Derek exclaimed.

"Whoa! Look at that," Alex said, fascinated. "What planet is that?"

"It's not a planet, it's a death trap," said Cindy, her voice drowning in fear.

"It's a human kitchen," said Jade, her voice rising. "They're going to serve man."

"Mmmm, kiddie casserole," mused Marlene,

practically urging my sister to have a conniption fit. "Say your prayers, shipmates."

"We're all gonna die!"

"The hell we are!" Derek said angrily.

"Okay, okay," I said, trying to calm everyone down. "Getting into a panic is not going to help anyone."

"Well, what do you propose we do? Sing *Koom Bi Yah*?"

"Yeah, I'm not too crazy about getting a probe stuck up my butt."

I turned to Alex and stared. "For real? A butt probe?"

"Hey, I've seen worse things."

"Where?"

"I'm a gamer."

A butt probe. I didn't expect Alex to say something like that. Well, after what we went through, it could be a possibility. I just hope he's wrong.

"Well, I can't guarantee about the butt probe thing, but I think we'll be better off if we just try to stay calm."

"Yeah, yeah," Jade chimed in. "Like Alex said, maybe they just wanted to tag us or something. Maybe they'll just take us back home and wipe our memory and we won't remember a single thing about all this. Yeah, maybe that'll happen. Right, Jarvis? Am I right?"

Jade was rambling. When she rambles, that means she's scared. Completely terrified. Anyone could see that. Her voice was shaky and her eyes were squinted, preparing for the tears that were sure to come. Cindy may be delicate and frail, but Jade wore her emotions like a billboard. I ignored the suffocating urge to embrace her and cry with her. But I had to be stronger than her if I wanted to protect her. I was her big brother. Out here, I was all she had. But inside, I was just as scared as she was. Sometimes I hated to be the tough guy. I'm not that good at acting.

"Stay with me, Jade," I said to her. "Ponies, ponies, ponies."

Everybody looked at us with curiosity.

"Dude, what the...?" Derek said.

"What does that mean?" Cindy asked.

"It's just a chant that our family has to bring us back to our senses – to wake us up. It brings back a positive memory."

Marlene just eyed us like we were crazy. "Ohhhkaaay."

For what seemed like the next half hour, the ship seem to be decelerating in speed as it entered the atmosphere of the planet. On entry into the planet's air space, a red-hot hue spread over the skylight of the ship. The friction alone caused the ship to shake and rattle so much that I was sure some of the alien cages would start plunging to the floor. But as soon as it got to an unbearable pitch, the shaking suddenly stopped. The ship just sailed through the sky, light as a feather.

It aggravated me that I couldn't see where the ship was going. All I could see was the black ink of space gradually transforming into an expanse of blue with puffs of lavender clouds whizzing by. From the swarm of butterflies that was overtaking the space in my stomach, I could tell that the ship was settling down to land. It dipped and bobbed at unexpected intervals making the other extra-terrestrials screech and groan unhappily. Whether they got airsick like humans did, I couldn't tell, but the air within the cargo hold increased its fetid odor to a new sickening degree. Thank goodness we threw up before we got in there.

I could feel the ship losing its speed and finally, it seemed to have stopped...or did it? Even though the purplish clouds refrained from zooming by, they seemed to be rotating away from us.

"Are we still moving?" Cindy asked aloud. A quick second later, the sky stopped rotating and something else appeared. A gigantic building, smooth and slick like polished granite, rose beyond the side of the ship. It curved away from us so I assumed it was an enormous circular building. It shimmered in the sunlight like brushed metal and had a small gathering of tracking lights down two rows along its sides. They pulsated with a rhythmic glow as the building rose to another 400 feet into the sky before it stopped growing. Then slowly, the lights stopped pulsating and the ship made an abrupt shake.

"The ship must've docked," Alex said. "Just like in Alaska, they're bringing in the catch of the day. Maybe we should start considering ways to cause them indigestion?"

Jade wailed into my arms. Dismayed, I gave a look at Alex.

"Would you mind not referring to us as food?"

"What? It's just the way they work. At least that's how it looks. These aliens go around the galaxy collecting other aliens for food, cleaning them and inspecting them, making sure they're fit for consumption."

My mouth fell open as Jade squeezed my arm and wailed again.

"Dude, do you even hear what you're saying?" said Derek. "You're talking about us like we're a bunch of happy meals."

"Really," said Cindy. "Have a little compassion."

"But the universe isn't about compassion," Alex said in his defense. "It's about survival. Every creature has their own way of doing it. Lions hunt gazelles, some flowers absorb the juice out of insects, humans pretty much kill everything and anything they want, and these aliens obviously scan the galaxy for whatever tasty vittles they can find. I guess this is what we get for thinking that we're at the top of the food chain. We're no longer the head cheese, we're the appetizer."

Tasty vittles?

Even though Alex had a penchant for stating our predicament in such a brutally honest format, no one could argue with him. We figured that he could be right. Maybe this was the end of the line. Maybe we were just six unlucky teenagers who would never see their graduation…or their 21st birthday. There was so much more I wanted to do in life: write that book about the living statues, fall in love, have a family, buy a house with two dogs and a sand-bottom swimming pool, and, of course, get my theme park built that would rival Disneyland. Now it was apparent that my dreams were just that – dreams. Nothing more.

They were just desires that would never be fulfilled.

My eyes almost glossed up with tears thinking about the life I wanted and would never have until a teeth-chattering thud rocked the ship. Aliens and creatures everywhere suddenly went wild as a loud humming vibrated the air around us and a portion of the hull as big as a supermarket revealed itself as a door. It melted into the side of the inner ring of the ship as a gigantic upright circle, but it didn't swing open. The circular shape rotated counter-clockwise, picking up speed and unscrewed itself backwards away from the hull. As soon as it was clear of the ship, the door rose up and an army of hovering machines glided into the corridor. The machines or drones had a similar mushroom shape and sour demeanor as our previous smaller captors except they were the size of small cars and much more...buff. They flowed into the ship like a horde of busy bees immediately beginning their work of lifting the enormous, alien-filled cages and taking them out through the opening.

"It's dinnertime," said Alex forebodingly.

"Maybe if we cluck like chickens they'll let us go," Jade said aloud.

Cindy, Derek, and Marlene looked at her oddly.

"What?!" they all said at once.

"Maybe they don't like chicken," Jade paused for a moment, then shook her head. "Yeah, I guess that's a dumb thought. Everybody likes chicken."

"Jade," I said to my little sister, "just breathe, ok?"

Our cage suddenly tilted to one side and we were lifted into the air. Cindy and Jade began screaming as Derek cursed. I looked up and saw huge robotic clutches wrap around the edges of our small roof. But the drone paid us no attention. It casually lifted our cell box and drifted toward the round opening, buzzing and beeping in its creepy computer language.

"It's got us," Jade cried out. "We need to do something!"

"Everybody, jump up and down. Maybe we can get out of its grip!"

We accepted Alex' suggestion and began jumping up and down. The drone escort must have been surprised at the unexpected shifting of weight because I heard it moan as it fumbled its hold on our small prison box. Unfortunately, what seemed to be a good idea turned out to be a very bad one. When the drone exited the ship, it entered into the main port which was a frightfully deep, vertical shaft. I caught a glimpse of the scary, gaping shaft below us that was buzzing around with a flurry of flying machines. My heart leapt as one end of the cage slipped from the drone's grip swinging us wildly to one side.

"Stop jumping, you guys!" I shouted, but jumping was no longer possible since we were all thrown off our feet. We slid down to the lowest corner of the cage into a heap of twisted bodies. We were jumbled into a grotesque version of Twister. Derek's foot went into my back as mine went into Alex' face. Amid the scramble, I could hear the drone becoming frustrated with his cargo. The pit below was screaming our names.

"Oh, God, please don't drop us," I whispered as I peered into the deep shaft. As if it had heard me, the drone lost its grip and dropped us. A weightless sensation consumed our bodies as we became airborne plummeting into the open chasm. The crowd of flying machines was enough to interrupt our descent, however, through a series of crashes and collisions toward the bottom floor.

The machines sputtered, crumbled, and broke as we fell several stories down into the crowded shaft. Other aliens screeched in excitement as we plummeted, but finally, our cage hit another cage on the bottom floor. It tipped over sideways once more then slammed down on solid ground destroying its shape and spilling our bodies onto the cold floor. It was literally a miracle that everyone came out of that fall alive and with no broken bones.

"Aw, man! Is that what it feels like to go through a washing machine?" I groaned. "Is everybody okay? Jade?"

"I'm alright," she said groggily. She was plopped spread-eagled on Alex' stomach. I couldn't help but crack a smile when I saw Derek's face land right in between Marlene's legs.

"Alright, buddy, show's over," she said pushing him away with her foot. Derek leapt to his feet and made a grimace of disgust.

"Thank God!"

I felt around to check if every part of my body was still intact and in one piece. I had a couple of scrapes here and there and I knew a bruise would soon form where Cindy elbowed my rib cage, but other than that, I was good. We landed in what looked like dank, musty, and eerie storage area that was stacked with empty cages. Some of them were damaged or completely destroyed with burn marks, deep claw scratches, and other grim indications that their inhabitants had a hard time escaping. The airplane hangar-sized room was quite dark and it was difficult to make out the farthest corners of the space. Grungy lighting and the mishmash of neglected cages made the area feel like it was unimportant or forgotten. However, my eye was attracted to one area of the room that emanated a faint glow. There, on a floating, rectangular bed-like device was someone I did not expect to see.

"Is that...?" I started to say, bewildered.

"Miss Cadzow!"

I wasn't the first to see her. Cindy spotted her instantly and rushed to her side. I can imagine that most students would think twice about coming to the aid of their school principal, a person whose sole purpose is to suspend, detain, and punish all who disturb the sanctity of her kingdom. Although Miss Cadzow was harsh, she was fair, and used mercy when necessary. Therefore, she was feared, but very well respected. So when I saw her laid out on her back on a heavy, metallic slab that resembled a sarcophagus my heart went out to her. Was she dead? Was this some kind of unearthly funeral rite? Why would they treat her body so ceremoniously?

"Is she dead?" Marlene had asked aloud what everyone was thinking. As we gathered around the floating cart, I noticed that her body was actually floating three inches above the surface of the interior and a light blue haze completely surrounded her body. Derek proceeded to do what I thought about doing but declined to do so: he reached out to touch her.

"I don't think that's a good idea, Derek," Alex stated. But, of course, that only prompted Derek to ignore him. He moved his fingers toward Miss Cadzow's arm where spark of blue light flashed around his fingers causing Derek to jerk his arm away. We all jumped but Derek hardly seemed fazed by the electric jolt.

"What was that?" Jade asked.

"I don't now," Derek replied. He tapped the air around Miss Cadzow's body and as he did so, fizzy static hissed and buzzed around his fingers like tiny fireflies. "Weird! There's like a force field around her. Feel it."

"Uh, no thanks, Derek. I like my fingers raw, not fried."

"I wonder if she can hear us," Alex said as he studied her. "Look, she's still breathing. She might just be unconscious."

"But why would they put her on this slab of metal instead of with us in the cage?"

"Maybe it's because she's older than us," I stated.

"Or maybe it's because she's the principal of our school," said Cindy.

"Or maybe it's because it's none of your business!"

The new voice boomed from behind us and nearly made all of us jump ten feet into the air. We stumbled over each other to flee from the startling voice, then stopped short when we saw that we were surrounded by a small troop of bulky, teal-colored robots. These robots were beyond high-tech science fiction! I guess it's kind of odd to admire their design when they're about to capture us, but I have to admit, these robots were fierce! They had a bow-legged stance but stood completely erect with an unusual firearm in their grip. They had two S-shaped arms, two bow-curved legs, and their head was shaped like a small scythe with the blade section heading down toward their back. Their design favored sweeping curves throughout their body like whoever created them figured out a way to capture the human anatomy through curved structure instead of straight lines.

Then there was the source of the new voice who was not a robot, but an alien, and a freaky one, too. He was a huge, towering creature that must have been about ten feet tall. It had a very elongated face that sagged with thin tendrils on either side of its raw, wrinkled face. Beneath its steely blue headdress were two slits of yellow light that peered unkindly down at us. When he took a step toward us, his rugged, earth-colored fabrics that hung from his massive shoulders ruffled away to reveal a belt of packs, electronic devices, and a highly unique suit of clothed armor clasped around his extraordinarily muscular body. His expression reminded me of a bad-tempered drill sergeant that was deformed by a radiation mishap. And just like everyone else, I froze in terror.

Cindy screamed, Derek cursed, Marlene gasped, Jade

passed out in my arms, and I was speechless.

"Whoa," Alex said in awe. "That's one big alien."

When I finally built up enough courage to speak I sounded like an owl.

"Who...who...who are...who are you?" I stammered.

"Someone you need to start worrying about," said the intimidating creature, its voice sounding like boulders rumbling across a bass drum.

"Why? What are you going to do to us?"

"We don't want to be eaten," my sister blurted out.

"Really?" the alien said, apparently amused. "What makes you think I'd want to eat you?"

"He said you were," she pointed at Alex who instantly turned whiter than rice. The towering alien glowered at him.

"Misinformed, aren't we?"

Alex gulped.

"That's why we're here, isn't it?" he asked in a small voice. "To be served?"

"I'm not surprised at your menial level of intelligence, considering that you're only younglings of your species. But the concept of digesting your flesh is unbelievably primitive." Interesting manners for such a fearsome looking alien.

"Then what do you want with us?" Derek asked.

"You'll soon find out," said the alien flippantly. "Os-Gouvox?"

Immediately a tall, silver and scarlet-colored, streamlined robotic figure stepped out from behind the imposing alien. It held a long, staff-like weapon or device that was made of curving blades and digital lighting. He looked like he might have been some kind of robotic warrior.

"Yes, Gatekeeper," the robot declared stiffly in his electronic voice.

"Take these new creatures to their enclosure by land craft. They are too delicate to send on a normal transport. I need you to see that they are delivered safely and without harm."

"As you wish, Gatekeeper."

The robot then did a bow and an odd salute where it brought its slender hands up to its bulging chest in one smooth motion. But once the Gatekeeper began coming toward us, the other kids and I shrank back not knowing what was going to happen. The Gatekeeper approached Miss Cadzow's floating bed, made a few taps to the side in a synchronized fashion, waved his palm, and proceeded to guide her device out from the storage facility.

"Wait," I said unexpectedly, surprised at the volume of my own voice. "Where are you taking her?"

The Gatekeeper barely turned his head as he marched away from us with several of his mechanical guards.

"She has information that must be extracted," he replied as a grimace of reluctance graced his face.

"What does that mean?"

But I didn't get an answer. I was just too lowly for him to devote anymore time to. Os-Gouvox watched the Gatekeeper make his solemn exit and then slowly turned to face us. I didn't know why but it was at that moment that I knew there was something wicked about this living figure made out of shiny metal and bolts. I could sense it. He glared at us with a cold, hollow stare that made my stomach flip.

"Welcome to Zuu."

Chapter 5
NUVU JOINS THE CREW

I love going on vacation. It's a real treat to go to new places and landscapes, taste new foods that I've never eaten before, experience the association of different people, and to just enjoy the excitement of being away from home. Unfortunately, the recent string of events is killing my adoration of far off places. I want nothing more than to be back in the humdrum life of suburban paradise and watch reruns of crappy anime cartoons while munching on potato chips. Boredom never sounded so desirable as it did then. I would have settled for algebra homework in place of being manhandled and caged up (yes, caged up again) by bow-legged robots that ignored every single insult and plea for help that escaped our lips.

The aggressive, humanoid machines stuffed us into another cage that was much smaller and lighter than our previous cell and proceeded to put us on a yacht-sized, triangular-shaped vehicle that hovered in mid-air. Along with the warrior robot that was called Os-Gouvox and several teal-colored robots, we were given an unusual ride through the base. The gigantic building that the ring-ship brought us to reminded me of a shipping port except everything was situated vertically. Hundreds upon hundreds of machines of various sizes, colors, and designs maneuvered quickly up and down enormous shafts where more cargo was shuffled around in a hectic manner. It was disturbing to see that most of the cargo were different cages full of live aliens. There were also outrageous plants and trees being transported, inspected, and dispersed by flying robots that moved so fast it was a wonder that they never crashed into each other.

Another thing that bothered me was that these machines were so human-like. Yeah, they talked and moved around like normal people, but did they have a soul? Did they sympathize with the creatures that were being imprisoned here or were they just doing what they've been programmed to do? Did someone control them? I must've been thinking out loud cause I heard Alex suddenly speak my thoughts.

"I wonder if that big, ugly alien is controlling these robots somehow?"

"I was just about to say that!" I said to him. "Brilliant minds do think alike."

Speaking of minds, I noticed that my head was really starting to hurt. I started to notice little white specks dancing in front of my eyes and when I tried to focus on one, they would be gone. A dull, harsh pain would radiate out from the back of my head and then desist, then flare up again when I thought about it, as if thinking about the pain would just make it worse. Man, where's Tylenol when you need it?

Our hovercraft glided into a tunnel and quickly began to pick up speed. After a quick two seconds, a thruster lurched the vehicle forward and sent us hurtling out into a bright and fantastic landscape. Huge, crescent-shaped mountains loomed over a sprawling bluish and green field that stretched miles into all directions. Bright, amber-colored stones jutted abruptly from the ground and reached for the sky that was drowned in a light purple glow and speckled with dark, pink clouds. There was so much saturated color on this planet that I felt like I was looking at a movie screen that needed the hues adjusted. I rubbed my eyes and slowly took it all in again. It was still unimaginably beautiful.

"Wow," Cindy said in awe. "It's beautiful."

"Yeah," Derek said unhappily, "I'm sure it looks better from the other side of these bars."

I glanced around at our cage then became curious as to where we came from. I looked back to the tunnel from where we had emerged from and was startled to see its tiny opening miles away. We were flying across the ground at a superior speed! It just didn't feel like we were going that fast cause the hovercraft was so smooth. I focused on the tunnel and saw that it was only one of several openings at the base of a monumental rock that was clearly the height of 5 Transamerica buildings stacked on top of each other. The top of the vertically angular rock was a small metropolis of metallic pylons, curved buildings, and...I had to blink, shake my head, and look again...*several* ring-ships!

"You guys, look," I said excitedly. "Look up there! That's where we came from. They have more than one."

Everybody tore their gaze from the enchanting landscape and craned their necks skyward to see what I was pointing at. I heard a small collection of gasps and grunts of surprise as we laid our eyes on the alien's shipping port. There must have been about 6 or 7 ring-ships docked on the city-in-the-sky. Three massive towers of the futuristic base were threaded through the diameter of the ring-ships and it was reasonable to assume that one of those ships invaded our school and brought us to this crazy planet.

"Can you believe all of this is happening?" Cindy said to us as the shipping port faded into the distance. "We've actually been abducted. How are we going to get back home?"

"But this *is* your home."

Our attention was stolen by Os-Gouvox who was standing directly in front of our cage staring intently at us. He made his statement with such conviction that it seemed we had insulted him.

"You will never see earth again. Zuu is your home now."

"Please, sir," I pleaded sincerely, "we just want to go back home. We have families, we have parents who are worried about us."

"You will address me as Os-Gouvox," he said, completely ignoring me. "I am a Sarok, an overseer of this planet. The Gatekeeper and I are your masters and your complete obedience is required for your own survival."

"So, what are we? Slaves?" Marlene asked.

"The term "slave" implies that you will be required to work. Fortunately for you, your roles do not include hard labor." Os-Gouvox turned to look out at the head of the hovercraft. "In case you were wondering, we do not speak your language. You only hear English through the linguistic implants that were injected behind your ears."

My hand involuntarily brushed the back of my ear where that conveyor contraption burned a piece of hot metal into my skin.

"So that's what that is," Alex mused. "Ingenious!"

"Sure is a painful way to learn a new language," added Marlene.

"They were implanted so that you may listen and obey orders when they are given to you. Insubordination is unforgivable and will be dealt with quickly and without question. You will be placed in a region that closely resembles your home world and you will be viewed by the Eszok for study."

"The Eszok?" said Jade uncomfortably. "What's an Eszok?"

"The Eszok are the rightful rulers of the universe and wish to study your species for reasons I do not need to know. However, I find it particularly annoying how inquisitive you human creatures are."

"If you find us so annoying then take us back to earth," Derek shot back. "You have no right to keep us here."

"Actually, we do. As I have said before, the Eszok rule the universe. You just didn't know it yet."

"That's bull…!"

Derek suddenly charged toward Os-Gouvox from within the cage, but Os-Gouvox hardly flinched. He stretched out his staff through the bars of the cage and shot a wave of electrical bolts into Derek's torso. Derek crumpled to the ground while everyone elicited a chorus of screams. The air crackled and hummed around Derek's body as he convulsed erratically. Then the electrical bolts disappeared.

"Derek!" Jade screamed, rushing to his aid. She knelt down and turned him over onto her lap. His eyes were half-closed, turned upwards. He was drooling, delirious, and his whole body went slack.

"Derek, are you okay?" Cindy whimpered. Derek's eyes just lolled around in his sockets, not looking at anyone in particular. Poor guy didn't even know what hit him. *I* didn't know what hit him. But whatever this creepy robot guy did to Derek with his staff made everybody his subjective peon. In just those few moments, Os-Gouvox had made his position known – Don't mess with me!

"Is that all you've got?" Derek said, almost incomprehensibly. "Come on, I'll take all three of you." The words left his lips like that of a drunken wino. I had to hand it to him, he may not be the brightest crayon in the box, but he has guts. So I tried a different approach.

"Please, take us back home, we beg you," I said sadly, but I couldn't even believe myself. I'm such a bad actor.

"I'm afraid that's just not possible. As irritating as your species appears to be, you are astronomically unique. There's a reason why you are the only humans on Zuu."

"Which is?" I demanded, but was immediately interrupted by a high-pitched beep that sounded from the dashboard of Os-Gouvox's hovercraft.

"We are approaching your enclosure," Os-Gouvox stated as he walked away to face the front of the ship. Directly ahead of us were one of the giant crescent-shaped mountains, but as we neared its base, I realized that it wasn't a mountain at all. It was an aviary. An aviary of which I have never seen before in scale, size, or design. The caged mesh was a thick see-through material that was held together by a simple maze of massive steel bars and poles. I could barely see what was inside but it appeared to be real mountains and foliage. All the mountains on the landscape were in reality giant, city-sized cages where they kept their alien captives and the one we were heading to had our name on it.

The speeding hovercraft never slowed down as we approached the base of the aviary. I thought Os-Gouvox's driver had failed to apply his brakes but I noticed that we were headed to a circular opening built into a tall wall that encircled the base of the enclosure. I looked up and it seemed as if the aviary went up for miles into the sky. I couldn't even determine where the sides of the aviary ended upon the horizon. The aperture towards which we approached flashed a brilliant, bluish-white light just before our hovercraft zoomed through. On the other side of the opening was a virtual paradise. Real mountain ranges spanned the landscape and were covered with an abundant array of colorful plants and flowers. A huge, majestic waterfall fed the valley from the northern side of the enclosure and emptied into an enormous, crystal blue lake. I was surprised to see other forms of wildlife as well. I spotted deer grazing in a meadow, flocks of birds sailing through the misty sky checkered with crossbars of the aviary. Giraffes, monkeys, bears, hippos, and other wild animals that must have been captured by the Eszok - they ambled throughout this alien-made environment completely oblivious to the fact that they were light years away from their real home.

"Wild animal park, eat your heart out," I said aloud. It was ironic, really. A race of creatures imprisoning another race of creatures in an environment that resembled their own world...like a zoo, except the humans are the ones under scrutiny. I shuddered at the thought of how low the Eszok must consider our race. As humans, we know we're not in our natural environment cause we know we've been stripped away from our home planet. So no matter how cozy and earth-like you can make our new home, it can never feel like our real home. They must think that we're too unintelligent to know the difference. Boy, were they wrong.

Our hovercraft drifted across a number of small hills of vegetation before it came to a small clearing that was scattered with giant boulders and several small trees. Os-Gouvox steered the craft into the clearing and guided it to hover a few feet above the ground. He grabbed his staff and made a broad gesture in front of our cage. As if by magic, our cage rose into the air and floated delicately over the side of the hovercraft. When we came to a soft stop six feet over the ground, Os-Gouvox waved his staff again and the bottom of our cage dropped out spilling our bodies unkindly into the clearing.

"Welcome to your new home," Os-Gouvox announced. "You have everything you need to survive – food, water, and shelter."

"What, no TV?" scoffed Marlene.

"You can't just drop us off like old luggage," I said, my voice sounding a little more frantic than I liked. "We'll die out here."

"You will not," Os-Gouvox said without hesitating. "The Eszok designed these enclosures so its occupants will survive for many years. You will thrive…if you mate with each other."

Everybody looked around at each other and instinctively made the same sound.

"Ewww!"

"You are interesting creatures, and the most valuable on Zuu. You are one-of-a-kind. We will have need of you in the future."

"For what?" I said, but my question went unanswered. The snooty robot turned his back on me and started pushing buttons along the dash of his hovercraft. "You can't just leave us here. We don't belong here! WE ARE NOT ANIMALS!"

It was like I was speaking to the wind. Os-Gouvox's hovercraft had lifted and sped away before I even finished my plea. My mind was racing on about what to do, what to say, and what to find to survive in this weird wilderness. I wondered if watching that Survivor show would have taught me some techniques on how to survive out in the wild world of nature. I had no idea how to make two sticks and a rock spark to make a campfire. Where would we find food? Would we eat wild berries and fish for the rest of our lives? Are we going to live in caves like Neanderthals and make clothing out of animal pelts? Were we going to be forced to (gulp) mate with one another? I couldn't stomach the thought. We stood gaping at each other, alone and dumbfounded, completely unaware and lost in a paradise world.

"Well, this sucks," Jade said unexpectedly. I thought she would be in a frail mood, but ever since we discovered that we weren't going to be eaten, she seemed a little more together.

"My parents always said I belonged in a zoo," Marlene joked. "I guess they got their wish."

"How can you joke at a time like this?" I groaned.

"I think this whole experience is opportunistic. It's all how you look at it. If I live through it, that's cool. If I die, that's cool, too. Better to be killed off by an unknown alien life form on a distant planet instead of a typical car accident or a boring natural disease. How many people can duplicate that? I just think of it as a grand exit to an otherwise dull and uneventful life."

"You're sick," said Cindy bluntly.

"It's pronounced 'eccentric'."

"The only grand exit I'm interested in is the one that leads back to earth," I said. The moment, I finished my sentence, something weird happened. My head felt like it had swooped downward and upward in one swift motion, but when I looked around I saw that I hadn't even moved. The sense of sudden motion within my head made me feel like I had just ridden a roller coaster and I was now stumbling out of the exit gate. I staggered next to Alex but managed to hold my balance.

"Whoa, dude, are you alright?" Alex said, bracing my arm.

"Yeah, yeah, I…I don't know. I guess I'm a little light-headed. I'm alright," I said as the world stopped spinning. The truth was, I wasn't alright. There was now a significant throbbing at the top of my head. It wasn't particularly painful, but it wasn't very comfortable either. I just knew that it didn't feel right and I wanted the sensation to stop.

"Jarvis, your nose is bleeding," Jade said with concern. "Did something hit you?"

I didn't believe her at first because I hardly ever get nosebleeds without a reason. I don't have sinus problems and I definitely don't remember getting hit in the face in the last few hours. Bruised ribs, yes, but a blow to the face? No. I lifted my hand and wiped a meaningless trickle of blood away from my nostril. It was hardly anything to worry about. I was more worried about the throbbing in my head.

"Hmm, that's weird. Did any of you guys feel weird when we left earth?" I asked everyone. "I mean, did you feel a little dizzy right when the ship went into warp?"

Everybody shook their heads.

"I thought I would feel a little off, but when I think about it, I didn't feel anything," Alex said.

"I thought you guys would feel a little something," I said, feeling somewhat isolated.

"You know what?" said Derek. "Actually, I did feel a little something."

"What? What did you feel?"

That was when he did what any dumb jock would do. He farted.

"Oh, never mind," he said with a smirk. "All better now."

Some people laughed but I just rolled my eyes at him, considering that he was just a bad joke himself.

"I'm glad you find our little situation so amusing, Derek," I said to him with a straight face. "But it wasn't nearly as funny as when that animatronic guy shot lightning into your gut. That was a real hoot."

Derek's smile immediately fell.

"That's ok," said Derek undauntedly. "When the time is right, he'll get his." He made a fist and punched it into his hand. "I promise."

"For real, Derek?" my sister said. "I don't think a simple beat down is going to take that guy out."

"No, Jade," I said in a mock supportive tone. "Let the caveman do his thing. Let's see him get his butt kicked again. If I could do it, I'm sure a robot could, too."

"Jarvis!"

"What did you say, loser?" Looked like I hit a nerve.

Derek didn't want to be reminded about our little scuffle which seemed so long ago, but in actuality, was only yesterday. "Who kicked whose butt?"

"I'm just saying, if you want to win a fight, you don't do it by lying on the ground throwing your fists around like a little brat."

"Dude, you want to start something NOW?" Derek took a few ominous steps toward me. I didn't know what I was saying. I should have just shut up when I had the chance, but I was so irritated by him making a joke of our dire predicament. This was serious stuff. We could die out here, and here he is farting and making light of it? *Really?* He came toward me with his chest puffed up like a proud Rhode Island Red and balled up his fists. "Don't think I'm going to back down for round two."

"You guys, knock it off," I heard Cindy say.

"So beating me up here, stranded, on another planet, is going to help us...how?" I said.

"It won't," Derek growled. "but it'll make me feel a lot better when your head is between my hands."

"Yeah, right, you'd probably rather have it between your legs!"

That did it. Derek was on me before I could even get my hands up. He tackled me to the ground and as we wrestled, dirt and rocks were kicked up into the air. He tried to put me in a headlock while I tried to pull him off me. I bet we looked like a couple of third graders fighting over who won a checkers game.

"Derek, stop it!" Jade yelled. "Jarvis, get off of him!"

I could tell Marlene was looking on with an uninterested leer.

"Testosterone rears it ugly head once again," she said.

At one point, Derek had me on my back and Cindy and Jade took that moment to pull him off of me. Alex ended up restraining me, while the girls tried to pacify Derek.

"This is stupid! Stop! Why are you guys fighting?" Alex shouted at us. "Simmer down!"

"Tell that to this crazy nut," I said, dusting the dirt of my clothes. That stupid jerk made me bite the inside of my cheek and I could taste the metallic flavor of blood on my tongue. Great! Now the inside of my cheek will be sore for days. I looked at Derek and the others and just saw a blur of shapes and colors. My glasses were gone! It's amazing that they've stayed on my face this long without getting knocked off. Now this little tiff with Derek could have broken my good pair of eyes and render me blind for the rest of my stay on this screwed up planet. If I find that he put so much as a scratch on my glasses, I'm going for round 3, even if I am going in half-blind. I groped around for my glasses, fuming about Derek's brutish demeanor, when someone kindly handed my spectacles to me.

"Oh, thank you."

When I put my glasses on, I was shaken to see myself grinning right back at me. I jumped back, astonished and breathless.

"What the...clone! Clone!"

It was! An honest-to-goodness, real live clone…of me! How did they do it? They must have snatched some of my DNA on the ship when we were on that conveyor belt contraption thing. It was disconcerting to see another me, almost like watching yourself in a dream. I scrambled backwards as my clone laughed to himself and waved to everyone with a slightly goofy attitude. I heard everyone gasp in shock except Derek who used his favorite cuss word to express his surprise.

"Awesome!" exclaimed Alex. The clone of myself leapt from its spot and landed on a ten-foot tall boulder. This clone must have been granted superhuman powers cause there's no way I could've jumped that high.

"Oooo, newbies," it said with my voice. As if witnessing a real, live clone wasn't strange enough, something even stranger happened. It changed! As it stared at us, the clone of myself morphed into a creature that resembled a chimpanzee except its head was unmistakably feline with huge, teal-blue eyes and long, spear-headed ears that split in two. Beige, smooth fur covered it's entire body and was mottled with small areas of black and blue and its tail, which was much longer than its crouched body, displayed a thick tuft of fluffy hair at the end. It stared at us with an over-exaggerated sense of curiosity and when it spoke, a row of sharp, small fangs flashed in contradiction to its eager behavior. Naturally, we all screamed.

"Back! Get back!" Cindy shouted while running to the back of the group. But the creature didn't seem to understand or care about our apprehension of his arrival. He landed boldly on the ground in front of us and studied us with wide, inquisitive eyes.

"Where you from, newbies?" the creature asked in a friendly, squeaky voice. No one said a word. We were still getting over the shock of its transformation.

"How..how did you do that?" said Alex finally.

"Do what? This?"

The creature looked at Alex and instantly morphed into a clone of Alex, dark eyebrows, tan skin, and all. Alex blushed as the creature spoke in his voice, "Me is an Echolakian. We morphers."

The creature morphed back into its furry self and took another step toward us, prompting us to take another step back. We didn't know what we were dealing with.

"It's a freakin', talking, body-snatching space cat," said Derek.

"It's a shapeshifter!" Alex corrected him. "I can't believe these things actually exist." It was now obvious that Alex was one of those socially elusive guys that found more pleasure in role-playing games than in human association. I remember seeing him in the yearbook a year ago as being part of a chess club, which is a notorious synonym for World of Warcraft lovers. He already admitted to being a gamer. He was probably beginning to dig this crazy planet just as much as Marlene. Cautiously, he took a step closer to the little creature. "So, you call yourself morpher?"

"No," the creature replied. "Me morpher. But me name

is Nuvu."

"Hi, Nuvu. I'm Alex. We're from earth."

Nuvu cocked his head curiously.

"Earth? What earth?"

"Um…it's our planet. Is there more than one?"

"Do not think so. Not heard of it." Nuvu raised his hand and touched Alex lightly on his arm. He seemed to be a little confused. "Where is fur?"

"We don't have any," Alex chuckled.

"You are cold?"

"Not really. That's why we wear clothes." Alex flapped the edges of his jacket. "See? Clothes."

Nuvu inspected his fabric then turned to the rest of us. "You animals look funny."

"Speak for yourself, Pikachu," snapped Marlene.

"Is they your clan?" he asked him.

"My clan?" Now it was Alex who looked confused. I guess he didn't know how to answer that one. "Well, no. Maybe. I don't know. We're all human. We come from the same planet."

Nuvu suddenly turned to Alex and stared at him. I didn't know it was possible for his eyes to get any wider, but they did. They got scary big. I thought they were going to fall out.

"You? You human? All of you?" he started to tremble with excitement, his huge, pointy eyes shivering with energy.

"Yes, we are."

Nuvu jumped ten feet into the air and did an impossible

display of flips, somersaults, and cartwheels. He squealed and sang as if it was his birthday and received the greatest gift in the world. The six of us just stood and watched dumbfounded.

"Alex, what exactly did you say to him?" Jade said.

"I don't know," Alex said, grinning happily. "Maybe he's never seen a human before."

Nuvu finally calmed down and skidded to a halt in front of us. He seemed elated to lay his eyes upon us.

"Me found you!" he said breathlessly.

The chirping of the birds on their leafy perches overhead was all that broke through the abrupt silence of our group. None of us had expected this little alien feline to say something like that. Found us?

"What do you mean found us?" I said. "You've never seen us before. Did you know we were coming?"

Nuvu looked like he was about to say something, but one of his ears flicked backwards and he slowly turned to face the valley before us. He stood motionless as if he was about to pounce on something. Then he turned to face us. His face, once full of eagerness and excitement, was now owned by a look of utter fright.

"They is coming," he said dreadfully. His tone literally made the tiny hairs on my arm stand up. I had no idea his voice could sound that deep. He could change the sound and tone of his voice as fast as he could change his looks. I looked past his head into the valley beyond. Nothing but picturesque landscaping that you'd see on a blissful postcard from Yosemite or Hawaii saying, "Wish you were here." Nothing seemed out of the ordinary. What was this thing so afraid of?

"Who is coming?" Alex whispered to Nuvu.

His question was answered when a small gathering of large, capsule-shaped ships emerged from behind the tree-lined ridges in the valley. They floated toward us, a mini-army of speeding, winged blimps that were producing a low humming almost similar to the gigantic ring-ship that invaded our school. As the ships approached, Nuvu scurried behind Alex's legs as the rest of us found ourselves huddling together as well. I had to admit that I was very intrigued about what was coming our way. What could be worse than what we went through already? I heard Nuvu make a little whimper and gulp hard. He pointed upwards to the gloomy ships and clearly stated the name of our new visitors.

"Eszok."

Chapter 6
A VERY BAD FIRST IMPRESSION

Honestly, I didn't expect to see the vile reprobate that hosted our kidnaping to visit us at such an early moment in our arrival. We didn't even have time to put on our make-up! Well, I suppose it's better this way. We can get the formalities out of the way so we can spit in their face and begin to devise a way to escape the clutches of our captor...or captors. I still wasn't' sure if this Eszok was a single creature or a group of creatures. By the looks of our new visitors, I'd say it was a group of beings and they must call their whole collective the Eszok. I found myself staring with uneasy trepidation at the floating capsules that began to descend to the ground only meters away from us. Fear tingled and danced across my skin as the nearest capsule halted a full three feet above the ground releasing a stream of exhaust from both ends of its elongated body.

"Jarvis?"

The fear in my sister's voice was obvious. I swallowed hard and struggled to keep my heartbeat at a decent pace so I could at least appear to be calm. I think I failed.

"It's okay, Jade," I said unsteadily with almost a puppy's whimper in my voice. "They just want to see what we look like."

"Then I hope this is just a photo shoot."

As soon as the words left her lips, the front of the capsule's surface popped forward and folded over itself a number of times releasing light wisps of blue smoke from the interior of the ship. The demure humming of its movement ceased as it revealed the innards of its contents to us. I was momentarily distracted as Nuvu scrambled behind me and tied himself around my legs, staring at the visitor's ships with eyes that resembled mini-planets.

"Eszok," he said again, basically introducing them to us.

The capsule opened up to what looked like a viewing platform from which dark, lumbering shadows milled about aimlessly. I held my breath as one of the shadows came into the light and revealed a sinister and deformed creature that was clearly unfriendly. The first thing that struck me was the fierce glare that projected out from underneath its thick, furrowed brow that made a vertical V-shape from the bridge of its nasal openings to the back of its head. It was dramatic and so drastic that it made the poor creature look like it was forever angry or disgruntled that someone had bashed its face in with a heavy saucepan. It's foggy white and pupil-less, beady eyes were set in a tall, oval-shaped skull that was humanoid and covered with pale, languid skin. They were ferociously thin but covered themselves with bulky clothing that were adorned with lace, shiny objects, rich fabrics, and other fashion articles that I've never seen before. They must've been about 7 feet tall and their lanky arms were way too long for their bodies. For some reason, I felt a sense of sadness for them because they seemed so frail and crooked. But there was something in that cold gaze that told me they did not need or want my sympathy.

There was a wickedness present in them that made me want to run and hide. I had no idea who or what they wanted to do with us, but at this point, I knew whatever it was, it could not be good.

"That is the ugliest alien I have ever seen," Jade said, pretty much summing up everyone's thoughts.

"And to think, it had the nerve to reproduce," said Cindy. "What kind of universe do we live in?"

Cindy cowered next to Derek and whispered over to Nuvu who wrapped himself around my knees.

"Nuvu, make them go away."

But I could feel every muscle in Nuvu's little body trembling uncontrollably.

"*You* make go away," he said. Then he jumped into Alex's arms and buried his face in his chest. Alex peered up at me then turned his gaze to our new visitors.

"Why is he so afraid of them?"

I looked at him with a lost expression.

"I guess we're about to find out."

And instead of staring back at the Eszok like little mute hamsters, I took a deep breath, waited for my stomach muscles to settle down, and decided to speak first.

"Um...hi. Hello."

My voice sounded so small that I wondered if they had even heard me. Evidently, they did because they all stopped moving and snapped at attention – all eyes were on me.

"Um, my name's Jarvis. I'm from Earth. Uh, you probably

already knew that, huh?"

The eerie aliens refused to respond.

"We were wondering...um...could you...uh, could you...please...send us back home? I don't think...I don't feel we belong here."

The transplanted elm trees that surrounded our enclosure rustled in the wind, but the aliens still didn't make a sound.

"Maybe they don't understand you," said Jade. "We're the one with those ear implants, not them."

"They have to understand us," I said back at her. "They're the ones that made them."

I continued to press on, hoping the sincerity in my voice would ensure our freedom.

"We're just a bunch of high school kids. There's not much we can do for you. We don't know any government secrets or anything. We just want to go home. Can you do that for us? Please?"

There were a few moments of silence when I felt that they had actually listened and were considering options. The empty silence was disrupted by a small rock that landed lightly at my feet. As I bent down to pick it up, an odd assortment of hissing sounds emanated from the Eszok's capsule. I stood back up and looked at the stone, thinking that maybe there was something special or unusual about it. That was when another small stone struck my left arm, followed by the annoying symphony of muffled hissing. Marlene instantly read my mind.

"They're laughing at us," she stated bluntly. "They think we're some kind of freak show."

"Throw it back at them, Jarvis," Derek shouted. "They're the freak show!"

And without warning, Derek picked up a good-sized stone and chucked a beautiful pass straight into the Eszok's compartment, striking an unlucky observer square in the face. Unpleasant squealing echoed from the capsule as passengers in the other capsules seemed completely surprised. Derek proudly dusted his hands off amid the sudden commotion.

"Winning pass of 2018," he said smugly. "That's for you, Coach Williams."

"Boy, are you crazy?!" I shouted at him.

"Oh, no. Not good. This not good," Nuvu moaned, holding his head in his hands.

"They want a show? I'll give them a show," Derek gleamed as he threw another rock at an unfortunate, slow-moving Eszok. "Winning pass against the Cucamonga Cougars."

Nuvu went ballistic. He had to stop Derek before the fool started to enjoy himself.

"No, stop! You must not do this!"

"Hey, if they're going to throw rocks, they're going to get them right back."

Derek pitched another stone and hit one of the poor creatures right in its beady, white eye. It jerked its hand up to its injured eye where blue liquid began to gush between its slick fingers. Nuvu tackled Derek and tied his hands together with his rope-like tail and shouted in his face.

"STOP THIS! You must not to do this! They will take you to Grarg!"

Derek was just about to knock our little friend senseless when the small armada of flying capsules began to depart. One by one, the pill-shaped ships shut their viewing platforms, powered their ultra-modern engines, and drifted over the top of the trees. The Eszok had had enough excitement for one day. The sound of their whirring engines faded away as the sound of Derek and Nuvu's struggle became more pronounced.

"Get off me, you little creep!" Derek groaned as he pushed Nuvu away.

"The Grarg. They take you to the Grarg!"

"What's the Grarg?" Cindy asked.

"Fighting. Lots of fighting."

"So it'll be like a theme park for Derek then," I said, still not knowing exactly what Nuvu was talking about.

"Shut up, Jarvis," Jade spat. "This sounds serious."

Instead of arguing with my little sister, I was going to ask Nuvu about this Grarg business, but I was interrupted by the loud arrival of a large, snail-shaped pod that came soaring into the clearing like a flying buffalo. It was armed with an arsenal of thick, wide cylinders and projectiles on its sides and resembled a scary conch shell ready for battle. Pure white and blotches of black sheet metal covered its bulbous carriage as massive prongs and wires of dark steel hung out from beneath its body.

"What the hell is that?" Alex shouted.

"Probe!" Nuvu yelled. "Run! RUN!"

We didn't need to be told twice. We scattered like a human firecracker, fleeing in completely different directions. However, one of us didn't move fast enough. The probe came directly toward Derek and caught him without even trying. The dark steel prongs from under its carriage reached out and pinned Derek to the ground. The prongs slithered around his immobile body and rendered him helpless within its python coils.

"Oh, God," he screamed. "You guys, help! Get me out of here!"

Nuvu heeded his call first by leaping onto the coils of the probe just above Derek's chest.

"Hurry! We must free him!" he shouted as he started tugging on the huge mechanical tentacles. Like a whip, Nuvu's tail snapped out towards my waist and wrapped itself around my torso. I didn't know how to help Derek being in this position, tied up like a burrito, but it didn't matter at this point. I was in trouble, too. The probe was already heading into flight and was taking Nuvu and I along with Derek's body. A sense of panic swept over me in an instant. Derek got himself in this scrap and now I was literally being dragged along with his punishment. Talk about déjà vu.

"Jarvis!"

I heard Jade scream my name and rushed toward my hands

and squeezed them with an unholy grip. The probe hardly resisted and began to take all four of us for a ride. Jade reached further up my torso, my face at her belly button and her face buried in my stomach. Next thing I knew, Alex grabbed a hold of Jade's waist and Cindy had grabbed onto Alex's waist. With all this added weight, the probe refused to slow down. It lifted us higher into the air, a human chain dangling from its chassis, and began to fly towards the entrance of our enclosure.

"Hey, you're not leaving me behind!"

Marlene ran up behind the flying probe with the human tail, leapt valiantly into the air, and just barely clutched onto Cindy's leg. The probe slowed to just a fraction of its original speed from the unexpected added weight, but its sleek engine powered up and sped across the natural landscape while Cindy screamed at the top of her lungs.

"I hate heights," she hollered.

"I hope you hate dying more," Marlene shouted from below. "Don't you even think about letting go!"

I could just imagine how strange we looked: six kids hanging from a flying conch shell. Only in outer space, folks. As we tightened our grips on each other's torsos, the probe sailed across the valley and headed straight toward the entrance that our robotic escorts brought us through only moments before. The same bright flash suddenly filled the circular opening and our ride went straight out onto Zuu's open landscape. The probe picked up so much speed that our human chain was now practically horizontal with the ground level below us. I could hear a couple of screams and grunts while our bodies swayed with flag-like precision in the air. I just knew someone was going to lose their grip and end up as a morbid tree decoration on the spiky woods down below.

After several minutes of being connected to each other in a dangerous high-speed flight, it was a miracle that not one of us fell to our doom. Our probe zipped over a rocky landscape that seemed to meld into a stadium-sized dwelling. The center of the building sunk in towards the bottom like a deflated cake and from its middle loomed a gigantic, ramshackle building that jutted out into the sky in all directions. It looked as if the building was frozen in an explosion with a countless assortment of tubing, vents, pipes, and slabs of dark metal sticking out of its lower region. Nuvu scampered through the metal coils of Derek's shackles and shouted down to us.

"Grarg! Let go! Let go!"

But the thought of letting go was absolutely absurd. We were too high off the ground!

And then Marlene fell.

I heard her voice trail off as we neared the edge of the low-lying building. However, there was no splat, no thud, or sound of crunching bones to signal her landing. I was relieved to only hear a slight grunt and a curse word. I looked up (or back, or whatever position I was hanging in) and saw that we were closer to the roof of the building than I thought. As soon as the others realized it was safe, they let go of each other one-by-one tumbling like a bunch of circus acrobats. I saw Nuvu unravel himself from the probe's coils where Derek remained captured.

"We will come for you," I heard Nuvu say before he leapt through the air and landed safely near our group.

The six of us stood on top of the odd building analyzing the outrageous structure that loomed in front of us. The teen-catching probe approached a small, flat area on the Grarg structure and hung motionless in mid-air as if it was waiting for someone to let it in. Sure enough, a strange opening collapsed in on itself along the surface of the Grarg leaving a passageway to enter. It did so without hesitating. The opening filled itself up again and the probe and Derek were gone.

"Derek!" Jade shouted, her eyes welling up with tears. "Where did it take him? What's it going to do to him?"

"Isn't it obvious?" Alex said. "He threw stones back at the Eszok. He retaliated. He's going to be punished somehow."

"Punished? Derek doesn't deserve this."

I couldn't help but give a huff in disagreement.

"I beg to differ," I said. Suddenly, Jade turned on me.

"Shut your mouth, Jarvis! You don't know anything about Derek!"

"Girl, are you serious? You dated him! I know enough. I know he likes to harass the general public to boost his morale. I know that aside from stealing kid's lunch money and starting pointless fights, he's obnoxious, self-centered, and aggressively stupid. What other pleasant qualities am I overlooking?"

"For one, his father beats him."

It felt as if sound had been sucked out of the air. Jade's statement forced everyone to freeze and listen.

"What do you mean his father beats him?" Cindy said quietly. "His father's a sheriff. That can't be true."

"Oh, no, girl. It's true. I've seen the battle scars. No one falls down the stairs that many times. I know football practice can be brutal but they're still wearing protective gear. He has bruises all over his arms and back."

"How did you see all these bruises?" I asked, knowing that their outings together could have been more intimate than I would have liked. My suspicions were confirmed when Jade gave me a "you-know-how" look. I cringed and shook it off. "Never mind!"

"Did he tell you his father was beating him?" Alex asked.

"Of course, not," Jade squealed. "He's a guy. He would never admit to being the victim. But I've seen how his father treats him, how he belittles and insults him, makes him feel like he's worthless – like he's not good enough. I've seen him get smacked once, but I had a feeling that he was holding himself back. I had no doubt that he would let loose on Derek once I was out of sight."

I immediately thought back to when his father picked him up from the principal's office on the day of our fight. He smacked him on the back of his head without warning. Was that merely a preview of what was really going on in the Simmons' household? Were things much worse behind closed doors? I had no way of knowing.

"So, in turn, he displaces his frustration with his father by making other kids his victims?"

Jade thought for a moment.

"Well…"

"So not only is he a thick-headed jock, he's a nutcase as well. For real, Jade, what in the world did you see in that guy?"

"I saw what was inside, Jarvis," she declared. "I wasn't quick to judge him like you. He's a good person stuck in a bad situation. He was in trouble. He just didn't know how to fight his way out of it."

Marlene nodded as she scanned the group.

"Kind of like the rest of us right now."

We glanced around at each other, wondering if we were all thinking the same thing. How could someone attack their own flesh and blood? It reminded me of a tragic episode I experienced in my personal life. No one attacked me personally, but I saw it happen. And I felt like it was my fault. But I didn't like thinking about it and, as usual, I pushed it out of my mind. We had a new problem facing us now and I was afraid of what everyone was thinking – that we save Derek.

In the back of my mind, I somehow knew that I would be faced with a moment like this: save the life of your nemesis. It's one of those self-fulfilled prophecies where if you concentrate on a certain act or event that *could* happen in your life, that act or event *would* eventually reveal itself as a reality. I always thought that type of psychology was very interesting, but right now, I wasn't digging it. I just wanted to go home and find myself waking up in astronomy class. And, unfortunately, the possibility of all these crazy events of just being an extremely vivid dream was no longer valid. This was real. And if things were really as bad as they seemed, then our main concern was how to survive and get back home.

The first step, though, is to keep the group together.

I sighed deeply and rolled my eyes.

"Fine," I said with a dash of defiance. "We save Derek."

Chapter 7
THE GRARG

"Ok, so how do we do this?"

"I don't know," I said, irritated. Why would Alex ask me that? I thought he was the one that had all the answers. He seems to be the smart one out of all of us. "I've never led a rescue operation before. By the way, we can't forget about Cadzow."

"Cadzow?" inquired Nuvu.

"Yes, she's our school principal who's currently taking the ultimate cat nap under the Gatekeeper's possession. Do you know how to get to the Gatekeeper's…base or compound?"

"Gatekeeper does not want to be found," said Nuvu simply. "Gatekeeper will find you."

"Ok, that's just creepy."

"Creepy or not, what does he want with her?" said Alex. "That Gatekeeper guy said that she had information that needed to be extracted. What does that mean?"

"Brain probe," Jade said flatly. "They're going to stick a small pole up her nasal cavity and suck her brains out."

"Now why would they do that, Jade?" Alex said. "It's clear that they're not interested in eating our brains. You got aliens mixed up with zombies."

"Not to eat them, to examine them."

"I don't think so. These aliens seem way too sophisticated to do something so primeval as pulling brains out through the nose. They could probably do something a little less invasive."

"Or more painful," said Cindy. "They don't seem to be very people-friendly."

"Whatever they want with Cadzow, it can't be good," I said. "So we need to save her somehow."

"Right, I agree," said Alex. "But we have to save Derek first."

"And we don't even know how to do that," I sighed. "Man, we're in trouble. Any bright ideas anyone?"

The group looked lost and confused. However, Nuvu popped up into view, his colossal eyes full of helpful advice.

"Yes," he said happily. "We slide."

Nuvu must have hit his head when we landed.

"We slide?" said Cindy, who was just as perplexed as the rest of us. "Slide on what?"

The furry and wiry creature hopped to the edge of the building and pointed downward.

"Slide," Nuvu said hopefully. I looked at the group who were just as startled as me.

"You're joking, right?" Alex said leering over the precipice. "The friction alone would set our butts on fire."

"Into Grarg. Only way in."

"What is he talking about?" Jade asked aloud.

As I glared down the sides of the bowl-shaped roof, I began to understand what Nuvu meant. This bowl acted as a deep foundation for the Grarg and there appeared to be large ducts or openings that led into the base of the bizarre structure near the bottom. The surface of the bowl was smoother than glass so sliding down was a possibility. But what, exactly, would we be sliding into?

"I don't know, Nuvu." Skepticism was all over my face. "It looks kind of dangerous to me."

As if avoiding danger was an issue anymore.

"No, it is safe. See?"

In one bold leap, Nuvu jumped off the ledge and was sent hurtling down the side.

"Nuvu!"

Cindy's scream was completely ignored as Nuvu rocketed down the steep slope of the Grarg's base. He seemed totally at ease and looked like he was actually enjoying the ride. A twist and a turn later, he waved back at us to follow him and then disappeared into a large air duct.

"You gotta be kidding me!"

"That's freakin' awesome!"

"That's freakin' nuts!" I rebutted. "We don't even where that leads."

"Well, he does," Alex said, pointing to where Nuvu slid inside the Grarg.

"We don't know who or what he is, Alex. For all we know he could be working for the Gatekeeper or that crazy mechanical dude, Os-Gouvox. He could be a shape shifting, man-eating alien leading us to his den for a late afternoon snack."

"Really, Jarvis? I think we're past the man-eating alien

thing. They're just not interested. Besides, did you see how scared he was when the Eszok approached us? He's terrified of them. He wouldn't boldly go into this Grarg thing if he knew they were in there. He's just eager to help us."

"I don't know, Alex," Marlene stated. "For someone who knows all about alien overlords and evil wizards you sure are trusting."

"Hey, it's either this or wait for another probe to pick us up."

The rest of us glanced at each other, realizing Alex' last line was the deciding factor.

"See you at the bottom."

Alex stepped off the ledge and fell like a rock. Although he was moving at break-neck speed, he was in full control of his body, as if he was just riding down the playground slide. Cindy groaned.

"Oh, God. I don't think I can do this."

"I can," said Jade with conviction. She stepped in front of us and lowered herself to take the monstrous slide of death. But I wasn't having it.

"What do you think you're doing?" I hissed at her.

"I'm going to save Derek. What are *you* doing?"

"Trying to keep us alive, Jade. We need to find a way to get back home."

"We can do that after we get Derek."

"How is Derek more important than our survival?"

"So you're just going to leave him here?!"

I hesitated for a moment. I knew I wasn't that cruel. So I changed the subject.

"You're my responsibility, Jade. Not Derek. He got himself in trouble. That was his fault."

"Do what you want, Jarvis. I'm gone."

And before I could even snatch a lock of her hair, she zipped down the side of the Grarg.

"Jade! Jade!" I shouted. I knew she could hear me, but there was no stopping her. She had already made up her mind. Her body rushed down the smooth surface and into the dark air duct.

"Dagnabbit! Why are little sisters so hard-headed?"

"Aw, what the hell?" Marlene said flippantly lowering herself onto the ledge. "There's a first time for everything."

"There's also a last time for everything, too."

I think Marlene was just as bad as my sister. She'd do whatever she wanted regardless of what you say to her. Except Marlene will do it without any thought of her own well-being. That kind of worried me.

"Hey, it could be a new way to go."

"Don't say that."

"Like Alex said, Jarvis," she said putting her legs over the side. "It's either this or the probe."

She pointed to our left where a different probe, bigger and much more fiercer than the previous one, was making its rounds on the perimeter of the Grarg. It was still too far away to see us but if we hung around long enough, we'd be its next catch of the day.

"See ya."

Marlene pushed herself off the ledge, sliding down the side of the massive bowl and into the air duct within a matter of seconds. I turned to Cindy who looked paler than Marlene.

"Ok, Cindy, we gotta jump. We can do this. It's just an enormous version of a playground ride."

"I get sick just riding the swings," she moaned. She grabbed my hand and I recoiled on contact since her palm was moist with sweat. But I sympathized with her fear and refrained from pulling away.

"You ready?" I asked.

"No," she whimpered just as the giant probe spotted us. A hum of electrical power filled the air as it suddenly jolted into our direction.

"Jump!"

It was a shock to find out just how fast those probes were. As the slick surface of the concave roof ran up our backs, the "Mama" probe was only inches away from our heads. It felt like we were sliding down an oil slide as the angry coils of the probe swished back-and-forth behind our heads trying desperately to capture us. Once we neared the bottom of the bowl, our speed suddenly increased! It didn't make sense at first because normally an object would slow down because of friction and come to rest, as science has proven. There was a strong, forceful suction that pulled us into the duct. Once we were inside, we were practically airborne and found ourselves sliding upwards instead of down. We fumbled over each other like two stuffed animals tumbling through a wind tunnel.

Our journey came to an abrupt end when our bodies flew upward and crashed into a meshed ceiling. A huge fan roared in our ears from the other side of the monstrous screen as we were pretty much glued to its surface along with debris and skeletal remains of other unlucky flying creatures.

Then a hand grasped my wrist and began pulling me to the right. I grabbed Cindy's wrist with my other hand and within a few moments, the others had dragged us both to safety. We stood on the ledge catching our breath, staring down the long wind tunnel we had just survived from.

"You know what?" Cindy smiled. "That was actually kind of fun."

"Well, cherish the moment," I said, my stomach doing still surging from side-to-side, "cause we are *not* doing that again."

After hearing her spineless moaning about slides and getting sick on swings, I was surprised to hear her say that. I was also surprised to hear a loud, earth-shattering roar overwhelm the roar of the fan. All of us jumped and shrieked, urging Cindy's growing bravado to take a nose-dive.

"What was that?" I shouted.

Nuvu turned and said something to the group but no one could hear anything over the loud roaring of the fan. He scrambled further into the tube that we were standing in with an upbeat and skittish gape. The rest of us hesitated as another terrifying growl ripped through the tight space of our dim surroundings. Alex, who still possessed an eagerness to venture into the unknown, followed Nuvu without question. Jade had Derek on the brain so her blind loyalty surpassed her fear and urged her on. Marlene didn't care where she was going, just as long as she was going *somewhere*. That left Cindy and I, the two scaredy cats, at the back of the line again. I was beginning to see a pattern.

"Ok, Cindy, we're going to have to grow some backbone," I told her as we made up the tail end of the group. "We can't always be bringing up the rear."

"I know, I know," she whined. "We have to be strong and courageous."

"Well, that and the chances of being picked off like lame sheep in a herd are higher when you're at the back of the group."

Cindy gave me a sideways glance.

"Nothing like a little pep talk to keep the mood light."

My ears perked up at her first attempt at sarcasm.

"Oh, so she got jokes? I'm sorry, little lady, but I'm not very good at sugar-coating reality. I tell it like it is."

"So, what do you think this Grarg thing is?"

"I don't know but it looks like it's someplace where people and other beings are taken against their will," Alex stated with his voice of discernment, which I now found slightly irksome. "Since the aggressive probes that proceeded to immobilize our friend, Derek, brought him here, I think it's safe to assume that this building *is* the Grarg. And as Nuvu pointed out earlier, there's lots of fighting that goes on here. So, I'm assuming that Derek will be thrown into some kind of fighting arena with other aliens."

Cindy and I looked at each other dumbfounded. Everyone else was stunned as well.

"Have you been here before, Alex?" I asked him. "You sound like a documentary voice-over."

"Just an educated guess," he said modestly, shrugging it off.

We trekked further into the dismal passageways of the depressing Grarg. Every corner we rounded looked exactly like the last. I could tell we were getting in deeper cause there were different sounds coming from the grates in the walls. Strange screechings and squawks and grunts and moans came from other prisoners all around us, but that giant roar we heard earlier had stayed silent. Then my ear focused on a voice. It was a familiar robotic voice, unfriendly and devoid of any emotion.

"Sssshhhh," Nuvu said as we moved past a wide grate. Unlike the other grates we passed on our journey, we could see through this one. It was at shoulder height and on the other side was that cool-looking, triangular shaped transport that Os-Gouvox gave us a lift on. Funny, it looked much more appealing when you're not caged up on its deck. I actually wouldn't mind having one parked in my driveway someday. But instead of admiring its streamlined angles, I became focused on its militant, mechanical driver.

Os-Gouvox had stepped off the vehicle and had landed into some kind of loading bay. There were several other unusual robots loading and unloading cargo from weather-worn minor ships that were docked in the bay. These robots seemed somewhat different from Os-Gouvox in that they showed some degree of human nuances and manners. They were very adamant about their work and kept eyeing Os-Gouvox as if they were afraid of him, like he was their boss from hell. Os-Gouvox paid them no attention since his gaze was transfixed on a tall figure that loomed over him. It was the Gatekeeper, but it wasn't really him. It was a giant hologram. The alien's body fizzled and was full of white static, almost like a television image. I guess they didn't have HD on this planet yet. As we walked by the air vent, we could catch what they were saying.

"...is not where they're supposed to be," I heard the Gatekeeper's hologram say. "The scouts sent a probe to capture one after it attacked them and brought it to the Grarg."

"Yes," Os-Gouvox said respectfully. "Unit 4 notified me of its capture. I came here to retrieve the specimen myself. From what I understand, these are very important creatures."

"The most important species this planet will ever see, Os-Gouvox. Their very existence determines the future of this planet. I can't have my prized possessions tainted in any way."

"I understand, Gatekeeper."

"Do you? Shall I remind you of our precarious condition the next time you raise your staff against one of my humans?"

The uppity robotic figure paused before he responded. It seemed that the Gatekeeper didn't like Os-Gouvox messing with his cargo. He must've somehow seen Os-Gouvox stick Derek with his staff earlier on the transport.

"I...I was merely illustrating his inferiority."

"Unacceptable! You will not cause these creatures any further undue harm. It's bad enough that one of them has been taken to that disgusting Grarg and the rest are missing."

Os-Gouvox humbly bowed his head and crossed his digits in front of his face. From what I could tell, it looked like some sort of sign of submission.

"Yes, Gatekeeper."

"As a Sarok, you have a duty to capture and return them to their enclosure before the Eszok Hi'are arrives. If you don't return them in time, Cadzow may have to suffice."

"Cadzow?" Os-Gouvox seemed slightly confused. "But Cadzow is..."

"An excellent substitute and I do not feel that I have to warn you not to question my actions!"

The Gatekeeper glared at him so severely that Os-Gouvox felt impelled to avert his eyes.

"Yes, of course, Gatekeeper. It is *your* decision."

"Are your instructions clear, Sarok?"

"Find the humans and return them unharmed."

"Before the second sun rises!" the Gatekeeper added angrily. "You must understand that in order for this planet to survive they must be contained by that time. I trust you will not fail me."

Os-Gouvox bowed again and crossed his fingers in front of his face again.

"I exist only to serve you, Gatekeeper."

The Gatekeeper's three-dimensional hologram flickered then disappeared without a sound. Almost immediately, Os-Gouvox flung out his staff and released a bolt of energy at the same exact spot where the Gatekeeper's hologram was just standing. All of us jumped back as we watched him parry the staff above his head and slam one end of it upon the ground. Many of the robots in the loading bay paused in their work and turned to watch him.

"Say what you will, Gatekeeper," he said to himself. "I will deal with these beasts my way!"

I heard Alex gulp.

"That's really not a good thing to hear, is it?" he whispered aloud.

"Can we go now?" Cindy hissed.

Cindy had the right idea. As Os-Gouvox exited the loading bay into the Grarg, we shuffled further into the maze of air ducts hoping and praying that we'd never run into that homicidal bucket of bolts. I guess we didn't hope and pray strong enough.

It's an absolute miracle we didn't get ourselves hopelessly lost in the Grarg's air conditioning system. There were ducts that were freezing and others that were sweltering hot. After awhile, I began to think that Nuvu was lost himself, leading us blindly into a never-ending maze.

And then our path ended.

The air duct led straight to a massive vent opening that was located above a huge, circular chamber. The chamber looked like an enormous arena where several concentric rows of suspended cages surrounded a large space of dirt and alien remains. Then we heard the roar.

"RRRAAAAWWWRRRR!"

We saw where it had come from and it wasn't pretty. From our high vantage point, we could make out two grotesque alien life forms in the high walled arena. One was a burly, two-legged, towering creature that was covered in brown, raggedy fur and sported a long, thick trunk from the top of its head. I could've sworn it was a two-legged elephant. It was currently up against a smaller, arachnid-like creature with five, scaly legs, no visible eyes, huge horns, and a bad temper. Even though I couldn't make out where its face was, it hissed incessantly at the taller creature and was in an uncontrollable rage. The creatures and aliens in the cages were rowdy and excited, cheering on the battling creatures like they were watching a boxing match. Directly above the concentric rows of cages was a stark white circular level that consisted of nothing but robotic figures and machines that displayed no sense of enjoyment. They were in a closed box section walled with a thin layer of glass and were busy tapping buttons and moving tiny devices on a table that doubled as a computer screen. I couldn't really understand what was going on.

"What in the world is this?" Jade whispered loudly to the group.

"It is the Grarg," Nuvu stated. "Bad captives are caught and brought here."

"Bad captives?" Alex turned to Nuvu. "So Derek is a bad captive. They're going to make him fight that?"

He pointed to the monstrous creatures that quarreled in the arena.

Nuvu nodded sadly. "He must fight...then die."

"The plot thickens," Marlene said, slicing through the dread with her deadpan drawl. The crowd below us suddenly threw a rage of excitement when the mammoth biped creature gained a victory over his opponent. The winning contender used its muscular trunk to grab the opponent's body and brought it down forcefully to the arena floor. Pinned and dazed, the spidery alien released its final squeals just before its opponent smashed its head flat with its hefty foot. A sound similar to that of a gigantic cracking egg filled the room as a greenish-yellow ooze splattered upon the floor. The sound made me cringe, Cindy gagged, but the crowd of caged aliens roared with approval.

"Interesting," Alex said to himself. "This fascination with violence must be a universal phenomenon."

"Yeah, I guess humans aren't the only ones cursed with

this imperfection," I said as the aliens in the audience cheered with their odd, warped voices.

Amid the incredible noise, the bellow of a weird, foul sound blared above our heads. We covered our ears and looked up to see an extraordinary contraption suspended high above the arena floor, the box level of robots, and our vent opening. It was a spherical machine that possessed a macabre assortment of racks, pulleys, conveyor belts, and gears that sprawled across a ceiling that couldn't be seen. Among the unearthly branches of this nightmarish device were a number of aliens clasped tightly in the grips of different probes. The probes themselves were actually a part of the machine as the bulk of their shells fit snugly into specific alcoves of the machine. The probes were identical in size, style, color, and design but each one held a different prisoner, including one that everyone had recognized.

"Derek!"

Jade's shout was completely drowned out by the rowdy audience, but Nuvu and I covered her mouth anyway. Derek showed no sign of hearing my sister, but he was obviously more concerned with escaping from his unfortunate predicament. The machine hummed a wicked sound and rotated downward to the floor. It stopped about ten feet above the ground when one of its probes uncoiled itself releasing its prisoner into the ring. Derek tumbled clumsily out of its grip and scrambled to his feet ready to defend himself. A hush fell upon the crowd as if someone had simply turned down the volume. Some observers slowly stood up and appeared to be in awe of what they were seeing.

"A human!" one of the creatures shouted.

The crowd quickly developed into another uproar. The robots that were in the glassy white level seemed slightly surprised at Derek's presence in the arena, but they merely nodded to one another then continued to twist nobs and tap buttons on their dashboards again. It seemed as if Derek's appearance stimulated a frenzy of cheers and jeers from the audience, but it was the bellow of the elephantine champion that demanded the attention of the room again. The frightening roar made Derek jump comically into the air. He spun around and caught sight of the massive alien that stood only meters away in front of him. I could easily read his lips from where we stood.

"Oh, my God!"

It was then that I was truly concerned about Derek's welfare. I couldn't stand the guy, but I didn't want him to die either. No one deserved to be trampled to death by a two-legged elephant. Derek was a well-built athlete, formidable, and agile. But in comparison with this monster, he looked pathetically vulnerable. And with what Jade told us about his personal life, he seemed almost pitiful. A sting in my heart hit me when I thought what this creature could possibly to do him.

The giant beast suddenly charged him causing Derek to burst into a panic. He took several steps backwards and stumbled over the broken carcass of an indescribable animal that had lost a previous battle. We felt the vibrations of the alien's hooves slamming against the ground as Derek rushed to his feet and ran. Fortunately, the bodies of previous losers were not disposed of and the giant rib cage of an unlucky contender was settled into the sandy arena floor ahead of him. Derek dove in between the rib cage and scampered to the other side just as the alien elephant bore down upon him. Poor Derek looked like a frightened little mouse fleeing from a hungry housecat. I had to restrain Jade from running out of the vent escape and blowing our cover.

"We have to do something," she cried. "It's going to kill him!"

"Not yet," Nuvu said.

Derek screamed and cursed at the rampaging beast as it attempted to break its way through.

"Get away from me!" he screamed.

The frustrated pachyderm from planet X then wrapped its thick trunk around several ribs of the rib cage and pitched the whole thing into the air with one thrust. With Derek inside, the rib cage soared across the arena and landed with a thud on the other side of the ring. I know it may sound cliché, but literally, the crowd went wild.

Derek's body tumbled out of the wreckage and I had feared the worst. He looked completely lifeless. The alien elephant bounded over to Derek and lifted its gigantic foot to crush him out of existence. We screamed as it brought its foot down…and cheered once we saw that it had missed. Derek had swiftly rolled onto his right side narrowly escaping the prospect of being the creature's new footwear. He rolled back and the alien elephant raised and lowered his foot again, missing Derek's body as he rolled to his left. The creature roared in frustration nearly bursting my eardrums.

Derek's contender raised his foot again, but this time, and quite by surprise, Derek did something smart. Before he rolled back to his spot, Derek briskly grabbed one of the large broken ribs and stabbed it into the ground with the tip sticking straight up. The alien didn't have time to react or change his footing. It brought its hoof down to crush Derek and instead impaled itself onto the broken rib. An ear-splitting squeal similar to nine inch nails scraping across a chalkboard echoed throughout the arena as the alien reared back in pain.

Now that he had the upper hand, Derek grabbed another gigantic rib that was almost shaped like a spear and headed for the creature's other leg. He gave himself a running start, held the rib like a javelin, and then threw it directly into the alien's knee. The creature bellowed again, along with the rapturous crowd who was enjoying the battle immensely.

With both of its legs injured, the alien elephant wobbled backwards into the slick innards of the creature it had destroyed earlier, slipped on its entrails, then fell flat on its back skewering itself on the dead creature's pointy horns. The earth shook under the weight of the creature slamming onto the ground. I even saw Derek have to balance himself after the shaking stopped.

The crowd exploded into a unified cheer.

Derek had won. He stood in awe of what he had done, gasping to catch his breath. He was stunned, speechless. Whereas Jade was practically in tears having screamed and jumped after every move he made in the fight. She was so out of breath, it was as if she was in the battle herself. My attention to my sister and Derek was quickly disabled when a bullhorn wailed above our heads again. Nuvu jumped into action.

"Quick! Get Derek now," he shouted as he jumped out of the vent and into the bright, white level of robot controllers below. "Before new alien comes, get Derek now!"

The horn that we heard signaled that a new contender was to be chosen and caused the Grarg machine to roar into motion. Huge wheels and booms rotated as cylinders pumped and probes circulated above the hanging cages. The noise was deafening along with the shouting audience. All I could think of was getting out of there to save my hearing.

Jade was two steps behind Nuvu and when she jumped down into the crowd of working robots, the reaction was just as I suspected: pure panic. The robots burst into a melee of confusion when they caught sight of humans entering the room. They were already surprised at the sight of one human in the arena. Imagine their surprise to see five more specimens squeezing in between them in their pure and untainted environment. I just hoped none of them had the same agenda as Os-Gouvox. I began to wonder though, what was so special about us? There must be a hundred different species on this planet, yet everybody goes ballistic when they see a human? Why is that?

My mind stopped wandering when I noticed several short and stocky creatures clambering down the sides of the arena wall. I couldn't tell where they came from. It was like they just appeared. We were about to climb over the side of the pristine robotic workstation into the arena when Nuvu saw them.

"Kergs!"

I didn't know if that was an alien curse word or the name of the aliens, but their appearance caused Nuvu to move double time. He nimbly jumped over the heads of robots to get to Derek.

"Derek! Derek!" Jade screamed climbing down the wall toward the arena.

Derek heard Jade's call and turned to look up in our direction. He looked lost and bewildered, very similar to that frail young man that faced an angry father just the other day. Jade's voice was the guiding light that brought a genuine smile to his face.

"Jade!" he shouted. He couldn't get to where Jade was fast enough. He leapt over debris and body parts to get closer to her.

Nuvu pounced onto the wall that surrounded the arena and let his tail drop along the side so Derek could climb it.

"Derek, climb up on Nuvu's tail," Alex shouted.

Derek caught sight of Nuvu's tail just as he took notice of the stocky creatures climbing down into the ring after him.

The thick-skinned and short-legged aliens were adorned with a dark blue hood that covered theirs heads and shoulders. Their skin was amber and wrinkly and they had gigantic hands that were twice the size of their head. I couldn't really make out their face cause they were so agile and quick. When they landed on the ground, they dove into the sand like it was a swimming pool. It was as if the sand was water when they moved through it. They burrowed underneath and came straight towards Derek who was, once again, in another run for his life.

Huge mounds of sand maneuvered themselves around the bodily remains within the arena and were quickly closing in on Derek's position. Although Derek was a seasoned athlete, his running speed could not match that of these burrowing creatures. I was sure his upper body strength would bring him up to safety in no time, but could he reach Nuvu's tail in time? His hand reached out to grab Nuvu's ten-foot long appendage, his fingers merely inches away from their destination. But they never reached their target.

A stupendous force harnessed itself around Derek's midsection and violently pushed him backwards. He was tackled by something that came up out of the sand.

"No!" Jade screamed.

At first, Derek seemed dazed when he landed flat on his back. He looked down at his waist at the half-size alien and saw the snarling countenance of what Nuvu called a Kerg glaring up at him. He clenched his fist and struck the creature's face, but even

I could hear his fingers crunch on contact. The Kerg didn't even flinch. His face must've been made out of stone. Derek cried out as a startling flash of light struck the middle of the arena floor. It was a familiar energy blast that originated from a familiar weapon – the staff of Os-Gouvox.

Every individual in the room – robot, alien, and human – responded to the blast. The robots suddenly began to fight their way out of the workstation. I guess they were just as scared of Os-Gouvox as the aliens were. He did appear to be the head robot in charge of everything. And it seemed to me that he reveled in everyone's fear of him. He stood on the opposite side of the arena where he stood calmly assessing the situation. His eyes, which were large slits on his headpiece, now had bright, red dots peering out of them. The way he was pointing his staff directly at the Kergs - it was obvious that he meant business.

"That human goes with me," Os-Gouvox announced. But the Kergs had no intention of obeying him. The Kerg that tackled Derek picked him up like a bean sack, threw him over his shoulder, and scowled at Os-Gouvox without a hint of reverence.

"Come and get him," it growled. The Kerg slammed its giant fist into the ground causing a massive sinkhole to form in front of him. The other Kergs jumped into the swirling sand and disappeared before Derek's captor jumped in after them. We caught one last look of Derek reaching out to us and calling out but the flowing earth swallowed him up and he was gone within seconds.

"DEREK!"

Jade's scream gave away our location immediately. A blinding blast exploded on the arena wall in front of us. Os-Gouvox had seen us.

Our group high-tailed it out of the arena by climbing back over the wall into the raiment white workstation, but I had to pry Jade's fingers from the top of the arena wall as she continued to cry out for Derek.

"Jade, come on! We gotta go! That robot's coming after us!"

"No! Derek! He's gone!"

Tears were rolling down her face. I've never seen Jade act like that before. She was completely distraught and I felt a rise of panic in my chest partly because a mad robot was after us and partly because I felt like I was losing any feeling of control I had over the situation. My sister was going to get us killed because she was crying over some half-wit kid.

My thoughts were shattered when another energy blast from Os-Gouvox's staff exploded above our heads. However, this blast was different as it seemed to have been deflected from an invisible force shield. I suddenly felt a claw-like grip wrap around my arm from the most bizarre alien I've seen yet.

"Both of you, this way! Now!"

The alien ordered us to leave with such force that we felt more than impelled to obey. The voice snapped Jade out of her crying fit and brought her to the reality that Os-Gouvox was indeed shooting at us. Os-Gouvox then leapt up onto the alien's cages and was making his way toward us like a creepy, mechanical crab, scaling the swaying holding cells with much ease.

With a face that resembled a kabuki theatre performer, I wasn't ready to argue with this new creature that came to our rescue. It was about my height, lithe and thin, and dressed in a long, flowing cloth that was imbued with light orange and brown earth tones and textures. There were beads, leather-like bands, and stones fashioned into its garments and around its neck and it was covered with shimmering tattoos that echoed technological designs. But its face is what made it so odd. I could have sworn it was a mask but I know I saw its lips move. The mask was fixed underneath a headpiece that resembled the cap of a shitake mushroom. And hearing that its voice was definitely feminine, I had briefly assumed that she was a wild woman from another world. It occurred to me that it wasn't the wisest thing to listen to a strange alien, but when you're being shot at by a bloodthirsty mechanical man, the only thought that matters is finding a way out.

Jade and I rushed up the stairs and up onto a promenade that stretched around the arena area. There were robotic figures of all sizes rushing this way and that, sounding like a car construction factory, but our group stuck close together, practically scared stiff among the parade of machines that scuffled around us, not knowing which one of them was among Os-Gouvox's entourage. When the alien that saved us appeared to the rest of the group, Nuvu leapt into her arms.

"Mioli! Oo-sa-bee!" he squealed. Apparently, they had met before.

"Nuvu! Un chana ga kek!"

"E-sinki!"

After that odd exchange of unrecognizable words, Nuvu took off down the promenade and turned left into a wide corridor.

"Follow Nuvu!"

The alien ordered us again and everyone obeyed with no questions asked. Like a herd of frightened sheep, we moved as one throng past angry and confused figures, tall and short, thin and fat, all members of a robotic society. After seeing the incredible variety of artificial intelligence on this planet, I began to wonder if there were whole worlds that consisted of nothing but robots.

Our escape route down the corridor seemed safe enough until a whirling sound accompanied by an explosion erupted above our heads. Debris from the ceiling rained down upon our heads but the cinders did nothing to slow us down. Os-Gouvox was on our butts and would not stop until we were in his cage again...or hanging lifelessly as a hunting prize on his hovercraft. I took a chance to glance back as we turned a corner and saw him and two of the teal-colored guard bots with the scythe-like heads flanking him on both sides. They had their built-in weapons aimed at us and did not hesitate to fire at will. Lucky for us, they were bad shots.

Another left turn brought us to the loading bay we saw earlier from the air vent in the wall. The other "worker" bots had disappeared and had left Os-Gouvox's transport completely unattended.

It was obvious what the alien wanted to do, but she told us anyway.

"Board the ship!"

"You want us to steal Os-Gouvox's car? Are you crazy?" Alex blurted out. "He probably has some kind of protective device on it."

"Look out!"

Jade's scream caused everybody to duck just in time as a beam of purple light shot across our heads and ended the shelf life of several cargo containers. But the alien that Nuvu called Mioli did not cower. She rushed toward the robot that shot at us from the transport and raised her hands in defense. The robot aimed his bulky weapon at her and fired again. Although his aim was true, the blast did not touch Mioli. Her hands put up a sort of protective barrier that deflected the blast and shot it right back at the bot blowing him to pieces.

"Whoa!" I exclaimed, "how did you do that?"

"It's nothing compared to what you'll be able to do."

Huh? What did that mean?

I hardly had a second to form a question about her comment when another blast exploded just feet away from our...well, feet.

"In the ship! Now!" Mioli shouted.

"I'm gone, sista!" I ran up the gangplank in a flash.

The rest of us followed with Mioli bringing up the rear

almost magically deflecting the shots fired from Os-Gouvox and his guards. That was when I saw that she was holding some kind of hand pads that projected a force field around her arms. She was moving fast enough to deflect the blasts by warding off every single shot.

Once the gangplank lifted up off the ground and sealed itself shut, Mioli jumped onto the controls, flipped some switches, hovered her hands over some blue lights, and immediately turned the ship into "get the h-e-l-l out of here" mode.

We all clasped onto a part of the transport and braced ourselves for the sudden jolt of speed we knew was coming. The sleek carrier hummed and vibrated smoothly then floated quietly off the floor and pointed itself toward the huge loading bay door and the wonderful outside world. A barely noticeable "ting" pierced the air as the scenery around us changed in the wink of an eye. The bright, crisp breeze stung my skin as the sight of unusually shaped trees and mountainscapes zipped by calmly. Thanks to our freaky looking friend, we had escaped without a scratch.

Chapter 8
THE WAY THINGS ARE

There was no way to tell how far we had traveled in Os-Gouvox's "car". It was faster than any car I had ever seen or heard of. Maybe it was more appropriate to consider it as a plane, but it wasn't truly airborne. It just hovered several feet off the ground like a hovercraft. But hovercrafts on Earth don't do 0-200 mph in 6 seconds like this one did. Although I was somewhat confused about what kind of vehicle we were riding in, I also didn't care. What was important was that it took us out of harm's way before harm could even touch us.

God bless this ship!

Almost 20 minutes had passed after we had left the Grarg and no one had uttered a word. Whether it was the shock of seeing Derek being dragged underground by goblin aliens, being shot at by malicious robotic life forms, or being at the mercy of some strange alien creature that knew how to drive Os-Gouvox's car, our minds had to take more than a few minutes to figure out what was going on.

I began to consider our little group of kidnaped kids as a small band of reluctant refugees. Here we were, officially on the run from some motorized men that wanted to either destroy us or return us to that grim reaper they called the Gatekeeper. What did the Gatekeeper want to do with us? He mentioned that we were too delicate to send on a normal transport to our enclosure and that we would soon find out why were taken from Earth. Did we ruin our chances of finding out by leaving our enclosure? Or did we save ourselves from a danger that would've cut our lives short?

Then I remembered Miss Cadzow. Poor Miss Cadzow. I felt guilty that I had completely forgotten all about her. Poor thing looked like a corpse about to be led off to her gravesite. Thank goodness she was alive! She probably had better survival skills than we had. Everyone at Langhorne High knew about Cadzow's high-ranking position in the US military. She was somewhat of a hero during the Gulf war and received a number of medals for extraordinary performance in the line of duty. What she did exactly is somewhat of a mystery, but the fact remains that she was trained to survive in situations like this. We're just high school students who barely know how to survive puberty.

Cadzow was now in her early 60's, but she didn't look a day over 40. Her smooth, taut, milk-toned Asian skin did not submit to old wrinkles or crow's feet. She wouldn't allow it. It was either her restrictive lifestyle or her infamous diet of wheat grass shakes, chicken, and walnuts that kept her looking young. Her most noteworthy trait was her ill-humored behavior toward kids that would step out of line. She was notorious for ripping into people when they did something wrong, but she exercised mercy when mercy was due, such as the case with Derek and I. People considered her to be a mean, old hag, but I think she was just asserting her position as the law of the school. She maintained order and made sure you stayed within that order. How could anyone not respect that? Man, I hope she's ok.

My thoughts of Miss Cadzow's welfare made me think of Derek's predicament as well. I just couldn't bring myself to accept his death as something real. I felt like I was watching a movie. I've never seen anyone actually die before except maybe that little dog my mom ran over a few years ago. Even then I didn't see him actually die because the little stray was taken to the animal hospital where he was put to sleep. Derek was taken away in an instant. Just sucked down into the netherworld of an alien planet. I could hear Jade's sobs over the hum of the hovercraft but she stopped sniffling a while ago. Maybe the thought of his death was starting to sink in. Or maybe she just decided to be her positive self again and entertain the possibility that maybe Derek wasn't dead. Whatever the case, Mioli must have been reading my mind because without warning, she casually turned away from the guidance systems of the hovercraft and faced everyone on deck.

"Your friend is not dead," she stated without a hint of doubt. "He was taken by the Kergs."

The sound of Mioli's voice seemed to awaken people's senses as we all began to mosey out of our secluded spots on the hovercraft and gather in front of our new guide.

"Kergs? Is that what those creatures were that pulled him underground?"

The watery crackle in my sister's voice told me she had been crying silently to herself.

"Yes," replied Mioli. "They took him to their caves though

I do not know why. The Kergs do such strange and suspicious things. They live in the honeycomb caverns of this planet but they will sometimes emerge to the surface to cause trouble, skirmishes and such, and take items back down into their caves such as your friend from the Grarg."

"But, why? What are they going to do with him?"

"Who's to say? The Kergs do things like that because they feel they are stealing from the Eszok. They will do anything to sustain their constant enmity with the Eszok. They hate their presence on their planet."

"So this isn't the Eszok's planet?" asked Cindy.

"No, they are merely using the Kerg home world for their own purpose in detaining as many alien species as they can find."

There was a short pause.

"Who are you? How do you know so much about all this?" asked Alex.

"Forgive me. I am Mioli. I am the matriarch of the Kembeqri. I mean you no harm."

"You're not working with that crazy robot that's trying to kill us?"

"Robot? What is a robot?"

"Are you kidding me? That guy made of steel and metal who has a vendetta against us."

"You mean Os-Gouvox? I am sorry but you use terms I am not familiar with. He is known as a zoid. He and all of his kind are called zoids."

"Whatever," I said. "We just need to know if we're safe with you."

Nuvu scampered up onto my shoulder and kindly patted me on the head.

"Is ok. Mioli good alien. Very good."

I guess that decided it then. If the space monkey liked her then I guess she was ok in my book. Nuvu leapt off my shoulder and transformed himself in mid-air into a beautiful, vulture-like bird that exuded sea-blue tail feathers and a transparent wingspan that had tiny, white circles all over them. He flapped his delicate fairy wings and landed at Mioli's feet, making her look like a heavenly and benevolent savior from a mysterious world.

"You have nothing to fear from me. Nuvu and I are old friends," she said with just the right amount of angelic softness to convince everyone. "The only thing you need to fear is the Zuuminion. They will never stop hunting you."

"The Zuuminion?" said Jade. "Now, what's the Zuuminion?"

"I will explain everything. It looks like we've arrived at my habitat."

For the first time in the last 30 minutes, I put my head up and noticed our surroundings. The scenery had completely changed. We were no longer on the plains of a vast field of boulders and warped, sparsely grown trees. Instead we were in the middle of a wildly overgrown forest. Trees with trunks as wide as houses jutted out of the ground at different angles reaching for the planet's sunlight in unorthodox fashion. They grew at 30°

angles twisting their way up towards a sky that was practically blotted out by its dense canopy of turquoise blue foliage. Although other trees were shaped like mile high carrots, their sheer size and grandeur presence were more intimidating than the giants of Sequoia National Park.

As our hovercraft rounded the exposed roots of a massive twisted tree, the entry port to Mioli's habitat appeared. The caged surface of her enclosure stretched up beyond the treetops and faded into the leaves above. One tree had grown so close to the entry port that it damaged one side of its circular entrance, deforming its shape and invading its surface with a lemon colored vegetation. Unlike our enclosure where a blue flash preceded our entry, there was none when we entered Mioli's realm. It appeared that this entry was in disrepair and forgotten and the security device no longer worked. At least, that's what I had assumed.

Our mode of transportation glided at a considerably slower speed traversing the imposing landscape that surrounded us. Mioli lowered our vehicle in a clearing that was unusually flat and devoid of plant life, as if it had been cleared for flying vehicles.

I thought that was kind of weird. This wasn't Mioli's "car". She stole it, yet she knew how to drive it. We're in this immensely dense space forest that's more convoluted and twisted than brain tissue and, BAM, a nice, little landing strip for the stolen car. I don't know why but I turned to Alex. I was beginning to acknowledge a connection with him, that we had the same insights on certain situations such as this one. As if on cue, he looked at me at the same time with a hint of apprehension in his eyes.

"This doesn't feel right, does it?" I asked him.

"No, it doesn't," he said flatly. "Mioli, how is it that…?"

"I know how to pilot a Seership if I'm not part of the Zuuminion?" She sounded as if she had been insulted. "Because my people designed and built these ships with their own hands. Anything that has been built by my species is imprinted in our blood. Even if we've never seen it before, we'd know how to control it if it was created by my people."

"And your people live here, in a forest, where there is an endless supply of high tech spaceships and hovercrafts?" asked Alex sarcastically. I guess he could hear the fishiness in her story, too.

"I was adopted by the Kembeqri long ago, when I was a youngling. I was separated from my species when the Eszok brought my family here. They were taken to the Eszokian Hesh, a type of artificial home world for the Eszok, but I escaped and have avoided the Zuuminion's detection my whole life."

"So what is the Zuuminion?"

Mioli's tone changed immediately from informative to accusatory in three seconds flat.

"How can you not know what the Zuuminion is by now? Is it not clear? The Zuuminion is our enemy."

"Um, could you be a little more specific?" Marlene asked.

"Os-Gouvox, the Gatekeeper, all of their zoids; they are the Zuuminion. They control and oppress every living creature on this planet using the machines my people created. Under the rule of the Eszok, they have manufactured a literal army to operate this planet and keep hundreds of alien species as their prisoners."

"Why would they want to imprison so many different aliens?"

Mioli turned to Cindy with a sense of foreboding in her voice.

"Because they are looking for something that emanates from all species: an all-powerful viku."

"A what?" said all five of us humans.

"A viku," Mioli looked around at us, surprised that we didn't know what the sam hill she was talking about. "You do not know what a viku is?"

Silence.

"Then I have much more explaining to do. Nuvu?"

In bird form, Nuvu spread his amazing wingspan and fluttered a few feet from Mioli's visage. "We're going to need a different transport. Do you mind?"

The shape-shifting creature flitted down from the Seership and landed in the clearing below us and started rounding circles. He was pounding the dirt with his claws and scratching the stones with a sense of urgency. Suddenly, Nuvu lurched forward and fell face first on the ground. His body bubbled and stretched, shedding countless feathers. He squawked and his mouth froze in mid-squawk and his jawbone shrunk to almost nothing. Four appendages began to grow along his sides that resembled split hooves of a giant deer. His body rose upon its masculine, brawny legs and widened out while sprouting a long, split tail. What he ended up becoming was practically indescribable - before us stood a massive, furry beast with a head similar to that of an anteater. His body was abnormally muscular and had a broad back that was wide enough for us to ride on - all six of us.

"We must head toward my clan's settlement. We have much to talk about and there may be probes scouting this area. I'm positive they will be looking for you." Mioli made her way toward the exit ramp of the Seership. "Come. Nuvu knows the way."

Needless to say, more than a few of us were very reluctant to climb on the back of a giant and bizarre animal that we've never seen before. Then Alex reminded us that it was merely Nuvu in one of his many forms and that feeling of anxiety seemed to fade away. Nuvu seemed to be a young and innocent alien that was eager to be our friend. His genuine interest in assisting these new creatures called humans baffled me. I couldn't understand why we were so unique and important in the eyes of the Zuuminion and why Nuvu was in our habitat in the first place. As far as I know, there's no creature like him back at home. What was he doing in our enclosure? Was he put there by mistake? If so, I was kind of glad the Zuuminion made that mistake. Nuvu took out a lot of the mystery of our first few hours on Zuu and made a gallant effort to save Derek's life. He was worthy of our trust. So when he changed into a larger-than-life beast of burden, I was considerably comfortable following Mioli onto the crest of his back. He had his left hoof raised where we could easily climb onto his back and straddle his soft spine. Alex, Marlene, and Jade climbed on without complaint but Cindy's nerves still held her back. Through some brief coaxing, Cindy finally made her move and climbed aboard.

Nuvu, who was now our enormous mode of transportation through the forest, made little grunts and snorts on our journey. I asked him if he was okay carrying everyone, but it appeared he could only speak when he's a certain type of alien. The journey itself was a surprisingly calm one. There were no robots – well, zoids - chasing or shooting at us, no monstrous aliens looking for a fight, just a relaxing ride through a magnificent strange forest. Birds that sang the most unusual songs glided gracefully above our heads. Creatures with scaly skin, shaggy hides, and bulging eyes glared at us from every corner of the forest but resisted any attempt to make contact with us. They just watched us from afar, just as mesmerized by our presence as we were with theirs. It was shocking that such a familiar setting could be so outlandishly weird. The landscape was similar but the styling, the sounds, the smells, and the colors were completely different and brilliant! It was more beautiful than any forest I've ever seen on earth.

It was clear that Cindy was not as receptive to the forest's beauty as I was. Her eyes darted back and forth at the slightest sound and she kept biting her nails and spitting them out on the ground, practically leaving a trail of breadcrumbs.

"I don't get it, Cindy," I said as I twisted around to speak to her. "You're a cheerleader. You get thrown thirty feet up into the air, do flips, splits, and almost defy the laws of gravity. You're a stuntwoman afraid of her own shadow. What's the deal?"

I could see Cindy squirm slightly from embarrassment.

"I don't know. I guess it has something to do with my mother."

"You're mother?"

"Yeah, she always pushed me to do cheerleading. It was her thing, not mine. She won all these awards and scholarships when she was my age. I guess people who live in small towns back east have nothing better to do over the weekend except to go to high school functions. I guess it's like going to the movies for them. They're either going to a game, a dance, or a dinner hosted by the Birchwood High Cheerleading Squad. They organized everything so everyone in town knew who they were. Being a cheerleader was like being a celebrity."

I could hear the disdain in Marlene's voice. "Isn't it, though? I thought you looked down on us mere mortals?"

"No! At least I don't. I know Brittney and Samantha are stuck up snobs, but most of us can't stand them anyway. They give the rest of the squad a bad name."

"Hmph, whatever," grunted Marlene.

"But what does your fear of the world have to do with your mother?" I said.

"Well, I wouldn't say I have a fear of the world," Cindy said, then gave a shrill yelp when a flying, glowing insect buzzed past her head. She then continued, "I guess I just wasn't prepared for it. My mother wanted me to be one of the best cheerleaders in the state, go to the nationals, and all that. So she trained me, disciplined me, put me in classes from the time I was 6. I guess I was kind of smothered in a bad way. Cheerleading was first, life and growing up was second. I think I did a head stand the day after I was potty trained."

"How did your dad feel about all that training? He wanted the same thing?"

"My dad died when I was very young, I think I was 10 or 11." I noticed Cindy's voice drop an octave lower. I looked back and saw that she looked distracted, her gaze kind of spacey. Her voice began to sound sad and I could tell immediately that her father was a sensitive subject.

"Um, you don't have to talk about..." I started to say, but she didn't stop.

"He had a massive heart attack. He wasn't even that old. I don't remember that much about him. One of the two main things I remember about him was that he gave the most amazing hugs. He was kind of thick so it was like hugging a giant teddy bear - warm, fuzzy, firm, confident, secure. I remember when some boy at school threw a chicken nugget at my head and everyone laughed at me. I cried all the way home. But when my dad hugged me, I forgot all about it, and he took me out for ice cream. I don't ever remember my mother doing anything like that."

"You said that you remember two main things about him. What was the other?"

"He always called me Little Feather."

"Little Feather? Was your dad Native American?"

Cindy giggled a little bit. "No. It was just that my mom was called the Eagle Queen because she could always fly so high when they tossed her in the air. Even though my dad said I could grow up and be whatever I wanted to be, he still called me Little Feather whenever I was in uniform."

"That's sweet," Jade said quietly. "My dad used to call me JJ Fad. I think it was some old music group from the 90s."

When Jade would mention my father, it was another delicate subject, especially for me. If Jade had known the truth about our family history, she would not be so chipper in divulging certain details. There were events in our past that I hate to talk or even think about. I was afraid that Jade would lead into more subjects about our father, so I changed the subject to something else.

"There's a lot of things I'd like to call you, too," I told Jade brusquely. "Too many to pick off the top of my head right now."

Jade sighed, annoyed that another bicker battle was imminent.

"Thank you, big brother, I can always count on you to remind me of my troubled childhood memories," she said sarcastically. I didn't know if she was joking or not, but it still irked me when she said "troubled". From what I could remember, Jade was a spoiled brat.

"What are you talking about?" I snapped at her.

"Well, it's not like you've always been the perfect big brother, Jarvis. My first day in high school was no picnic. It wasn't like being on another planet, but I did feel out of place, like I didn't belong. Everyone was so much bigger and more confident than me. I thought I'd never fit in. You could've been there to help me find my place."

Seriously, I had no idea where this was coming from. Jade never needed me for anything and this is the first time that I've actually heard a pinch of humility come from her own mouth. She's always been so self-involved and pretentious, but maybe the previous events of our journey to Zuu gave her insight to her faults and gave her the desire to change her self-righteous demeanor.

"What could I have possibly done to help you find your place at a high school?" I said, completely bereft of any emotion. I wanted to believe she would be a modest, humble human being, but I had a bad feeling about this little testimony.

"Nothing," she said. "Absolutely nothing which is what you're so good at doing. I just followed mom's advice to just be me."

"That sounds painfully corny," Marlene mused.

"I know, but, girl, it's true. Once you stop comparing yourself to others, you become you. How do you think I became so fabulous?"

And she's back!

"It's pronounced 'deluded', little girl," I said. "You're only 16. You're too young to be fabulous."

"So speaks the jealous tongue," she replied with her nose in the air. I could have smacked her.

"Do you guys always fight like this?" Alex asked.

"Yes!" said Jade.

"No!" I said in unison.

"One of the benefits of being an only child," Marlene said to no one in particular. "One less person to annoy you."

"I envy you, Marlene," I told her. "Less stress, more bliss."

"Yeah, bliss," she said unexcitedly. "Sitting in a big, empty house by yourself while you're parents are out on another one of their petty romps to Solvang, Club Med, New York, the Bahamas, or France. Of course, they say it's business but who goes to Disneyland on a business trip? Just imagine the countless music videos you can mindlessly observe while stuffing your pie hole with Monster drinks and Top Ramen and no one could give a crap about when your birthday is or who your friends are. Sometimes I wonder if they even realize they had a kid. Yeah. Complete and utter bliss."

Marlene was just morbid. From what I could tell, there's nothing you could do to make her enjoy the sunshine that could be shining right in her face. She's just moody.

"Well, don't burst with excitement."

"I know what it's like to have your parents gone away all the time," Alex said to Marlene. "They're never around when you need them. It's like they don't…"

"I wasn't asking you to sympathize with me, trophy boy," Marlene barked suddenly. "My point was that life sucks and you can't do anything to make it better!"

Everyone's hair stood up when Marlene made her outburst, even mine, and I don't even have hair! But Alex was the only one who seemed to be unfazed.

"So hiding behind black and putting powder sugar on your face is one step toward making your life better?" he retorted, but with a hint of concern. All Marlene heard was a challenge to her style of dress.

"SHUT UP! At least I don't dress like a prep boy wuss from the 80s!"

"It beats looking like a funeral zombie. Besides, Old Navy has fantastic deals on long sleeve shirts. It would be a crime to ignore them. It's one of those little perks in life that you willfully turn away from."

Even though she was sitting two people behind me, I could hear her suck her teeth and huff in desperation.

"You're freakin' hopeless."

"No," said Alex seriously. "I'm hopeful."

Well played, Alex. I'm beginning to like him more and more. He keeps his cool AND is cool. Marlene stayed silent after that. I was kind of grateful, too. It was kind of embarrassing to get involved in all this silly bickering in front of a noble alien. Yeah, I guess I would call Mioli noble. She seemed wise and trustworthy, almost proud of whom she was. I began to wonder what her life was like hiding from the Zuuminion every single day. Along with Os-Gouvox and those relentless probes lurking everywhere, it's a miracle she even survived this long. What kind of life is that to constantly be on the run?

"You're a very loud thinker, Jarvis," she said suddenly. My heart stung in my chest and it felt like it was burning.

"Wh...what? What do you mean?" I stammered, thinking the worst.

Did she hear my thoughts?

"I can hear your thoughts."

Crap.

"You're kidding, right?"

"I can't hear your precise thoughts, but your brainwaves emit a vibration that I can sense. It's unusually strong in your species. From those waves I can get a good idea of what you're thinking about."

"So, you can read my mind?" I said fearfully. I never liked the thought of someone being able to read my mind. A person's thoughts were his own, a private treasure chest that has no key to unlock it. Everyone has their own viewpoints, ideas, or secrets that they may not want to share with the world and I've always felt that it's their right to keep it to themselves if they wanted to. They may also have dark secrets that they do not wish to relive again. And it's for this reason that I felt offended at the possibility that she could read my mind. I DID NOT want to answer questions about my past.

"No, my species can sense your feelings, but we cannot read your mind. There is another alien species that can."

"Which one?"

"It doesn't matter. Os-Gouvox and the Eszok eradicated their species long ago. They were considered a threat and were quickly destroyed."

"That's horrible," said Cindy sadly.

"They were destroyed because of their viku – the ability to read minds."

"Mioli," said Alex, "what is a viku?"

"Every alien species in the known universe has a unique viku. A viku is an ability that only the species from that planet possesses. In the case of my adoptive clan, the Kembeqri, they can control the movement and growth of vegetation."

"So they literally formed the growth of this forest with their abilities?"

"What nature could create in a matter of centuries, they created in a matter of days."

"That's amazing!"

"In the case of my own people, the Koz, we can engineer and control incredible machines that can't be duplicated anywhere in the known galaxy."

"Like that hovercraft, that Seership, we were on?"

"Exactly."

I thought about if for a moment, but nothing was coming to mind.

"So," I said timidly, "what about humans? What is our viku? We don't have any special abilities."

Mioli looked at me curiously, as if I had said

something unusually stupid.

"I've already told you, Jarvis," she said ominously. "Your mind."

I blinked. "My mind? Are humans the only species that have a mind?"

"Of course not. All species have a mind. I've been on Zuu all of my life and have encountered hundreds of different alien species. But there's something unusual about the human mind. I could feel your presence in the Grarg. I knew you were there before I even saw you, all of you. But, Jarvis, yours was the most powerful."

"Probably cause he has a big head," said Jade, killing the mood.

"Shut up, Smurf," I told her, then turned to Mioli. "What do you mean mine was the most powerful? What did you…sense?"

"I don't know. I am Koz so we can actually sense what a person's mind is thinking, just not in detail. Your mind carried a very difficult signature that was hard to process, but it was strong. Humans are extremely rare in the galaxy. I don't know much about you. You're a very mysterious species."

"Mysterious? What's so mysterious about a bunch of teenagers? We're harmless."

"OW!"

Cindy yelped and made me jump.

"Who was that?"

"Something stung me," said Alex as he rubbed the middle of his back. His face was pinched in pain.

"What was it? A mosquito?" said Jade. I couldn't believe it. Did she just say that? Did she forget where we were? When we turned to look at Alex, a small insect that resembled a flying kitten with miniature wings and giant eyeballs zipped out from behind him and flew past our heads.

"A peepsnoot," said Mioli with little interest. "They are a nuisance, but are harmless."

"Felt like a syringe sinking into my spine!"

"A syringe? What is a syringe?"

"It's just a needle-like thing," I said quickly. I didn't want Mioli to get off the subject. I wanted to know more about this viku stuff. "Listen, about this viku business, are you saying that even humans have some kind of ability, that we have a kind of extraordinary brain power thing?"

"It has been known that the viku of some species become stronger, much stronger, when they are taken from their home world. But that is a rare occurrence, even more rare than the existence of humans. Maybe through time, your viku will manifest itself. Have you felt any different since you left earth?"

"Nope," replied Jade.

"No," Cindy responded.

"I wish," grunted Marlene.

"Just a bad bug bite," said Alex.

"Um, no," I lied. I hated to lie. But I didn't want to admit that ever since we were in the ring-ship, I've been feeling a little… weird. It's not like having a cold, indigestion, or gas. But it was like my awareness of things around me had been heightened. My headache was beginning to become unbearable and throbbed incessantly now. I got dizzy spells that seemed to last only a split second, but would leave my head spinning. They would change my mind somehow. I could sense where things were located, how people felt, what time it was without looking at a clock, what certain creatures in the forest were doing even though I've never seen them before, and I even had a slight idea of where Miss Cadzow was. I couldn't explain it, but I knew that she was no longer in the alien compound where we first saw her. There was also something else about her that I couldn't quite put my finger on, as if my perception of her was somehow altered when the Gatekeeper took her away. He said she had information that needed to be extracted. What on earth did that mean?

After I responded falsely to Mioli's question, I knew it was stupid to lie. She already told me she could sense the contents of my thoughts. Although she was facing away from me, I saw her glance back at me with an air of understanding.

"I see," her voice soft yet filling me up with guilt.

She knew I was lying.

Our trek through the Kembeqri forest lasted for another few minutes as Mioli told us about the different species of aliens on Zuu. Words could not describe how fascinated I was with how many alien races that actually existed. There was a species whose viku granted them the ability to shape rocks into whatever form they wanted with their bare hands. Another had the ability to move at a speed so fast that you could barely see them. There was also a species that had the ability to change its physical size at will. It could be as large as an elephant or tiny as an ant with just a single thought.

I found all of this stuff to be incredibly awesome! I had no idea there were other life forms in the universe, but discovering that they could do all of these things was immensely intriguing. I say that cause Alex used the term "immensely intriguing" and I felt that he had summed up my feelings exactly. I was beginning to think that this guy was one cool dude. He was just about as cool as me.

Almost.

My body felt a sudden shiver when Mioli jerked her heard backward and released an odd, terrifying howl. It sounded like a cat being eaten by an owl and it made the hairs on my arm stand up.

Her otherworldly caterwauling was gradually overcome by a disharmony of other whoops, howls, and hollers that seemed to come from the highest corners of the treetops. I looked up and saw thin, gangly figures climbing and crawling down the giant gnarled trunks of the countless trees around us. They resembled humans but appeared to have skin made out of tree bark. As they neared our convoy, I could barely make out their faces. Instead of eyes and a mouth, they had hollow openings that were in a different location on each individual, and they had more than two legs, some had three or four. Even the shade and value of their "bark" skin were a variety of dark earth tones. I could see how these aliens could escape the detection of the Zuuminion since they could melt right into their environment without ever being seen. But Mioli stuck out like a sore thumb, a glowing sore thumb with a flashing light on her head.

Without even turning around, I could see in my mind's eye Cindy trembling like a dry, autumn leaf. I found it interesting how the rest of our group expected the unexpected to happen and no longer cowered when it did. Sadly, Cindy was a late bloomer.

"Do not fear them, human," Mioli said to Cindy right when I was about to calm her myself. "The Kembeqri know nothing about violence. They are the most gentle and life-loving species I have ever known. Their home will keep you safe from the Gatekeeper and his Zuuminion."

"For how long?" Cindy asked with uncertainty.

"That remains to be seen. We will discuss things further, but you must be in need of nourishment. Surely, humans must require sustenance to survive as all creatures do. Are you hungry?"

"YES!"

The response was practically involuntary. Our mouths answered the question before our brains even received the message. It's amazing how you don't realize how hungry you are until someone mentions food. We were so busy trying to stay alive and figuring out where we were that we didn't have time to stop and have a snack. So when Mioli mentioned something about eating, my stomach lurched and my salivary glands were ready for action. Where's lunch?!

Our next meal was only a few hundred meters away – straight up. Yes, these people lived in the trees. It's one thing to look like one, but they also lived in delicate dwellings that spanned the breadth between the forest's trunks and treetops. Some areas had wide walkways that looked like stretched out tree bark while some pathways were just trees on their side with a path cut into them. The trees also sprouted an incredible variety of the most unusual flowers and vegetation I've ever seen. Different flowers grew at this level that didn't thrive on the forest floor. Tree branches twirled into fantastic shapes that resembled peacock feathers and oriental fans and doubled as shelters, common areas, and walkways. It was like a dream in an unrealistic paradise! I never could have imagined trees to grow into such wondrous forms and believe me, I have a wild imagination. I am an artist after all.

We arrived at the main level on the back of Nuvu. The creature he had turned into could climb trees like a gargantuan beetle. He straddled the trunks of three trees and kept his back level so as not to upset our seated position. Very gradually he alternated his legs upward and raised himself into the treetops. It was like riding a living elevator.

Once we reached a wide hallowed out treetop, Nuvu touched down and crouched low so we could depart. After the last passenger descended, he made a deep, guttural grunt and transformed himself back into his simian-feline form, cute and cuddly once again.

The Kembeqri wasted no time in being gracious hosts. We felt like royalty after they gathered around us and inspected us like we were some kind of weird aliens, which, I guess, we were. Cindy wasn't too crazy about them invading her personal space, but the rest of us had no problems with the Kembeqri checking us out. It was a surreal meet-and-greet. The Kembeqri didn't speak. They just made clicking sounds accompanied with the creaking of wood, as if a rocking chair was trying to communicate with us. Their sprawled fingers lightly brushed against our clothes and faces like a blind person feels a person's face to identify who they are. As their fingers contacted our skin we felt a subtle surge of electricity being transferred into our bodies. It was a warm, tingling sensation that no one was expecting or was afraid of as it seemed to have made us more comfortable with their presence.

We were then led to a common area that was nestled in the top hollow of an enormously wide tree whose branches spread up and outward to reveal the magnificent soft sky that was now exhibiting a light pink shade with several serene planets floating above us. The one thing I noticed about this planet was that the sky changed colors throughout the day, from a cool, light purple, to a periwinkle blue, and now it was turning into a light burgundy color. Artists would love this place!

As we made ourselves comfortable on a gathering of

moss-covered stones, Mioli and a small group of Kembeqri began bringing us a selection of plants, flowers, mushrooms, twigs, and leaves. They were placing these items at our feet then looked at us expectantly. I wasn't really sure what to do at this point. I glanced over at Alex to see what he was thinking and sensed that he was just as confused as I was.

"Is it some kind of offering?" I asked him.

He looked down at the collection of flora and fungi at his feet and gulped.

"No," he said disappointedly. "It's lunch."

Again, the realization of where we were in the universe hit me again. Why did I expect burgers and fries for lunch? I was at least hoping for some kind of dish with hot meat. But these aliens may be offended by the consumption of flesh. On the other hand, since they ate vegetables were they considered cannibals? After all, they were live vegetation, too. I guess dishes were optional as well. They just grabbed stuff off the trees and threw it at our feet. No kitchen necessary. This was what you call "roughing it".

"I already miss my mother's fried chicken." I said.

Nuvu cocked his head curiously and looked at me. "Fried chicken?"

"Yeah, it's a type of food humans eat on earth."

"What 'fried' mean?"

"Cooked in really hot oil. The bird is cooked in really hot oil and becomes crispy."

Nuvu looked at me as if I had committed a heinous crime.

"You cook bird in hot oil? Alive?"

"No, the bird is dead. It's ok, really. It's not like the bird was going to become a doctor or lawyer or anything."

"Well, I guess it would be rude to not eat it," Marlene said as she cautiously picked up a royal blue mushroom. She looked it over as if she was trying to fool herself into thinking that it actually looked delicious. "Besides, I like mushrooms."

We all stared at her as she gave a nervous laugh. No one else laughed. She paused, closed her eyes, and took a bite off the mushroom - total Alice in Wonderland scene.

Marlene chewed slowly expecting the worse, her eyes squinted shut to endure the disgust. Then the muscles in her face loosened, she opened her eyes again and looked at the mushroom. She took another bite, a much larger one. Her face was a mix of confusion and satisfaction. We held our breath as she turned to us to give her verdict.

"It's a marshmallow."

No way. A marshmallow? I had to try this out for myself. I swung down to look through the pile of plants at my feet and found a small number of the same blue mushrooms that Marlene was now stuffing her face with. I picked one up and it felt as light as air, like it wasn't even there. I squeezed it but it didn't give in like the squishiness of a marshmallow. It was solid and soft similar to a bagel. I closed my eyes and took a bite off one side, slicing my incisors through its plump surface. Once I began chewing, my taste buds began singing and dancing. It was sweet

168

and sugary just like a marshmallow, almost better. The texture of the mushroom changed in my mouth and made it delightfully gooey and tasty.

"You gotta be kidding me? For real?" I said, fascinated with its flavor. The others were eating their mushrooms, too, and the same look of pleasant bewilderment spread across their faces.

"I hope you like it," said Mioli humbly. "Those shrooms grow wild in the forest. However, my favorite is the snoki moss."

Mioli pointed to a batch of greenish-yellow moss that was stuck on a piece of bark on my pile of weird plants. I pulled off a tuft of the lacey, sticky material and stuffed it into my mouth.

It was cotton candy.

"This is crazy!" I said to Mioli with my mouth completely full of the stuff. "It tastes like cotton candy!"

Mioli seemed to be taken aback and cocked her head.

"Kott in...candy? Is that a good thing?"

"Oh, it's a wonderful thing. Guys, you should try this stuff!"

But everybody was too busy digging in their own piles and chowing down to even look at me. Cindy had a giant piece of tree bark sticking out of her mouth that she said tasted like beef jerky. Jade was scarfing down small, thick flowers that she swore were made from chocolate. Alex was nibbling on plant stems that he said tasted like pineapple and Marlene had already finished off 5 mushrooms. She was now working on the snoki moss and fuzzy, thick leaves that tasted exactly like potato chips. It was the most incredible meal I ever had!

"I wouldn't mind being a vegetarian on this planet," Alex said with a mouthful of branches.

"You're telling me," Marlene responded while shoving down a bouquet of flowers.

"Oh, so the bride of doom *does* know how to smile?"

"Yeah, so what? You going to mark it down on your happy calendar?"

"Maybe," Alex said with a slight chuckle. "It's a good look for you."

I thought Marlene would shoot him a poisonous glare but instead she just rolled her eyes and shook her head. If I didn't know any better, I'd say that Alex just hit on her or gave her a very weak insult.

Throughout our meal, Mioli went on to explain how things were on the planet of Zuu. As she had mentioned earlier, she was the matriarch of the Kembeqri species, sort of like a representative that reported to the Gatekeeper or Os-Gouvox about the activity within their enclosure. The Zuuminion did not visit the Kembeqri at all because they felt their viku was unnecessary for their purposes. So they were neglected and forgotten. That was pretty much why the entry into their enclosure was unguarded. Every alien species that lived on the Zuu planet was kept in an environmental enclosure but their cages were not always enclosed spaces. Some species were kept on isolated islands away from other aliens. Creatures that flew were not kept in cages but their primary food source and living habitat was built to sustain them in only one area. There were also alien species that were sustained in bodies of water that contained nutrients that provided their survival. There were even pockets of air on the planet where the chemicals in the atmosphere were controlled so that different aliens could breathe air that was similar to their original planet. If any aliens left their enclosure for a prolonged period of time, they would die.

I just couldn't believe a whole planet could be the home to so many different aliens. But I realized that even Earth, our home that must be more than a million light years away, is a planet that sustained millions of different life forms some of which haven't even been discovered yet. The only difference is that all the life forms on Zuu were brought here by a ring-ship and against their will.

Although aliens thrived in their separate "worlds", they were still prisoners, privy to the cruel intentions of the Gatekeeper and the all-powerful Eszok. The captives on this beautiful and technologically advanced planet had everything they needed to survive, but they were still captives. They did not have the freedom to go where they wanted or to mate freely. Mioli also mentioned that the Eszok frequently made the aliens part of their sadistic experiments that would leave poor subjects disfigured, mentally altered, or dead. It was as if every alien was kept in their own cages until the Eszok needed them for a new experiment, kind of like lab rats waiting for their turn to be dissected. She said she didn't know what the experiments were for or what they were trying to accomplish besides finding an unusually powerful viku. All she knew was that they had been doing it ever since she's been on the planet. After hearing about the ways of this world, I should have gulped down two more helpings of bubble gum flavored berries knowing that it could easily be my last meal. But the gravity of the situation made my headache much worse and I quickly lost my appetite. Everyone on this planet was a steer waiting to be slaughtered. These Kembeqri better have a serious escape plan in the works.

Chapter 9
ALEX HAS A VERY SERIOUS PROBLEM

After our first extraterrestrial meal, I realized that we were the first kids to eat in space. We were the first kids in space, period. I still couldn't get used to the fact that we were no longer on our home planet. Our feet were grounded yet here we were, on another planet, in another solar system, in another galaxy. It occurred to me that figuring out a way home was next to impossible. We're teenagers, barely making it through the grueling trials of high school SATs and teen angst. We aren't prepared to pilot a hyper-spatial super craft or whatever they call it to get back to our home world. I wouldn't even know what direction to go in.

Mioli and a small number of the Kembeqri volunteered to show our group where we could find water, more food, and where we would be sleeping for the night. In the back of my mind though, I wondered, how long would we be staying here? Was this going to be our new home? The thought bothered me. In fact, the act of thinking was starting to bother me. My head hurt! It pounded with an annoying vengeance as if my brain was trying to push its way out of my skull. My body was also beginning to feel a little odd, like my skin was a hindrance or a tight package that I needed to break out of. I noticed an unusual sensation since we had left the Grarg and I couldn't figure out what I was feeling. It was as if there was a small ball of fire forming in my chest smoldering and tickling me in my rib cage. There was no pain but

I felt restless and calm all at once.

I focused my attention on my surroundings and tried to put myself in a more relaxed state. One thing I noticed about Zuu was that there were two suns that shed light upon this world. One was brilliant and hot, much like earth's sun, the other was smaller and less bright, kind of like seeing a glowing moon out at daytime. At this time, the smaller of the two was settling in the north and caused the sky to melt into a glorious shade of orange. Along with two or three planets and a wispy, blue nebula that could be seen through the planets' atmosphere, the skyscape was ultimately picturesque. I had to get an unobstructed view of its glory.

The Kembeqri formed superior pathways in the treetops that led all the way to the crown of the trees. I gladly followed one path and made a twisting trek up between fantastic displays of aromatic plant life that was both ethereal and comforting. The flowers seemed to breathe a peaceful mist into the air as I passed them, making my agitated insides settle beneath my skin. Their blossoms followed me as if they were watching me. My pathway ended by narrowing itself into a large branch that hung above the other branches. After I climbed onto a smaller branch, I made myself comfortable and gazed out above the Kembeqri forest.

The view was nothing short of breathtaking! I was on top of a virtual sea of greenish-blue trees that rippled delicately under a light, refreshing breeze. Beyond the forest, giant mesh cages where other aliens were imprisoned could be seen through the confines of the ominous Kembeqri habitat. The cross-hatching of the giant cage was so distant and light, that I almost forgot it was there, altering the beauty of the surreal skyscape beyond it. Soft, lavender clouds drifted through its gargantuan metal frame without a care in the world. But it was there, keeping all life within its shield, holding its captives ready for whatever the Eszok had in mind for them.

"Quite some field trip, huh, Jarvis?" I heard a voice say. I looked down the pathway I had come up from and saw Alex walking towards me holding half of one of those baseball-sized melons I had earlier during our vegetarian feast. The other half was in his mouth delivering the unmistakable flavor of Jolly Ranchers down his throat.

"It beats going to the museum," I replied. "Only problem is that there's no end to the trip. I'm ready to go home now."

"How could you want to go home now? This place is fantastic! I could stay here for years and never get bored. There's so much to discover here."

"I have to admit this place is beautiful. If it wasn't overrun with a mechanical army that wants to put our heads on a wall, I'd consider coming back for Spring Break."

"You might still be here on Spring Break."

"That's a depressing thought."

As much I hated to believe it, I had to entertain the possibility that Alex might be right. We may be here until we expire. Here we were, six kids barely through high school, with no survival skills that would help us last 3 days outside of suburbia. A cub scout would at least have a fighting chance. At least they're trained at how to catch rabbits, tie knots, to start a campfire, and all that useful stuff you could use if you're stuck alone out in the woods.

But there *was* something that seemed to develop into a positive note.

I wanted to tell someone about the change in my senses ever since we landed on the planet. One problem was that I couldn't really translate what I was feeling into words. I just felt...different, and in a good way. I couldn't confide in Marlene who didn't seem to care about anyone including herself, or Cindy who yelped at the drop of a hat. There's no way I would tell my sister. I needed to protect her from the unknown and until I knew more about what was happening to me, I would disclose nothing to her. And although our situation on Zuu was becoming grimmer, I was beginning to feel more confident and courageous - almost as if I was developing a power of some kind.

"Alex?" I said.

"Yeah?" he said, chewing on the rest of the Jolly Rancher melon. He reached up and scratched the back of his neck.

"Do you believe in God?"

"Totally. Absolutely. I'm Catholic."

"So you believe that he created man, animals, the earth..." I spread my hands out showcasing the surrounding views. "..and all of this?"

"Who else could have put it here? I don't know what you

believe, but I don't think a big explosion made any of this. There had to be a designer. There are too many differences between us and this world. I don't think all of these living things came into being merely by chance."

"Neither do I, but do you believe any of that stuff that Mioli said earlier? You know, that viku-voodoo stuff? It sounds very Xmen-like to me."

"How can you *not* believe it, Jarvis? We rode on the back of a shape-shifting monkey-cat. We had lunch with a tribe of walking tree people. We're on the run from an artificial intelligence that literally runs the planet. I wouldn't be surprised if E.T. walked up to me and told *me* to phone home."

"But she said that even humans have a viku – that we have some kind of inherent power, too."

"Well, it has been known that humans only use a small percentage of their brain," he said as he massaged his lower back. "I think it's like 5 or 10 percent."

"What about the other 90 percent?"

"We haven't tapped into it yet."

"So there's a lot of potential waiting to happen. Maybe that other 90 percent determines what our viku is?"

Alex raised an eyebrow.

"Maybe."

Here goes nothing.

"Well, maybe that other 90 percent *does* wake up when our cognitive minds are taken from our home planet? What if it wakes up senses or abilities that we didn't even know we had?"

Alex looked at me perplexed and started scratching his back again.

"You mean like a self-defense mechanism that gets triggered in the mind?"

"Say what, now?"

"You heard of Sigmund Freud? That psycho-analysis guy?"

"Yeah?"

"He believed that the unconscious mind would enact strategies to ward off or deny unacceptable stimuli to keep the self-schema from being damaged. If your body hasn't been in a certain situation before, your mind will respond in a way to keep itself safe, protected."

The whole time he was talking, he looked like he was trying to catch a lizard crawling down his back. I thought maybe he was just trying to catch an itch, so I continued to ignore it and tell him my ordeal.

"I didn't tell Mioli this earlier but ever since we came to Zuu I felt like something was opening up in me. As if my insides were changing and are fighting to get out of me, but I can't figure out how to make them come out or what exactly I'm trying to get out. But now I have an idea of...um, Alex?"

Alex's itch now began to overcome him in a very ravenous fashion. At first, he was scratching the spot where the peepsnoot had stung him without even thinking about it. But I noticed that his hand was twisted around to his back the whole time I was talking to him. He looked as if he wanted to pull his skin off.

"Are you okay?" I asked him.

"My back," he said, screwing his face with discomfort. "It itches like crazy. I must be allergic to that alien's sting."

"But Mioli said those peepsnoots were harmless. Here, let me take a look at it."

I stepped down from my perch and skipped down to Alex who was now attacking his back with both hands. The poor guy looked helpless. It looked like his itch was all over his back, not just in one spot. I lifted up the back of his shirt.

"It's probably just a rash."

What I saw was not a rash.

The color of Alex' skin had completely changed color. His flesh had turned the same color as chili con carne and from what I could tell, the same texture of it as well. His back looked like that of a horny toad with a skin disease. The sight of it made my heart sting and my stomach turn. I gasped. How could a little insect do this? I felt my soul scream from within when a pair of glossy, gray eyes suddenly blinked open from his back and glared straight at me.

I wanted to console Alex, really, and tell him that it was nothing, just an insignificant rash or blister. But instead I jumped backwards, tripping over my own feet, and scrambled backwards screaming like there was no tomorrow.

Alex's scream overrode mine. His outburst was not from fear, but from pain. Excruciating pain. Tear jerking, stomach-lurching, make you want to slap your mama, genuine pain. It had to be because what I saw next almost made me hurl.

What appeared to be limbs or appendages shot out of Alex's back and placed themselves on the ground in front of me. 4 of the sinewy legs stretched to their full height and lifted Alex off his feet and about 3 feet into the air. Muscular crab legs had sprouted out of his back and forced him to take a ride while facing the sky whether he liked it or not.

I realized I was still screaming maniacally when the creature in Alex's back suddenly took off into the Kembeqri village with Alex howling on the other side. I did my best to follow the creature into the village where it ran into a number of the Kembeqri. The Kembeqri did not make any shrill noises or screams but they made a loud, excitable harmony of remarkable clicking sounds. Then the Alex creature (I hate calling him that, but I had to think of something) took Alex on a wild ride across the pathways of the village, up and down the meandering tree branches, and around the Kembeqri aliens. If I didn't know any better, I'd say it was looking for something. It didn't bother running away and it wasn't interested in attacking anyone. It just darted from one corner to another while Alex yowled in agony. I couldn't watch him suffer like this. I had to get help.

"Mioli! Mioli, help! It's Alex!" I yelled out to the wooded world around me.

Mioli emerged from a small hut that was shaped like a giant shell casing several pathways away. She quickly approached my area with the girls who had colorful braids entwined with grass stems in their hair…everyone except Marlene, of course. I guess she wasn't down with Cindy and Jade's girly hair fashions.

"Mioli, look!" I pointed to the Alex creature which was now crawling down the twisted trunk of a towering tree. "What's happening to him?"

I heard all three of the girls scream and give a yelp of disgust. I was expecting that. But I wasn't expecting Marlene's voice of concern.

"What in the world happened to him?"

"I don't know. He just said his back was itchy and then BAM! Some eyes and legs pop out of his back!"

Mioli stared at Alex for a moment whose parasitic passenger was taking him for an uninhibited romp in the treetops.

"A syringe," she said in a query. "Tell me what a syringe is."

"What? What does that have to do with anything?"

"When your friend was stung by the peepsnoot, he said it felt like a syringe going into his back. What is a syringe?"

"It's a needle," said Marlene. "A big needle that people in the medical field use on earth."

Alex's screams were getting louder and more grotesque, indicating his metamorphosis was changing his insides, too.

"God, make it stop!" said Cindy.

"A needle. That explains it. Your friend was not stung by a peepsnoot. They're sting is minimal. He was impregnated by a Mort Kuup."

"Impregnated?!" all four of us said in unison.

"Alex got busy with another alien?" Jade said in shock.

"I don't know what that means," said Mioli, "but the needle-like sting, the curved legs coming out of his back, and the eyes – they're all indications of being stung by a Mort Kuup. It's a type of fungus that grows on the trees. We must have passed too close to a colony while we rode on Nuvu's back. It could have stung any one of us."

Nuvu immediately felt guilty. I saw him gazing up at Alex's writhing body in the branches above and he made a sort of muffled whimper.

"Oh, Alex," he said sadly. "Me sorry. Me so sorry."

"Do not blame yourself, old friend," Mioli said consolingly. "It could have stung anyone. Even you."

Their moment was suddenly interrupted when Alex's body plummeted from the air and landed on its back right in front of us. We surged back and the parasitic alien glared at us from between Alex' shoulder blades. It's disturbing face was obviously insectoid and it now looked as if a pair of antennae was starting to grow out of his back. It released a hiss that was more fear-inspiring than a rattlesnake combined with the roar of a grizzly bear. We fell over ourselves trying desperately to get out of its way as it scampered on its 6 legs toward a central tree in the Kembeqri village. It quickly picked up speed, gasping in excitement, and then leapt upwards onto the tree. It tightly clamped its legs around the base of the tree's trunk abruptly cutting off the sound of the parasite's disgusting voice. Now Alex's back was solidly pinned to the tree with the six appendages gripping onto the trunk. His face showed nothing but pure terror and helplessness. I noticed Marlene's eyes were quickly tearing up.

"Why are we watching this? We have to do something."

The moment the words left her lips, members of the Kembeqri started to appear out of the trees and branches around us. Their bodies were the perfect camouflage. There were dozens of them around us and we didn't even see them cause their bodies blended in seamlessly with their environment.

The Kembeqri approached the tree that Alex was pinned to and spanned out in front of him like he was putting on some kind of concert. Alex's eyes were wide and filled with panic. He convulsed and mouthed words that had no sound. His face was wet with sweat and his skin was pale. I thought I was going to faint just looking at him.

"Alex!" Cindy cried.

Then something weird happened.

The Kembeqri straightened themselves up to their full height, stretched out their branch-like arms, necks, backs, fingers, and torsos in all directions and filled the air with a hum of warm energy. The air vibrated with a force radiating from their limbs and seemed to surge directly toward Alex. Alex's eyes rolled up into his head and his labored breathing quickly stopped. He began breathing normally, his mouth fell open slightly, and his rigid body slackened as if all his muscles had suddenly decided to rest.

"What's happening?" Marlene breathed.

"A sacred event," Mioli whispered reverently.

"A sacred event?" I said annoyed. "How can you call this a sacred event when our friend is hung up there like a Christmas tree ornament?"

"The Mort Kuup's purpose in life is to find a suitable tree to sustain itself. Once it finds a favorable tree, it clings to it for the rest of its life becoming one with the tree. This one in particular has become connected to the first and eldest tree of the Kembeqri forest. The Kembeqri are merely honoring its union and blessing it with a long life."

"But what about Alex?" said Marlene worriedly.

"It's as if they don't see him. He is its host. Once the Mort Kuup has made a complete meld with the tree, Alex's body will wither away and fall lifeless to the ground."

"My God!" gasped Jade.

"No!" Marlene growled in disbelief.

"I've seen this happen only a few times with other animals of the forest," Mioli continued. "I cannot tell if they are in pain or in total bliss. But Alex is alive, living off the tree through the Mort Kuup. However, his connection with the life force will be cut off when the Mort Kuup severs its bond and dies. He will be nothing but a shell of his former self."

"No!" I shouted surprising everyone, including myself. Mioli and the others jumped and turned to me. "We've already lost Derek. I'm not going to standby and let this stupid planet take

184

another one of us away. That is my friend. There must be a way to stop this from happening!"

I could tell Mioli was a little shaken by my outburst. But I didn't care. I was pissed. How could I let something as trivial as a fungus suck the life out of my friend so it could live its life stuck to a tree? Sure, it had spindly legs and a nasty attitude, but this where I put my foot down. I'm keeping this group together and alive even if it kills me.

"There may be one way," Mioli said after a few seconds.

"Tell me," I said sternly.

"Skeener eggs. I know that their yolk is extremely poisonous to the Mort Kuup. If applied correctly, the yolk may kill the Mort Kuup and spare your friend's life."

"What's the down-side?" Marlene said. Mioli's lost expression prompted her to explain further. "What are the side effects? Will it work?"

"I do not know," said Mioli "I never had a reason to disturb the laws of nature."

"Well, like Marlene said, there's a first time for everything," I stated boldly. "Where do we find these eggs? Around here?"

"Skeeners are located in a biome very far from here. They do not have an enclosure because they are flyers, monstrous airborne creatures that will attack anything that moves. They are located in the Xeeths, a maze of bottomless canyons in the south."

"How far is far?" I said, undaunted by the negative details of these mysterious birds.

"An hour by Seership. We may not make it back in time to stop the Mort Kuup's full connection to the tree. Your friend may be…expired by the time we return."

My gaze fell upon Alex's body whose peaceful expression, which now graced his face, contradicted the state of his slack body that had six insectoid appendages stretching out of his mid-torso and across a gigantic tree. I then noticed that thin tendrils of pink vines were seeping out of the tree's bark and wrapping themselves around Alex' arms and legs.

"The tree is accepting the Mort Kuup's host. It will be more difficult to sever the Mort Kuup's connection if the tree favors the host. A tree's bond with a host is permanent. It cannot be cut off."

"That's all I need to know." My mind was made up. "We leave now."

Chapter 10
TRAGEDY IN THE XEETHS

It may sound redundant to say that something had been bothering me for a while. From the moment we were kidnaped from earth, I feel it's fair to say that my day had been a little less than pleasant. Alex and Derek's day hadn't been so great either. There had been an unspeakable number of kinks in the last 24 hours of our lives. However, I wouldn't categorize what's been bothering me as a kink. I think it's more like a mental twitch.

As I mentioned before, my mind hasn't been the same since we left earth. The pain in my noggin is ridiculous now. I feel jittery, energized, and very unlike myself. What bothers me the most is that no one else has experienced the same sensations as I have, as far as I know. And now these sensations in my head were beginning to grow into something that I could physically feel in my brain. Isn't that weird? I mean, think about it. What muscle could you move in your brain at will? Try it. Flex your brain like your flexing your arm or twiddling your finger. Go ahead. You can't do it, can you? But I can. I think the sensation in my head was the formation of a new muscle or tissue in my head. I know it doesn't make sense, does it? But somehow I knew that's what it was. It wasn't a tumor or something painful. It just felt like a new toy that was begging to be played with.

So I did.

I voluntarily moved a new muscle in my brain by just

thinking about it and I felt the sensation of movement inside my head. I wanted to yelp in surprise of how unusual the twitch felt but instead my body froze. I couldn't make a sound cause I couldn't figure out where my mouth was. I couldn't move my hands to feel for my mouth cause I couldn't feel my hands. I looked down and my body was gone. I was a pair of eyes floating across the landscape. Really!

So this was what it felt like to have an out-of-body experience. Did that mean I was dying? Maybe I *was* growing a tumor after all?

I was expecting to drift away from Zuu and enter the pearly gates at any moment, but I never even left the planet. My soul or whatever spiritual part of my being had left my body and was making a break for it. How could I stop it? Below me, the countless massive enclosures of alien species zoomed by me in a blur. I didn't even have a chance to see what was in them. I sped by odd-shaped rock formations, purple lakes, and mountainous areas that were covered with fluffy, violet snow-like particles, and then ventured into an area that was very familiar. The tall, skyscraping, red-colored stones were scattered all around a blue-green colored and sandy landscape and there, looming above the wide plain, was the Gatekeeper's compound, our first stop when we came to Zuu.

Within seconds, my floating senses entered the compound, but my mind entered a different area of the complex. We had been in the lower levels of the Gatekeeper's enormous base of business but now I was higher, much higher, in his streamlined structure.

I entered a huge room that had incredibly tall windows that looked like tall buildings. The room was full of startling sunlight and was populated by a small army of robotic figures behind low, curvilinear consoles covered with a billion blinking lights. In the back of the cavernous room stood the Gatekeeper, arms crossed, face scowled, and obviously in a very foul mood. His disapproving leer was fixed on a large screen that floated several feet about his head.

"I told you not to contact me until you had detained the younglings, yet you speak to me empty-handed? Are you malfunctioning, Os-Gouvox? I have an updated model waiting to replace you if I deem it necessary."

"With much respect, Gatekeeper, it is only matter of changing strategy."

The sound of Os-Gouvox's digital voice echoed from his hollow hull and rang in my ears. I really did not like that guy.

"They are not as acquiescent as most species on Zuu," he continued. "They resist capture and do not understand their place."

"You were aware of that setback when we extracted information from Cadzow."

Cadzow?

"The Eszok Hi'are will be here after the second sun sets. You are out of time and excuses."

"I understand, Gatekeeper. I will make my delivery

before the allotted time."

Even though he was a robot, Os-Gouvox's voice was layered with frustrated shame. His air of conviction stank worse than sweaty feet.

"Find them, Sarok. Find them now!"

The Gatekeeper abruptly waved his hand across Os-Gouvox's image and made it disappear. The motion simultaneously caused the screen to float higher towards the ceiling where other screens gathered flashing unusual images from all over the planet. The Gatekeeper turned away from where I could see him, but then he stopped and looked up, almost as if he knew that I was there. It then hit me that I didn't know how to get back to my body. I didn't even know how I left it. But no worries, if it's just my mind that's in the room, how could the Gatekeeper see me?

"Jarvis?" the Gatekeeper said.

Impossible. How could he possibly know I was there? But he did. He was staring straight at me.

"Jarvis?" he said again, but not with his own voice. It was female. It was Jade's voice.

"Boy, wake up!"

Without a single blink, my surroundings had changed. The cathedral-esque walls of the Gatekeeper's control room had completely vanished along with the small army of metallic, working figures. The enormous room had been replaced by a never-ending outdoor plain scattered with unbelievably tall and crooked mountains. I had returned to my body, safe and sound, and felt completely calm. How on earth did that happen?

I sat there innocently on a seat on the Seership that was now rocketing over the Zuu landscape at phenomenal speed even though it felt like we were sitting still. I remembered that we had left the Kembeqri forest almost 45 minutes ago and while Mioli chatted with the girls, I had decided to play with my brain. What had started out as a harmless experiment ended up as an out-of-body experience that garnered everybody's attention.

"Jarvis, what's the matter?" said Cindy coming closer. I could tell she wanted me to answer in the negative. I decided to lie to keep her calm.

"Nothing," I said, not even convincing myself.

"Then why are you bleeding out of your eyes?" said Marlene.

"What?"

I put my fingers between my left eyelid and nose. I didn't notice it before, but now that it was brought to my attention, the warm sensation of thick liquid could be felt flowing from my tear ducts. It wasn't a lot but it was enough to freak me out…as well as my sister.

"Whoa," I said quietly. "That's new."

"What's going on, Jarvis? Did you get stung by that pee stick, too?" my sister said frantically. "I don't want to see legs popping out of *your* back. You're my brother. You're much smarter than Alex to let that happen to you."

"It's okay, Jade."

"No, it's not okay! We're not okay, Jarvis. We're not

okay! We're going to die here!"

"Jade, calm down," I demanded. I could tell I was losing her.

"We're gonna die here!"

"Jade!" I grabbed her by the shoulders and shook her. I didn't know what else to say to her make her calm down. Then one thing came to me.

"Ponies! Ponies! Ponies!"

The look on Jade's face was a mix of confusion and panic. It seemed the words didn't make sense to her and she had to stop and make sense of what I said. She looked at me, bewildered, but not completely lost. Her mouth fell open and nothing came out. She went from hysterical to calm in five seconds flat. It's amazing what three little words can do. Naturally, everybody looked at me like I was crazy, too. They weren't very hip to the "ponies" therapy.

"Ponies?" Mioli looked completely lost. "What are ponies?"

"What about Derek? What about Alex? They're both gone and now you're bleeding out of your eyes," Jade whined softly. "Jarvis, I can't deal with this."

I was immediately reminded when Jade would run into my room during those fierce thunderstorms we had when we were younger. She'd come in running with those little barrettes swinging around her head like African jewelry. After whining about the thunder being so loud, and not being able to wake up mom from her unearthly snoring, I would have to tell her that the thunder is nothing but God moving his furniture around. The lightning happens when he accidentally knocks over a lamp. Whether she believed me or not, I didn't know, but it made her fear of thunder and lightning subside long enough to put her back to sleep. Unfortunately, our current situation could not be explained away with godly house cleaning. There was no way I could know what was going to happen to us or Alex or Derek. I couldn't even explain what was happening to me. The one thing I was sure of was that I was much more scared than Jade was right now, and I couldn't let her know that.

"Jade, I know you're scared. It's okay to be scared. But being scared isn't going to help us achieve anything right now. We need to be bigger than we are in order to survive this, alright? Alex is counting on us to save him and Mioli believes we have a good chance of doing that. We can't let him down. So let's calm down and man up. We can do this, ok?"

Jade bit her lip to keep herself from crying. She nodded stiffly.

"What about Derek?"

The name vibrated down my back and made little hairs on my head stand up. What in the world...? I stopped and looked away from Jade and looked around at our environment, as if I was going to say, 'he's right there.' But he wasn't. He was nowhere to be seen, but I knew he was alive and well somewhere on this planet. I just couldn't figure out how to see him. It was a weird sensation that I could barely explain. But all I said was, "Somehow we'll get him back."

"Okay," she whispered.

Nuvu's tail appeared over her shoulder and guided her to a seat a few steps away. He reminded me of our dog, Kiska, an Alaskan malamute, whom we had to put down a few years ago. Not that he resembled a dog, but he was there to tranquilize any emotional frustration just by being there and embracing us.

"That was a good lie, Jarvis," said Marlene coolly. "Looked like it worked."

"I wasn't lying, Marlene."

"Dude, he's dead. You want to dig up the whole planet for his body?"

"He's not dead. I don't know how to explain to you how I know this but I can feel his presence. It's like he's literally breathing on my face, just like you, but I just don't see him."

"I think you're losing your mind." Marlene said, and she walked away in her usual funky mood.

"Do you really think he's alive, Jarvis?" said Cindy with a spark of hope in her voice.

"Without a doubt. In my mind, it doesn't make sense that he should be dead."

Cindy nodded understandably.

"Ok, I believe you. After we get this egg and save Alex, are we going to start looking for Derek?"

"Yep, then we find Cadzow and find a way to get back home."

"That's a lot of things to be looking for. Sounds like

we're going to be here for a while. But I'm glad one of us knows what to do."

Cindy smiled at me then went to sit next to my sister. I was left standing alone with Mioli who stood stock still glaring at me. Well, I felt she was glaring at me. I couldn't tell since she had that mask permanently glued to her face. She stood motionless. I looked her up and down wondering if she was about to slap me for lying to her earlier.

"What?" My voice was an uneasy squeak.

She came closer and leaned towards me.

"Your viku," she said ominously. "It's starting to manifest itself."

"I'm...I...I don't..."

"You said it didn't make sense that he should be dead. That's because you are internally connected to your own species. Your life and theirs is as one being."

"I don't understand."

"You will," Mioli said quietly, then walked past me to the front of the Seership. She gazed out across the towering columns of mysterious stones and stared at a clouded, dark horizon in the distance. "We've arrived. The Xeeths await us."

I had imagined the Xeeths to be similar to the Grand Canyon, but it was more like Bryce Canyon except it was on a much more grander scale. Towering, elongated mountains and boulders stretched up from the ground and reached toward the heavens. All of their tops were completely flat as if someone had sliced off all the tops at once. The stone was colored a grayish blue hue and was dusted with large clumps of that weird violet snow I saw earlier in my vision.

As we flew in the midst of the Xeeths, I understood what bottomless meant. In reality, nothing is truly bottomless cause it has to have a base or a foundation of some kind. But in this case, I couldn't see the bottom at all. These monumental rock towers went on for miles down into the belly of the planet resembling thick, craggy snakes reaching for the sun. Some of the pinnacles had fallen over into precarious positions forming arches, natural bridges, and natural pyramids. I felt that if I sneezed, I'd cause them to collapse. The howling winds that roared throughout the narrow valleys were accompanied by the distant screech of a very vocal and very irate creature making our apprehensive journey into the Xeeths even more foreboding.

"Nice place," Marlene said with a distinct tinge of fear in her voice. "A few more plants and I could move right in."

"It sounds like the canyon's breathing," Cindy said looking over the side of the ship. Nothing but blue mist could be seen below us giving the illusion that the rock formations were floating in the clouds. "Is it alive?"

Seeing that we were on an alien planet, I guess that was a valid question.

"Very much alive," Mioli stated. "The Xeeths are full

of life which desires to destroy it. Be on your guard. Eyes to the sky - Skeeners move at an unrealistic speed."

"We'll keep that in mind," I said scanning the rocky world around us. "How do we find these eggs of theirs?"

"The paramounts," Mioli gestured toward the tops of the stone pillars. "Their nests are always closest to the sun. It keeps their eggs warm as they hunt for fresh meat."

"Well, they're not getting my meat."

"Nor mine," said Jade.

"Nor mine," echoed Cindy.

"Nor mine," said Marlene.

"Not mine," squealed Nuvu.

Mioli turned inquisitively toward the group.

"I agree not to be captured as well."

"Fine," I announced. "We watch each other's back for the duration of our little 'shopping spree' here."

I made quotation marks with my fingers. Once again, it was obvious that I stumped Mioli with my earth lingo.

After several minutes of gliding silently in the dismal gloom of the Xeeths, Mioli reached over and tapped my arm furiously. She pointed up toward a particularly tall rock cropping that rose out of the Xeeth's gloom and stood proudly in the warm sunlight hundreds of feet above us.

"A lone nest," Mioli whispered. "In normal communities, skeeners guard each other's nurseries as if it were their own. But a lone nest yields two caretakers: a mother to hunt, a father to guard the home."

We all craned our necks toward the nest to see if there was any movement or a flutter of wings. There was nothing.

"So, where's the daddy?" asked Marlene.

"He's not here," I said. "That means this is our one and only chance. We need to get closer. Mioli, take us up."

Mioli guided the Seership closer to the lofty stone pillar.

"This is risky, Jarvis," she said, her voice layered with trepidation. "Skeeners are extremely fast. The father could be hiding and watching us now. We can't bring the Seership right next to the nest."

"Why not?"

"The father would be upon us before we knew it."

"So what do you suggest we do?" Cindy asked. "Sneak up on the nest?"

"It's the most wisest thing to do if we stay in the shadow side of the rock."

The Seership could only go so high without being seen in the bold rays of sunlight above the rocky plateaus of the Xeeths. So, unfortunately, a predicament revealed itself.

"Someone has to climb up to the skeener nest, don't they?"

Mioli didn't say anything. Her silence was an affirmative answer.

"I'll do it."

I heard the words but I couldn't believe where they were coming from.

It was Cindy.

"Cindy? Was that you?"

"Yes," she whispered. Her body stood firm and rigid and the look in her eyes said *don't mess with me, I know what I'm doing.*

"My father and I used to go rock climbing when I was little. I learned a little bit when I was in 8th grade. Besides, I'm more athletic than any of you. I'm built for this kind of thing."

"I hope you don't die for this type of thing, too," said Marlene.

"Are you sure about this, Cindy?" I asked. It was just so hard to believe that this was the same girl that was afraid to slide down into the Grarg. And now she was volunteering to climb the pinnacle of death, possibly putting herself out as bait for the carnivorous birds.

"Alex deserves a chance. If this egg is going to save him, we have to get it. Plain and simple."

I nodded.

"Then don't let me stop you."

The Seership hovered in a crevice that was partially hidden by a fallen boulder. It was a perfect location because our view of the shadow side of the nest's rock tower was directly in front and above us. Cindy proved herself to be an exceptional climber. She scaled the side of the stone pillar easily and without struggle. Her method of climbing was hand then foot, breathe confidently, and don't fall. After watching her for several minutes, I could tell that she was doing it without thinking. It was practically her second nature to be on the rocky wall.

I also sensed something else. I could feel how she felt.

People always say, 'I know how you feel,' but this was particularly different because I could clearly feel her heart beating next to mine, the speed of her heart rhythms vibrating against mine. Her irregular breathing pattern could be felt through my lungs even though I had no problem breathing normally. The strain of her muscles and the beads of sweat that rolled down her brow could be felt on my body as I stood motionless staring up at her. It was as if I were two people in one body. The sensation was terrifying, but it was also unmistakably natural.

Cindy was almost near the top when I felt a disturbance in her confidence. I peered up at her and noticed that she was looking at the other stone pillars around her.

"You guys," she shouted down to us. "There's more than one nest out here."

Mioli rushed forward and shouted, "Are you sure? You're not mistaken? If there's more than one nest then it's a possibility that you've already been spotted."

I could feel the sudden panic run through Cindy's body when a ghastly screech sliced the still air of the Xeeths. The canyon echoed the horrifying sound that pierced our ears. Mioli put the Seership in escape mode and bolted out of our hiding place.

"They've seen her! They'll be upon her in seconds!"

Cindy miraculously scrambled the last few feet up the side of the stone pillar and dove head first into the spiky black branches of the skeener nest. I just hoped to God that there was at least one egg in that nest and no skeeners!

Again, the repulsive scream of a skeener echoed off the canyon walls, except this time, it was accompanied by another. When I turned toward the sound, the blur of brownish-gold and purple tore a streak through the chilly mountain air. At first, I thought I was looking at a griffin, but it was more reptilian than avian. They resembled flying snakes with two lower appendages that harbored veiny muscles and a pair of diabolical claws. Their wings fluttered quickly like a hummingbird's. I assumed that was how they moved so unrealistically fast.

"Is that a …?"

But Mioli cut off Marlene's question with the obvious answer. "Skeeners!"

Mioli accelerated the Seership in Cindy's direction and I was shocked to see three skeeners preparing to land right on top of her.

"They're gonna get her!" Jade screamed. But right when the first skeener landed on Cindy's nest, Mioli slammed a button on the dashboard and a green shaft of light sliced through the air and struck the disgusting winged creature. The creature fell from the nest while the others scattered in opposite directions screeching their ugly little hearts out.

"I'm glad this ship comes prepared!" I shouted. "Cindy!"

A tuft of blonde hair blew up and out of the nest. Thankfully,

Cindy's wide eyes were staring straight at us from under it. She was unharmed and completely fine. What was even better was that she was clutching a large, smooth, purple stone with creamy specks all over it.

"I got one," she said breathlessly. "I got the egg!"

Cindy's happy moment was sadly short lived when a gigantic skeener popped up from behind the edge of the nest and snatched her up by her shoulders.

"No!" I shouted, but I was drowned out by Cindy's bloodcurdling scream. "Mioli, get her!"

Mioli stepped on the gas, or whatever she pressed on to make the Seership veer forward, and we trailed after the skeener that had Cindy in its claws.

"Can you shoot it down and catch Cindy?" I asked Mioli.

"Yes, as long as you keep the others off our ship."

"The others?"

I only had a millisecond to forget about them until two other skeeners landed on the Seership. They were huge and ferocious like raptors with wings. Come to think of it, that's exactly what they looked like except they had no forearms. Just a wiry, muscular serpentine neck that held a triangular monstrous head full of pointed teeth and a bad attitude.

"Shoo, shoo," Jade said as she tried to wave one off. But Marlene was much braver. She kicked one in the head as it snapped at her. It didn't help cause it kicked her right back.

"Mioli!"

The skeeners hovered over Marlene and Jade moving in for the kill, but a small furry creature jumped in front of me and blasted them away with a small weapon-like device.

"Fried chicken!" Nuvu squealed. The skeeners fled from the ship, but there were three others behind them closing in.

"Nuvu, you got another one of those?" Marlene said pointing to Nuvu's weapon.

A scream ahead of the ship suddenly stole my attention. Two new skeeners had attacked the skeener that had Cindy in its claws and were trying to steal its prey. The poor girl flapped around like a lifeless doll while the fierce creatures scratched, bit, poked, and wrestled with each other. Then the obvious happened.

They dropped her.

"CINDY!"

My scream echoed against the canyon walls. I tried to reach out to her with my mind but I got a blinding and thorough sense of utter terror. There was nothing I could do.

However, Nuvu did. Like a hot potato, he tossed his "space gun" to Marlene, ran to the front of the Seership, and leapt out into the wide, open sky.

"What the heck is he doing?" shouted Jade. "He can't fly!"

The moment she said it, Nuvu transformed himself into another skeener, except he was reddish-brown and smaller.

"Oh, yeah," said Jade dejected, "I forgot."

Nuvu spread his newly spawned wings and dove toward

Cindy's falling body like a rocket. The other skeeners aimed for her, too, but Nuvu got to her just before they crash-landed on a wide plateau covered with violet snow and some sort of wild blue vegetation.

Mioli steered the Seership away from the nest and headed down to where Cindy and Nuvu had landed. From our vantage point, I could see Cindy's body sprawled out on the unusually colored field upon the plateau, bruised but okay. I could see her raising herself up on her hands, and then she came to her feet. But a particularly adamant skeener reached Cindy before we or Nuvu could and successfully swooped down and snatched her up once again.

Nuvu witnessed the reptilian bird clutching Cindy as she ran towards him and transformed himself into a frightening, thick-skinned, hulking creature that was a cross between a gorilla and a lion. He released an earth-shattering roar that I didn't know was logically possible and sprang up onto all four legs. Just as the skeener began to lift Cindy off the ground, Nuvu leapt up into the air and met the skeener head on, tackling him to the ground. Cindy's body was slung straight up into the air, but was lucky enough to land directly onto the deck of our Seership.

Mioli guided the Seership closer to the plateau where the leo-like Nuvu and skeener tumbled in a vicious wrestling match. In one move, Nuvu clamped down onto the neck of the skeener, arched his neck, and tossed him over the side of the plateau. That skeener's flying days were over. Nuvu peered over the side and made that disturbing roar again, howling in victory.

"Nuvu!" I shouted. "Leave now, gloat later!"

Nuvu bounded across the plateau and jumped up onto the Seership innocently. He changed himself into his original form and approached Cindy.

"Cindy Ok?"

Cindy dropped to her knees and gave Nuvu a big bear hug.

"Cindy, OK," she said pecking him on his furry cheek. "Thank you, Nuvu."

I was also relieved to see Cindy was alive and well. I know Nuvu confirmed it, but I asked anyway, "Are you OK?"

"Yes, but I lost the egg. It was right in my hands and I lost it."

"No lose egg, Cindy," said Nuvu. He brought up his ropey tail that was curled up around a dark purplish object with cream-colored specks. It was the egg. Everyone gasped and cheered.

"Nuvu, you're incredible!" Cindy smiled, hugging him again.

Nuvu just smiled and blinked his massive, crystal blue eyes looking like the most modest Echolakian in the world. Then his countenance suddenly reverted back to the lion-like alien and roared loudly in Cindy's face. A split second later, we realized that he wasn't roaring at Cindy but up at the devious skeener that quickly snatched her up off the Seership.

"NOOO! CINDY!" I screamed.

How could that have happened so quickly? We just got her back and now her feet were dangling in the air again. It was as if I blinked and she disappeared.

The Seership tilted and veered toward the skeener that captured Cindy, but then something hard had struck the bow and almost knocked everyone off deck. Sparks exploded and the Seership lurched backwards.

"Mioli, what's going on? We have to..." I started to say. But I was cut off when Mioli stepped on the gas and shot forward.

"Os-Gouvox!" she shouted and pointed toward a low gathering of rock towers where a small, streamlined flyer began shooting a spray of blue lasers at us. "He's found us!"

What ensued afterward was a wild car chase in the sky. We played cops and robbers with laser cannons and soared around, over, and through the pinnacles of the Xeeths, causing considerable damage along the way. Explosions just feet away from our Seership blew away sides of the canyon causing us to retreat from Os-Gouvox's flyer.

Every move we made, Os-Gouvox premeditated our position and fired on us. Our Seership was severely damaged, we were unprepared to fight back, and Cindy had been birdnaped. I couldn't figure out a way to escape from this guy and I knew that Mioli's maneuvers with the Seership were not going to keep us alive forever. We were overwhelmed and I was completely and utterly pissed. I refused to let the Zuuminion capture me and my companions again. This is our life and it belongs to us!

The more I thought about the attack on our freedom, my head felt like it had expanded and an emotional bubble began to balloon inside of my gut, except this time, it was tangible. I could feel a sensation growing inside my chest, rising up through my neck, and burning in my cranium. I wasn't scared of this sensation at all. I embraced it, controlled it, and suddenly found myself spouting white hot fire straight out of my mouth.

"BACK OFF!!"

That was when I felt it, a superhuman surge of energy rushed through my soul. It felt as if something had exploded within me and came out through my mouth. I directed it toward Os-Gouvox's flyer and saw his mode of transportation burst apart. Raiment white flames and blue smoke consumed him and his crewmates. It was all I had witnessed before I felt instantly exhausted. My sight blurred and my legs gave out. Next thing I knew, the floor of the deck rushed toward me, and my world went black.

Chapter 11
MIOLI AND I HAVE A LITTLE CHAT

When I regained consciousness, I had turned blind. I blinked several times to adjust my vision but soon realized that there was nothing wrong with my sight. I mean, absolutely nothing. Not only did I quickly understand that it was now nighttime, but I also had perfect vision. My glasses were gone but the world around me was completely clear and colorful. The shades of night on this planet were imbued with deep purples and greens that glowed with a warm luminosity creating a serene and magical wonderland.

I sat up from a lying position where I was conveniently positioned next to a pathway that led through the Kembeqri village. The skin on my face felt oddly taut and dry. I brushed my fingers upon my cheeks and felt a dried, sticky material on my face. I pulled my hand away and saw red on my fingertips. It was dried blood. I had been bleeding from my eyes again. I racked my brain for a cause and inspected my head for injuries, but my skin seemed unbroken and I was in no pain. Furthermore, my throbbing headache that had been gnawing at my brain ever since I came to the planet was completely gone. My head was pain free. I also realized that I had been unconscious for the rest of the journey back from the Xeeths. I was completely alone.

Where did everybody go?

It was most likely that the Kembeqri were standing two feet

in front of me. They blend in so well with their natural settings that I didn't even bother looking for them. As for Mioli and the rest of my clan, their location was a mystery, so I tried something new with my newfound senses. I mentally reached out towards my clan to find out where they were. I thought about Marlene's fetish with the color black, Cindy's heroic actions, Mioli's wisdom, and my sister's ability to irritate me. Almost immediately, I could feel their presence a short distance away, similar to a soft buzzing or flutter on my skull that told me what direction they were in. Unfortunately, I sensed there was one buzz short.

Cindy.

I feared that she didn't make it back. I walked through the village and came to the wide clearing where Alex was pinned to the giant tree by the Mort Kuup. It pained my heart to see him motionless, almost frozen, stuck with his back against a monstrous tree that was presently sucking the life force out of him. The tree had no intention of letting Alex go. A million red and pink tendrils were now seeping into his skull and a cocoon-like membrane had formed around his torso and legs. His hands were splayed open as if he was trying to push away from his woodland prison but he had already become a part of the tree. The one aspect that was oddly comforting was his face for he did not seem to be in pain. With his eyes shut in a blissful manner, he seemed content and at peace. Maybe that's how we all feel before we die.

I tried to feel his presence with my mind, to receive a vibration of life from within his body. But there was nothing, just the rush of hollow wind that combed through the Kembeqri forest all around me.

"That is not the wind that you feel."

Mioli's words did not startle me. I felt her presence come near me a few moments ago, but I was concentrating on Alex's condition.

"What is it then? The voice of death?"

OK, I agree that it sounded a little morbid but I guess a little of Marlene's mind was stuck in my head.

"No, it is the movement of life," Mioli replied. "You can feel the rush of its energy flow through this forest. Your friend is now a part of that energy."

My heart dropped in my chest causing a lump to form in my throat.

"So, he's gone, isn't he? The yolk of that egg didn't work after all."

"It's too early to say. The fact that he's still able to breathe the air proves that something is different. Creatures are normally expired or dried up after being a Mort Kuup's host for this long. No, something very different is happening here."

It was evident that Mioli was just as baffled as I was about Alex's plant problem. But I also had more concerns.

"Where's Cindy?"

Mioli slowly lowered her head. Not a good sign.

"Lost," she whispered. "I could not see where the skeeners took her once Os-Gouvox attacked. I am sorry."

I expected to hear that. Os-Gouvox took us by surprise at the most inopportune moment. It was as if he planned it that way. I took a second to reach out to Cindy's conscience to see if I could locate her. There was barely a flutter, but there *was* something there. A pinpoint of light or movement in my mind that told me that she was still alive. But I couldn't reach her. Just like Derek.

"Our class is starting to shrink, Jarvis," I heard Marlene say. She had been sitting on top of a massive boulder that was glossy smooth and surrounded by a floral bed of dark magenta. She stared longingly at Alex with her legs pulled up into her chest as her head rested on her folded arms. "It's just you, me, and your sister now. Yippee."

I noticed that Marlene was slightly rocking back and forth obviously some kind of nervous tick she possessed.

"You okay, Marlene?"

"Be hopeful," her voice barely audible for once. "He said be hopeful. We're being picked off one-by-one and he said be hopeful."

I took a glance at Alex and then back at Marlene, realizing that there was some humanity hiding inside her empty soul somewhere. Alex had broken through her shell and now I had a responsibility to help her out of that shell.

"Alex is a smart guy, Marlene," I told her. "He has a positive outlook on everything. I'm sure he believes we can find a way home. I *know* we can find a way home."

"You're all talk and no…" Marlene faltered, then gazed down at me. "Actually, you *are* a show. That little puff of white fire you blew out of your mouth earlier. What was that about?"

"I …I don't know how that happened," I said nervously. "It just…it just happened."

"No, Jarvis. Floods happen. Earthquakes happen. Stuff happens. White fire spouting from your mug doesn't just happen. It's bad enough that we're on an alien planet but spontaneous combustion is just a little too heavy for me *and* for Jade. You seriously freaked her out."

"I'm sure I did," failing to hide the shame in my voice.

"If you're going to turn into some kind fire-breathing extraterrestrial, at least give us a heads up."

"I'll explain it to you as soon as I have someone explain it to me." Mioli stood several feet away staring at me. I nodded my head and she understood. She turned away from me and headed up into the treetops.

"Come with me."

To tell you the truth, I had no idea what was happening to me. The world around me had completely changed. It didn't change physically, but the way I reacted to my surroundings felt different. The way it felt and the sounds that emanated from my environment seemed to hit me as a physical force, their sound waves were as real as someone's hand tapping me on my back. The way the rays of their suns hit me; it was like I could actually hold it and bend it, not with my hands but with my mind. I sensed that there was a new universe that could be manipulated completely under my will. The thing that bothered me was that I couldn't understand why this was happening to me. All six of us came to Zuu on the same ship but I was the only one exhibiting these weird abilities. Pardon the pun, but why did I have to be the black sheep?

I'm always the odd man out, the last to be picked at flag football, the first to miss out on the last frozen juice bar served in the cafeteria line, but those matters seemed trivial compared to this. These abilities did not seem temporary. They were going to change my life forever. They would alter the way I viewed the world and myself. And could I control these powers or would they control me? That's another thing that really scared me.

After 10 minutes of walking in silence through the street-wide branches of the Kembeqri forest, Mioli led me up to the highest plateau of a grassy earth mound that swirled its way to an apex above the forest. The landscape of this planet sometimes reminded me of the fantasy worlds that I saw illustrated in those "fantasy world" magazines. I thought to myself when I saw illustrations of floating mountains and bug-eyed monsters, *wouldn't it be wild if a place like that actually existed?* Now here I am, traversing across a tree that's as wide as my school and receiving guidance from an alien whose real face is a mask.

At least I think it's her real face.

"It is not my real face, Jarvis. The atmosphere on this

planet is poisonous to me. It keeps me alive."

Mioli didn't even turn around. She had read my thoughts that quickly. I hate it when she does that.

"But I thought all the enclosures on Zuu had different atmospheres to support all life forms?"

"The atmosphere on Kozus could not be duplicated. The Eszok are not totally capable of recreating everything."

"Well, at least they can't read minds."

"I am sorry. As I said before, you are a very loud thinker."

"I guess I have a lot on my mind. Can you blame me?"

"Not at all. Your abilities have more than presented themselves to you. This is just the beginning."

"You mean there's more?"

"You will be able to remember anything that has been said, that has been done, what you hear, in very minute detail. You will be able to manipulate the movement of objects by just thinking about it. Also, you do realize that we had this conversation without even speaking?"

I stopped and realized that she was telling the truth. When I thought about it, I don't actually remember moving my mouth to form words in the last five minutes. And now that she mentioned it, I also realized the last few words I said sounded hollow like there was a small echo to them, as if they were being heard a long distance away without me having to yell.

Now, I was freaking out. I was using my abilities without even knowing it.

"Do not...freak out," Mioli said, in my head once again.

"Could you please stop doing that?" I said as gently as I could, but it came out more snappy than kindly.

"I apologize, but it is hard not to respond to someone who thinks so clearly. I cannot read your thoughts, only sense them." Mioli paused for a moment. "I sensed them when I was at the Grarg."

"Why were you there in the first place?"

"I was there to sabotage the Eszok's equipment. But while I was there, I felt a strong vibration come from you that was riddled with extreme frustration. I couldn't determine if it was controlled rage or a desperate sadness. The mix of emotional power that is within you is one that I've never come in contact with before. There is some kind of war going on inside of you, Jarvis."

"No, there isn't!" I spat out. "You don't know what you're talking about."

I couldn't understand why I was so angry all of a sudden. And at the same time, I did. She was getting too intrusive. I've spent my whole life blocking out a horrible memory and I've made changes to protect myself, my mom, and my sister from making that memory manifest itself. There was nothing I could do but to suppress the memory, but doing so made me increasingly impatient with people, quickly irritated, annoyed, and, I have to admit, frustrated. Sometimes, I felt it was so completely unfair to be loaded with certain responsibilities that I wanted to lash out and just give up. Forget about everyone and just think about Jarvis.

But the one person that kept me grounded was my mom. I felt I had a duty toward her. There was no way I could let her down. Not after what she's been through. I couldn't just throw in the towel and fall prey to my basic instincts. I had to be a better human. Unfortunately, I wasn't totally sure on how to do that.

Mioli had gone too far. That much was clear. I didn't want her sensing what was in my head anymore. The last thing I needed was another therapist to get me through the day.

"It appears I have reached a cutting off point," she said quietly. "Do not feel you must share everything with me. I'm merely a single being that wishes to understand another. We may even be able to learn things from each other."

I slowly turned to face her, somewhat intrigued that I could still get something valuable from her. She wanted to dig into my mind, so I needed to dig into hers.

"Like what?"

Mioli stopped walking and turned to me.

"Copy me," she said. "Do what I do."

Mioli raised a fist and punched the air in front of me. I stared at her wondering if she really wanted me to punch an invisible man. I did, feeling somewhat odd throwing my fist at nothing in particular. Mioli then punched the air again, kicked her leg up into the air, and landed into a fighting stance. I proceeded to do the same. Then Mioli punched, kicked into the air, spun around, and punched again. Oh, ok, so this is a fighting lesson? I did the same three maneuvers again, slightly surprised at how confident I felt in following her form perfectly.

"How was that?" I asked.

Mioli didn't answer. She punched the air, kicked into a tree, spun around, flipped backwards, twisted herself to swing her legs into a full circle, did a roundhouse kick, jumped over my head, slammed her fist into tree, and made a piece of fruit fall directly into the palm of her hand. She looked at me.

"Do what I just did in exactly the same order," she said.

My jaw fell open. *Yeah, right!*

"I don't...," I started to say.

"You saw what I did. Mimic my actions. Try it."

For real? Is she serious? My first thought was, *I fought Derek, not Bruce Lee. How can I imitate what you just did?* Then I stayed still, stared at her, and was shocked that I could remember every single move that she had just done. I just saw what she did and her moves were fresh in mind. All I had to do was move my body in response to what I had remembered. I took a breath and closed my eyes. Without hesitating, I punched the air, kicked the same tree, spun around, flipped backwards, twisted myself to swing my legs into a full circle, did a roundhouse kick, jumped over Mioli's head, slammed my fist into another tree, and made a different piece of fruit fall directly into my hand. What the...?!

I was breathless. I stared at the fruit that plopped so comfortably into my hand. My head was buzzing with exhilaration and electric activity. "How did I do that?"

"Your mind is beginning to remember things at an

accelerated rate. You can mimic every fighting maneuver from the very first time you see it. You could learn many things in a very short time without much effort."

"That's beyond awesome! I wonder what else I could learn? I could learn calculus, astronomy, physics, philosophy, music – everything! Within two semesters!"

"Not only that, you're mind seems to desire a humanistic aspect of learning. You want to know more about other life forms around you."

"Well, I can already sense the presence of …I guess, other humans. Are you going to tell me how I can read their minds, too?"

"That is something I cannot teach. It's like me teaching your tongue how to taste. You can't teach something what it was meant to do. The Koz are very aware of metaphysical forces and that is our nature. Our ability to sense your feelings seems very upsetting to you. Therefore, if you wish to keep your thoughts concealed, you can do it by focusing on yourself. Your thoughts can only be heard or felt by someone if you're projecting your mind to them."

"Projecting my mind?"

"It's just like speaking to another person except you're not using your physical body to do it. You did it only a few moments ago."

"Yeah, I guess I did," I said, but it sounded too easy. I wasn't really focused on Mioli when I said that I was freaking out, but somehow she caught that anyway. It's bad enough being an 18 year old trying to figure out where I stand in the universe and in my relationships with friends and family, now I can't even keep my thoughts to myself without being exposed. Saying 'this sucks' doesn't fully capture the foreboding possibilities of this new ability.

The horizon of the surrounding Kembeqri forest was finally reached as Mioli and I ascended the pinnacle of the towering mound of earth. We could see a huge vista of ghostly shapes in the distance. The vast, encompassing enclosures on Zuu resembled silver mountains peacefully lounging beyond the turquoise treetops. A flock of orange and white avian creatures sailed over our heads as a refreshing twilight breeze billowed through my soiled shirt and Mioli's loose-hanging smock. There was a large, bright sphere of light settling beyond the mountains of cages. It created a surreal sunset that caused the sky to melt from fuchsia to purple to a cool, dark blue splattered with stars and colorful nebulas. From this vantage point, I felt like I could touch the stars and become part of the universe. And now that my senses were heightened, I felt like I really could.

Little, squiggly surges of vibrant energy were wiggling down my neck and through my trapezius muscle, almost as if I was feeding off the universe. The sensation made me tremble and my teeth chatter a little. I wasn't cold yet I had the sensation that I was in the middle of a gigantic baseball stadium and the glare of a billion eyes were causing my muscles to vibrate intensely. My mind didn't know what to focus on first and I thought I was being pulled apart in 50 different directions. It didn't hurt, but for the first time, my thoughts felt like solid objects moving around in my head. A literal, three-dimensional puzzle was floating around in my head and I knew that when I mentally connected certain pieces together, I could perform a special ability. Suddenly, this viku thing started to make sense.

"An uninhibited connection to the universe usually clears the path to an individual's potential."

After the cosmic surge subsided, I heard Mioli's comment and looked at her.

"Is that something your yoga instructor taught you?"

"It is universal knowledge, Jarvis. Every species knows that there is life everywhere in our existence. You must draw upon that life force to help you identify your own. That is what identifies and strengthens your own viku."

"You end up discovering what you are by discovering what you're not."

The words left my lips without even thinking about them. I just knew them to be true.

"Exactly. You felt it, didn't you? The solid presence of your viku forming itself within your mind? The universe is helping your species return to its former self."

"How come I'm the only with a viku? The others should have it, too, then."

"They will, in time. But yours is developing much more

rapidly than theirs. It's hard to say why. It may be that the universe feels more attracted to your mind."

"It's probably because I'm always the oddball. I never fit in anywhere."

This may not have been the best moment for self-pity, but I couldn't help it. I had to face it. I was a weirdo. I never fit in with anyone else's cliques or clubs because I didn't act, talk, or do the same things that other kids did. I just didn't have the desire or the drive to be who they were. Although I enjoyed not being categorized with the common teen masses, it felt painfully lonely. Not knowing where you fit in had influences on what you should say and whom you should say it to. I always said and did whatever I felt and in doing so, I alienated myself from the rest of school society. I had very few friends and low self-esteem. I would never let my mom, and especially my sister, know exactly how unaccepted I felt. Sometimes, I even fooled myself by ignoring my isolation and engaged in friendly banter to whoever would notice me. It still didn't erase the fact that I was actually envious of other kids, envious of their acceptance by their peers. That was something I never had and Jade always reveled in. I guess I was envious of her, too.

"Where is Jade anyway?" I said, trying to change the subject.

"She's in the Kembeqri shelters. She was very upset by what she saw today."

"What happened exactly? What made me pass out?"

"Your viku spiked. You channeled a tremendous amount

of anxiety and directed it towards the source, Os-Gouvox. You caused his transport to explode in mid-air."

I could not believe it.

"You're kidding? Did I…kill him?"

"Os-Gouvox is a zoid. He cannot be killed, but he can be destroyed. Whether he exists or not remains to be seen. But if he survived, we will have another chance to obliterate him. Then I will wear his limbs as a trophy piece."

I knew Mioli hated Os-Gouvox as much as anyone would, but I didn't think she was ready to kill him, or deactivate him, or whatever you do to end the life of a zoid.

"I wish he was a living soul so I could kill him!"

Mioli's words shocked me. I didn't know her that well but her last words were contradictory to her calm demeanor.

"Um, a little harsh, aren't we?"

"Hardly. We are at war with the Zuuminion, Jarvis. Can't you see that? With your newfound abilities the Isagetti would have an advantage to win back our freedom. You merely need to watch a zoid of the Zuuminion in battle and be able to mirror every single move and strike he takes. You could be an unstoppable force, Jarvis."

"Whoa! Wait a minute now! Are you trying to get me involved in some kind of galactic war? The Isa-what? What are you talking about? I don't even know all of the Eszok and what they're all about. All I know is that the ones that are running this planet are a bunch of stone-throwing jerks. The Gatekeeper and

Os-Gouvox seem more dangerous than they are."

"The Gatekeeper works for the Eszok but he does not rebel. He gathers hundreds of different species for the Eszok and stands by silently letting the Eszok belittle, torture, and murder dozens of races in the name of domination and science. His heartless stance makes him a traitor to anything that breathes. Os-Gouvox has been programmed by the Eszok to feel nothing and to attack anything that defies Eszokian rule. They both must be destroyed and you, Jarvis, have the power to do it. You must help us."

"What exactly are you asking me to do, Mioli? I don't know how I did what I did to Os-Gouvox and now you're asking me to use my power as a weapon?"

Mioli seemed to catch herself and appeared to understand that she was asking too much from me.

"I am not a killer, Mioli. I'm sorry the universe is the way it is, I really am. Our planet isn't in any better shape, either. But don't ever ask me to kill someone. That's something I just can't do."

My senses had obviously been heightened because now I could sense the shame not only in Mioli's voice, but in her own body. It was like a shroud of nakedness had fallen upon my shoulders making me want to run and hide. But the shame was not mine, it was Mioli's.

"I...I apologize. It's just that I've never encountered a species with an ability as powerful as yours. But I understand that these powers are strange to you and you're probably somewhat overwhelmed."

"Ya think?!"

"May I teach you something?"

Mioli's question seemed a little rehearsed, as if she had waited for just the right moment to ask me this. I was cautious, but curious.

"What?" I said, looking at her sideways.

Mioli's robes fluttered with a delicate air when she placed herself next to me at the precipice of the lofty earth formation. She crossed her legs Indian-style and faced the horizon, draping her arms directly down the center of her body, one on top of the other. She held her head level then lowered her brow slightly.

"When one becomes lost in his way, it is best to let the universe guide you."

"And how exactly does one do that?"

I didn't mean to sound negative, but I couldn't ignore how cheesy that sounded.

"Please don't underestimate the life force of the universe, Jarvis."

"Ok, ok, It's cool," I said. "I'm keeping an open mind. Work your magic on me."

I crossed my legs maybe a little too enthusiastically, faced the horizon next to Mioli, and formed a V shape with my arms, one hand over the other, positioning myself in what felt like a yoga position. I did my best to clear my mind, threw away any preconceived notions of what to expect, and tried to convince myself that whatever Mioli was about to do would help me better understand and control these new abilities.

"Let's do this."

"What I'm about to teach you is a universal practice. Every species in the known universe has developed their own method of connecting with celestial energy. The Uka call it Shoku'un, the Faumese call it The Trance, the Kembeqri, my people, call it Ushan. It is a metaphysical state to help you reconnect with the soul of the universe."

"The universe has a soul?" I asked apprehensively.

"The universe is made up of not only stars and planets, Jarvis, but of billions of sentient life forms, each with their own thoughts and vikus. These billions of life forms create a vibration in the universe that is unimaginably powerful and enlightening all at once. By practicing Ushan you can tap into that power and reconnect, as well as strengthen, your natural-born viku."

"Really?" I had to admit, I was somewhat impressed. "What do I do?"

"Close your eyes. Block out what you see and just concentrate on what you feel. Focus on your mental senses. The vibrations of the universe can only be absorbed when you let down all your physical senses. Forget about the feeling of your clothes upon your skin, the ground that you sit upon, the air you breathe, and search for the warmth of the universal soul."

It sounded complicated. Mioli told me to ignore all these things that I never even paid attention to. Now that she told me to ignore them, I couldn't help but focus on them. So it took me almost a full ten minutes to actually relax.

I imagined myself lying naked on a beach in Fiji. Of course, there would be no one around cause I would be embarrassed, not relaxed if people saw me naked. I've seen pictures of Fiji and I remember the water being unrealistically clear. You could see straight to the bottom. I could just imagine how completely relaxing it would be to lie floating in that crystal clear liquid. Not have a care in the world and just float for hours, listlessly. I imagined the sparkles in the water forming into tiny, twinkling stars and colored the clear water with ebony ink. There I was, floating in space but able to feel any minute disturbance within the ripples of the water. It was absolutely incredible. I felt like I was really there.

My vision of peace was about to put me to sleep when I felt a very light tingle on the back of my head. It felt as if a tiny, cold ant was crawling up my back but I knew it couldn't be some kind of insect cause I felt it *inside* of my skin. The weird thing was that I relished its presence. If it really were a bug, I would've made a ridiculous scene. I hate bugs! But this creepy feeling inside my neck felt new and interesting and stimulating. I didn't want it to stop. I wanted more. And then, as if the tingling had heard me, it spread gradually down my back, flowed into my rib cage, up into my head, and deep into my spine. There was the sensation of being pulled back into a mist of powdered sugar and warm rain, the tingling using my skeleton as a carriage to carry me into its world. I was immensely saturated in the pleasure of this feeling, but then something happened.

A single, negative thought had somehow appeared to me while I was bathing in this new sense of bliss: how do I get back?

The light rain of warm sugar suddenly left me, and the tingling stopped. I opened my eyes and found that I was crying. Not tears of water, but of blood. Streaks of crimson dripped from my cheeks, but I didn't care. I wasn't afraid anymore because I knew what was happening.

"Your mind is beginning to remember," Mioli whispered. "It takes a toll on your body, but your human mind will begin to remember what it's truly capable of doing."

"So this is just temporary," I said, inspecting the smears of red on my fingers. "My brain is just warming up?"

"It's emerging from its overextended slumber. Your species has not been connected to its viku for centuries. It must have been lost or pushed back into its sub-conscience through years of evolution."

Could Mioli be telling the truth? It makes so much sense. Not only because it sounded right, but, because it *felt* right. I've never felt so confident about anything else in my life before. I am supposed to have these abilities because this is how humans were created. Even *I* know that we're not able to use our full brain capacity. However, now that I've been stripped away from my home world, my human body has triggered its defense mechanism and has dug its way into my conscience to manifest its natural-born viku. It was always there. It just needed to be reactivated. I guess it took a full-blown, extra-terrestrial kidnapping to do that.

"This is crazy," I said quietly to myself. Mioli, silent for a moment, turned to me. Then she gazed out at the horizon, seeming to have something else on her mind.

"This life normally is," she said.

Chapter 12
THE ZUUMINION

I found it amazing that I was even able to get 1 hour of sleep that night. After my little chat with Mioli that evening, my head was buzzing with all sorts of ideas, visions, thoughts, theories, and mathematical equations. I despise math yet I discovered that when I recalled a certain math problem from my quiz the other day, it was easily solved. I didn't even need a pen and paper - I just did it in my head. Man! Why couldn't I have had this brainpower during finals?

There were more than just practical facts swimming around in my head clicking together and making sense. There were these new senses that I had quickly developed that made my world more kinetic and more alive than usual. The life force in living objects like trees and plants hummed mildly all around me like a huge biological machine. I could sense where hundreds of creatures were located by branching out my mind like I was stretching out my fingers to feel the rain. What was really weird was that I could begin to understand the Kembeqri. I couldn't completely understand what they were saying, but I could translate their emotions through the sounds they made. When they were irritated, impatient, or excited they made a quick succession of clicking sounds. They creaked their branch-like appendages when they were interested or in a conversation. And they also moaned pleasantly if something pleased them. It was uncanny. Never in my life did I think it was possible to actually communicate with a tree.

Aside from improving my alien relations, I was still worried about Jade. I know that what happened at the Xeeths disturbed her and she couldn't come to terms with it, I mean, how would you feel if you saw your older brother shooting white flames out of his mouth? You'd probably tip-toe around his field of vision, too, not knowing when he would blow again. I reached out to her with my mind the following morning to see how she was. The Kembeqri were a little old-fashioned in some respects because they believed that males and females of our species should sleep in separate shelters. So since I was the only male left of our clan, I slept in a treetop shelter by myself. When I reached Jade's mind, it was similar to lightly brushing against cotton with thin fingers from my brain. It felt kind of girly, like lace and feathers –so weird.

She was asleep, but not sound asleep. Her dreams must have been filled with something dreadful because she squirmed and whimpered while she slept. I've never seen her do that before. Jade was a hardcore sleeper and snored like there was no tomorrow, just like mom. 200 tons of exploding nitrogen couldn't stir her from her slumber. But now, she couldn't even get slightly comfortable on her heavenly mound of Kembeqri-strewn pulmp stalks, an abnormally soft bed of shredded plants.

I was a lousy older brother. I made a promise to myself and to my mother to protect my younger sister, no matter what the cost. And here I am instilling an unnatural, ethereal fear in her while she struggled to keep her sanity in a hostile, strange environment. For once, I felt like the sinister enemy and not the valiant protector. How could I turn this around and prevent the past from repeating itself? The last thing I want on my shoulders is the blame for another family tragedy. Whenever I think about what happened to my…

No! Stop it, Jarvis! You told yourself to put it behind you and focus on the present. Now pull yourself together and take charge. There's nothing about your past that will help you or your sister get out of this mess. Now, focus!!

I bolted upright from my extravagant bed of shredded flora, not because of my concern for my sister, but because something foreign struck my newly discovered senses. There was no one else in my shelter but me, so the sudden presence of a physical danger hit me with the force of a speeding garbage truck.

My eyes darted around the room searching for the phantom menace that assaulted me. There was no one else in the room: just my natural bed, some weird Kembeqri home items, and me. But there something was in the air. Something very dangerous…and powerful.

I poked my head through the hollow of my shelter expecting to find some kind of mean, man-eating creature, but there was only a peaceful stillness that blanketed the Kembeqri maze of twisting trunk "streets". A hazy morning mist brought a damp beauty to its mystical floral atmosphere.

I crept out of my shelter and walked slowly onto one of the wide branches that were elevated high above the forest floor. There was a disturbing silence.

There was definitely something wrong here.

The Kembeqri were resting all around in the treetops above and around me. I could now sense where they were located and it was like I could see them without even looking at them. They were sleeping, or in a trance-like state that was similar to sleeping. For a moment, I wondered what a tree would dream about.

My cautious roaming sent me higher into the canopy of the ominous forest, branches of which harbored a large assortment of bizarre fungi that resembled horns bursting from their boughs. From this vantage point, I received a panoramic view of the Kembeqri forest and the valley beyond. The sky was a silvery mesh of light blue reminding me that even the Kembeqri lived in a caged world. But it was at this point that the danger I sensed this morning could be heard…and seen.

Less than a mile away, an object that looked like a massive column of steel was crashing its way through the forest. All types of flying creatures were fleeing into the skies, completely bewildered at the invasion of this violent intruder. I couldn't tell what it was doing but it seemed to be walking towards my direction destroying the environment along the way.

I took one step closer to get a better view then… CRASH! A huge, metallic arm the size of a city bus came down into my field of vision and annihilated the branch I was standing on. My world suddenly started spinning into a whirlpool of tree bark and countless leaves. I could feel the pit of my stomach open up as the ground below rushed toward me at frightening speed.

What on earth just happened?

I was about to die and I didn't even know how or why it happened. All I could do was scream my face off. My body flipped over itself in mid-air and then I hit something. At first, I thought it was the ground, but it was plush and feathery. My surroundings were buzzing by at break neck speed and I was still in one piece. When my equilibrium had returned, I saw that I was on the back of a gigantic, gorgeous blue bird with rainbow wings.

"Nuvu! Man, we need to give you some money for all of the lives that you've saved!"

As Nuvu released an ear-splitting birdcall, I turned backwards to see what had destroyed my temporary roost.

An enormous, rusty, steel contraption that towered over the trees was thrashing its way through the forest. Along its six arachnoid legs were an incredibly surreal amount of rotating blades, buzzsaws, pinchers, axes, chainsaws, and other weird-shaped blades that sliced through the trees like hot butter. The legs were attached to a gigantic central pylon that was taller than a ten-story building and was warped and swirled like a used Q-tip. What was so scary was not the speed that the "monster chopper" hacked through the formidable trunks of the Kembeqri enclosure or how nothing solid could stop its rampage, but that there were two of them hot on our tail. Nuvu dove deep into the damp realm of the monumental trees evading the destructive giants that were leveling the forest. Where they came from, I couldn't tell but I had a strong feeling that they were searching for six stranded teenagers.

In a few seconds we reached the Kembeqri village, an uneasy indicator that the monster choppers were too close for comfort. My first thought was to get everybody out of bed, but Marlene, Mioli, and Jade were already up. They stood looking anxious in the main plaza, almost as if they already knew what was going on.

"I could totally hear you in my head!" Marlene said as Nuvu swooped low to the ground allowing me to return to good ol' terra firma. "It was like you were right there in our hut, but you weren't. That was so cool! You heard him, too, didn't you, Jade?"

Jade didn't look very happy that she heard my voice in her head. She just looked me up and down as if I had peed on myself.

"I, I..I don't know what I heard," she lied.

"What did I...? Then you guys must know what's coming?" I said restlessly. "You know what I saw?"

"Yes," Mioli said. "They are devices of the Zuuminion called Rovers. Ultra-destructive and unstoppable. They must be searching for humans. We must leave, now, before they reach the village!"

"But where can we go? Wherever we go on this planet, the Zuuminion will find us. They run this place!"

234

"I understand that," Mioli paused. "That's why we must get you off this planet."

My heart virtually flew in circles around my rib cage.

"You can do that?"

"I can't, but I know a group of people who can."

"Who?"

"It doesn't matter who, Jarvis," Jade blurted out. "If they can get us off this planet and back on our own, we're gonna do whatever they want."

"But what about Cindy, Alex, Cadzow, and…Derek."

A visible struggle contorted Jade's face. She was completely at odds with her own selfish desires and what she felt was right. I was shocked to hear what she said next.

"Leave 'em! I can't take anymore of this space alien crap. I am too through! I want my green grass and blue sky back. I want out! I want to go home!"

"Jade, you don't mean that…" I started to say, but the sudden arrival of a large tree stump struck the tree above us causing everyone to scatter for safety. The Rovers were at the borders of the village destroying the beautiful trees as they clanked their way through.

"To the Seership!" Mioli yelled from somewhere in the fray. When the dust settled momentarily, I saw her robes dart out from underneath an arching tree branch and scurry out of the plaza. Marlene and Jade emerged out of nowhere running up behind her quickly catching up.

I got out from a cramped corner between two swirling branches and began to follow. But as I ran through the plaza, something above me caught my eye. It was Alex. His limp body still pinned painfully to the trunk of a gargantuan tree that was currently sucking the life out of him. As horrific of an experience that must be, his face showed nothing short of complete bliss, as if he was enjoying the most fantastic dream. I never thought I would feel a connection to someone so quickly. I don't have a lot of friends, but I thought Alex was a good guy. Right when I was getting to know him, some parasite decides to take him away. Not cool.

Even worst was that we had to leave him, leading the Rovers away from his area.

"We'll be back for you, buddy," I said out loud. I knew he couldn't hear me, but it made me feel better to say it and hear it. "I promise we'll be back."

I don't think I ever ran so fast in my life. Mioli was a tall, athletic, and healthy individual who had a knack for finding hidden passages through huge hollows of contorted, twisted trees. I felt like I was running through a kid's playground, skipping across branches, sliding down and through snaking trees, and even swinging across gaps on long vines. When I thought we'd never reach the ground in time, a glimmer of sleek silver glinted in the morning sunlight. The reflection winked at us, guiding us in its direction. The Seership was ready for action.

After Mioli leapt into the driver's alcove, she swung her hands across the dash clicking and flipping switches left and right. The Seership hummed to life and jerked upwards while the girls and I took a seat behind Mioli. It was at this moment that I felt an absence in our group, our clan, or whatever you want to call it. Our meager crew of kidnaped kids was cut in half by enduring circumstances that were clearly far beyond our control. And even though I wasn't exactly close friends with anyone else in the group, I sensed a longing for their company. Well, maybe not a longing, but I felt it was my duty to keep us together. Oddly enough, that feeling even included Derek. I guess I needed an argument every now and then to keep me on my toes.

The Seership climbed effortlessly above the thick canopy of the forest giving us the feeling that we had just emerged from a virtual ocean. Our position also provided a very disturbing view of our pursuers who seemed to have called out the whole interstellar armada to capture six kids. A humongous flying vessel that was 10 times the size of the Goodyear Blimp hovered directly in our flight path. It was flanked by dozens of smaller pill-shaped ships that were heavily equipped for battle. Steel appendages that resembled fire cannons and spindly machine guns adorned the hull of each ship and were all pointed at us.

"The Zuuminion!" Mioli exclaimed.

"Wow," Marlene whispered, "all this for us?"

I remember how Mioli mentioned that the Zuuminion was

the ruling organization that operated the Zuu planet. Although their practices seemed similar to a dictatorship, they acted more like wardens reigning over their captives and treated them like unintelligent sheep. From what I understood, this organization was populated completely by unemotional zoids and I could see the frantic urgency in Mioli's movements that displayed her fear in being detained.

"What do you want us to do?" I asked her.

"Hold on!" she replied.

Our ship sped directly toward the Zuuminion's massive lead vessel, then ducked down below it, prompting a quick and futile rain of laser shots from the enemy, and emerged on the other side. My stomach lurched once Mioli stepped on the gas and made the Seership shift into high speed. I knew we'd be safe once we were out of the Kembeqri enclosure and out of range. We zipped through the entry portal of the huge enclosure and soared out into the wide plains that gave the impression we had entered a completely different world. I had to remind myself that the enclosures were recreations of environments of a variety of worlds. When the cool snap of Zuu's original atmosphere hit me in the face, it was like a slap of fresh air compared to the damp humidity of the Kembeqri habitat.

It then occurred to me, how in the world did a ship the size of 12 city blocks get inside the enclosure with all of its entourage? As far as I could tell there were no openings or doors in the mountainous aviaries that could allow passage of something so huge. When I turned back to see if the Zuuminion was following us, I had received the answer.

One thing I've learned since I've been on Zuu is that the normally accepted rules of science and technology have been broken and expanded into a realm that I could barely comprehend. The huge airship had made its way out of the Kembeqri enclosure just by floating through it, as if it wasn't even there. It shimmered slightly, very similar to what the air looks like around the hood of a car on a very hot day. Every vessel that flew through the aviary experienced the same phenomenon where their outer hulls began to ripple before they traversed through the iron mesh.

"Their hulls are vibrating," said Mioli, once again frighteningly perceptive of what was going on in my mind. "Any solid matter can pass through another if it vibrates at the right frequency at the sub-atomic level."

Normally, the words that came out of Mioli's mouth just now would have been lost on me with my young teenage brain that was obsessed with comic books and theme parks. I could never get into science or physics because it was just as wicked as math. But now, I'm assuming that my mind had been expanded, grasping even the most difficult of scientific concepts as child's play. I even had the formula that made the transference of matter through solid matter pop up into my brain.

However, the flight maneuvers of how to evade from an armada on a speeding Seership were beyond me. It was clear that we were not going to have an easy route out of this.

"Mioli," I said, "I don't care what you do, but whatever you do, please, make sure you get us out of this alive."

And before I knew it, we were thrust into another high speed, high-flying air chase in the clear skies of Zuu. Mioli shifted gears and our Seership took off at ludicrous speed, the Zuuminion's drones following hot on our tail. Mioli guided our craft past a series of stone formations near the shore of an enormous lake. I glanced to see if we could make it to the other side but I didn't see a speck of land. Was this some kind of ocean? The waters were not blue, they glistened with a brilliant aqua green and in certain areas along the water surface were huge plumes of white smoke reaching for the sky. I couldn't understand what they were at first. They looked like spouts from extremely large alien humpback whales. As we got closer, I saw that the massive plumes of mist were sea sprays emanating from gigantic whirlpools in the ocean.

"What are those?" I shouted to Mioli.

"Water exchangers," she responded. "The water gets recycled on a regular basis to keep it pure and at the proper levels to sustain life."

Baffled, I stared at her. "But it's a whole ocean."

"Yes," she stated unastounded, as if recycling the waters of an entire body of water were just as mind-blowing as flushing a toilet. These Eszok were truly technical geniuses. However, my admiration of their engineering feats was short-lived when they again fired upon our Seership. Our vessel jerked to the right almost throwing everyone off their feet. A high-pitched beeping started and a green light bounced off the dashboard.

"Geez, don't you have shields on this thing?" said Jade.

"Not anymore," breathed Mioli. "They just disabled them. The next shot we take could knock us out of the sky"

And that's when I saw him. Os-Gouvox's transport zipped through columns of mist straight towards our crippled vessel as if he was just waiting for Mioli to say those words.

"Mioli, I wish you didn't say that out loud," I told her as I motioned behind us. Mioli glanced behind us and said something incomprehensible. I can only imagine that it was a curse word that our linguistic implants couldn't translate. She spun around and pushed a lever all the way forward and smacked a large, blue button. The Seership reared forward at yet an even higher speed. The sea below us looked like green silver and the towers of mist were obliterated from our view. Our feet must have been somehow anchored to the floor through molecular magnetism (another scientific possibility that I later discovered) because my body leaned backwards as the ship rocketed across the green body of water. I could feel my skin being pulled to the back of my head as tears squeezed out of my eyes. I thought I was about to lose consciousness until the extreme sensation suddenly subsided. The landscape around us gradually stopped speeding past us and the Seership made some unusual spitting sounds. The vessel rattled and hissed then halted in mid-air above Zuu's recyclable ocean.

"Umm.." said Jade quietly. "Was that supposed to happen?"

Mioli repeatedly tapped a button with exasperation, but

the Seership stayed silent. We were stranded high above an intimidating ocean surrounded by giant whirlpools and floating mist. I looked around to see if the Zuuminion had followed us even though we went into sonic speed.

"It looks like we're alone," I said as I scanned the environment. All I could hear was the deafening roar of the massive whirlpools below us. They were thoroughly impressive, but terrifyingly eerie since the bottom of them could not be seen. The nearest pit had to be at least 500 feet wide and it appeared to be the smallest in the family. I imagined what might be at the bottom of those daunting aquatic maws when the sound of a light hiss cut through the air. It must have been the sound of an air vacuum being broken as the monstrous Zuuminion vessel dropped out of sonic speed and stopped less than a mile behind us. The smaller fleet of armed flying vessels scattered around us within seconds after their supersonic flight. We couldn't shake these guys. I hate to sound cliché, but we were sitting ducks.

Before I could even think about what to do, a shot exploded in the air behind me. I ducked and shouted, coming face-to-face with the deck of the Seership. Two more loud pops exploded in the air and then was followed by Marlene's voice, enraged and completely out of character.

"We're not going down without a fight, you dirty space turds!"

The sound shattered the air like a mini-cannon above the dull roar of the waters below us. She was wielding the hand weapon that she used against the Skeeners earlier and was now firing at the largest ship. What the hell was Marlene doing?! We were clearly outnumbered and overwhelmed. She put our precarious position into virtual suicide by firing upon our pursuers who had us completely surrounded and at their mercy. Going down without a fight seemed like the only way to go. But if Marlene decided to go Rambo instead, she could have at least given us a warning.

"Marlene! Girl, are you crazy?!" I shouted.

I stayed stomach-down on the deck of the hovercraft, knowing it was a futile stance against fifteen well-equipped alien warships. But it felt safer anyway.

"They're not going to take me alive! No probes are going up my butt!"

And those were her last words. Sadly, the Zuuminion was in control here. Like Os-Gouvox said, disobedience would not be tolerated. A seemingly insignificant electrical bolt shot from a nearby warship and exploded at Marlene's feet sending her backwards suddenly at great speed. Her legs slammed against the side of the Seership, flipping her head-over-heels, and down into the watery abyss beyond.

"MARLENE!" Jade screamed. I was too stunned to even contemplate what I had just witnessed. There was no scream, no call for help - just the sight of Marlene's frail body, dressed in black, being hurled over the side. I can't imagine what was going through her mind as she plummeted hundreds of feet into the mouth of one of those nightmarish whirlpools. Did she regret taking a last stand against our pursuers? Or was she proud to deny her body for whatever reasons the Eszok tried so hard to capture it just to see it fall out of their hands? Whatever her last thoughts were, it didn't matter now. She was gone, along with her dark and witty sarcasm.

"They...they killed her," I said in shock, barely able to even form the words. I tried to reach out to her with my mind, but there was nothing but empty darkness.

"The Eszok have ways of retrieving what they want," Mioli said. "They wouldn't have gone all the way to earth just to dispose of her."

"But you said the Eszok killed hundreds of their captives."

"Yes, but only after they've outlived their usefulness or satisfied some perverted scientific curiosity they might have had. Marlene and the others you lost were never detained long enough to be tagged."

"What do you mean?"

"They're still valuable cargo. They may search for them for days if they're still alive."

A flutter of hope rose in my chest.

"So, there's a chance Marlene, Cindy, and...Derek could still be found alive?"

"It's their planet. The Eszok control the Zuuminion who are nothing but robotic minions. When they receive an order to find someone or something, they usually do."

"But what if I...?"

An idea suddenly revealed itself to me but Jade shuffled in

between Mioli and myself and pointed into the air.

"Something's coming! They're coming!" she said frantically.

From the starboard side of the largest flying vessel, a smaller pod-shaped vehicle emerged from an opening and elegantly floated into the sky. The oblong vehicle glided on a smooth course straight to our stranded Seership. It looked like a huge, hideous vitamin seeking a collision course with our ship. When the dull point of the vessel approached our ship, it slowed and split open like a blossoming flower to reveal its computerized insides. From its gaping aperture something similar to a metal gangplank extended itself to the deck of the Seership. Immediately, I grabbed a hold of my sister and I felt a surge of an unusual warmth flow up towards my head. There was no way I'd let them take my sister. The rest of our human clan had been taken away from me, but I'd be damned if I let these monsters rip my little sister away from me. She was all I had left. I couldn't lose her.

I scanned the deck of our Seership for the weapon that Marlene used to shoot at the skeeners, but it occurred to me that when Marlene went down into the whirlpool, she still had the weapon with her. I looked around for another weapon, but everything on the Seership was foreign to me. I couldn't tell if it was a spare part or a ray gun. The second I felt that the three of us were defenseless a group of gleaming and ominous shapes marched out of the mouth of the flying capsule. They were the same zoids that we saw at the compound earlier – tall, elongated figures of distorted metal that held a collection of vile staffs buzzing with blue electricity at its end.

"Jarvis," I heard Jade say. "We're trapped...Jar...Jarvis?"

Her last words were lost to me, being erased from sound. A tingle of cold ice went up my spine, along my neck, and into my head. I didn't understand what was happening or how it had started, but I knew that I didn't want it to stop. A sensation of unusual power flowed into my head and through my body. It made my skin suddenly hot but I could feel my insides shivering. This feeling was familiar, as recognizable as the feeling you get when you go down the first drop of a tall roller coaster. Then I realized I had just experienced this feeling recently, when Os-Gouvox had ambushed us back in the Xeeths. When I felt cornered, angry, and vulnerable, this power overcame me and I was able to do something that was not humanly possible.

Hmmm... maybe it was time for round 2?

I didn't have any weapons but I thought about just throwing whatever I could at these zoids. Sure enough, it was as though the universe had read my thoughts. The minute I thought about throwing something, a large crate of metal parts rose from the floor in front of Mioli and violently hurled itself at the nearest zoid, striking it in the chest and producing a shower of sparks.

Mioli and Jade looked at each other and said in unison, "Who did that?"

Normally, I would have thought the same thing, but it was crystal clear now – it was me. I had connected with an inner metaphysical energy that had always been inside of me and I was beginning to understand more fully on how to use it. My thought was the same as a physical act.

I wanted to tear apart the Seership and throw its entire clunky, heavy, volatile innards into the approaching zoids. As I rose to my feet, pieces of the Seership tore itself away from the helm and dashboard and rocketed into the poor figures that thought they had a chance to detain us. Huge pieces of the ship collided against the zoids and the ship behind them, tearing their limbs from their bodes and causing a plethora of minor explosions.

And then their leader appeared at the mouth of their ship, a slim figure of steel and rage that could not bear to be outmoded by a human teenager. Os-Gouvox rushed out of the ship and down the gangplank, the chink of his hefty robotic feet vibrating against the catwalk was ringing in my ears. Before I could even think about aiming a Seership thruster at his head, he swirled his fully charged staff above his metal noggin and pointed it directly at me.

"Not this time, human!" he shouted.

A blinding light engulfed my vision. Sound disappeared and a brutal, unsympathetic force wrapped itself around my senses. A void of darkness devoured my body and our mini battle had suddenly been defeated.

We lost.

Chapter 13
CADZOW'S SECRET

I opened my eyes and as soon as I did, I felt the uncontrollable urge to close them again. I had never experienced such bodily pain until now. Every cell in my body was on fire. A sensation similar to hot needles coated with rubbing alcohol enveloped my entire being. The urge to scream radiated from my gut, but I felt too lethargic to even open my mouth. I just closed my eyes and let the pain take me in and before I knew it, I had fallen back asleep.

I only discovered that I had fallen asleep when I awoke to the sound of Jade's voice, which sounded strained and weak.

"Jarvis," she said, as if she was just waking up from a deep sleep. It sounded like she had been knocked out for a couple of hours, too. "Jarvis, wake up. Come on, wake up. Open your eyes."

Jade sounded like she was on the verge of tears. I could understand why she would break down now. She had lost her home, her mother, her freedom (and her boyfriend, I guess) all in a matter of hours. It would be a lot even for a full grown adult to endure and she was only fifteen. I was actually amazed that she was able to last this long without losing her mind.

I suppose I didn't give her enough credit. She was a strong little girl. Sometimes a little too strong with her mouth and attitude, but if she needed to, she could stand on her own. She didn't always need me.

But I could tell that she did now. She sounded genuinely scared and fragile, qualities I wouldn't normally describe her with. This was the moment when someone with more life experience would put their arm around you and tell you that everything was going to be alright. Unfortunately, our mother wasn't here. Just me. The pleading in her voice signaled to me that she needed her big brother to make everything alright.

The fuzziness in my head was starting to dissipate as I forced myself to wake up. As my consciousness began to clear, I expected to be lying flat on my back on the Seership. When my eyelids slowly peeled open, I found my body was in a vertical position, hands raised over my head and my legs slightly pulled backwards. My wrists and ankles were bound in some kind of manacle that was made from pure energy. No metal or steel hardware held my limbs in place, just a pulsating blue ring of light around both of my hands and feet binding them firmly together. My body hung suspended in mid-air over a floating, black obsidian-colored disc that periodically flashed sprawling veins of orange electrical bolts across its shiny surface. Above me was a long shaft of light that came from a skylight seemingly hundreds of feet above me.

The room I was in was a cross between Frankenstein's lab and the captain's deck of the Star Trek Enterprise. The room was a huge oval filled with floating tables covered with unrecognizable storage units, tables, flasks bubbling with multi-colored fluids, glowing machinery with a hundred different silently moving parts, and monitors that were stationary holograms. The space was brightly lit from tall, narrow windows that lined one side of the lab. Everything was ridiculously clean and appeared to be sanitized to a molecular level. All I could see through the thin window openings were magenta clouds lazily passing by which appeared too thick to be at ground level. At one point, the clouds broke and I could see a bluish haze of a horizon line that was definitely too low to be viewed from ground level. I deduced that we were in a ship, a huge vessel of some kind - most likely the same ship that captured our Seership. The Zuuminion hijacked us like futuristic pirates and made us their valued booty. First, the octopods on planet earth, now the Zuuminion on planet Zuu. Kidnaped twice in three days. That's gotta be a record.

I become somewhat frantic when I suddenly thought about the whereabouts of my sister. After all, it was her voice that woke me up. I was so preoccupied in figuring out my location that I didn't even realize that Jade was right next to me. Less than ten feet away to my left, my sister hung limp over a twin of the electrified black disc, restrained in the same fashion as I was.

Her hair was a mess. Jade's wavy, cinnamon-hued hair stuck out in all the wrong places. Her clothes were disheveled, dirty, and it looked like one of her sleeves was torn off at the cuff. Not only did she have a cut on her hand, but she also had a purple bruise forming at the curve of her elbow. She was also missing a shoe.

"Jade," I said in a croaky voice, "what in the world happened to you?"

"What do you think? I put up a fight. I knew they were going to capture me, being overgrown robotic jerks and all. But, that didn't mean I had to go quietly."

"Are you alright?"

"Yeah," she glanced back at her restrained feet. "I'm missing one of my Jordan's, though."

My mom bought her those Jordan's just a year ago. Jade had been badgering my mother for a particular style for months but my mom could never afford to buy them. However, my mom had succeeded in paying off an installment loan and it freed up a decent amount of money. So my mom surprised her one evening and Jade went through the roof. The first week, she wore them to bed. Through week two, she coordinated her church outfit to go with her flashy new sneakers. For the past year, she wore them to school every single, freaking day. Frankly, I was quite shocked she wasn't having a conniption fit. Maybe she did and I just missed it.

"You seem unusually calm for a prisoner of an alien race of robots," I said, still seasoned with an air of weak breath.

"I think the fight has gone out of me now. That was my last hurrah. I just have to accept what's going to happen to us. We're in trouble, Jarvis."

"Ya' think?"

"I'm serious, Jarvis. This is it. The end. The finish line. The final flush. Dead at fifteen."

"Stop being so dramatic, Jade. We still have a chance to get out of here." I looked around the shiny, streamlined lab for other life forms or captives, but it looked like Jade and I were alone.

"Where's Mioli and Nuvu?"

"I don't know what happened to Nuvu. I haven't seen him since we've been captured."

Jade paused for a moment.

"I think they killed Mioli though. The zoids attacked her after Os-Gouvox electrocuted you."

The little energy I had left in me felt like it was knocked right out of me.

"They killed Mioli?"

"Mioli started a fight with Os-Gouvox. I couldn't understand what she was yelling at him, but he wasn't interested in talking. A couple of swings from that staff of his and Mioli was on the floor. He let some of his goons finish the job, beat her senseless, and then she was completely still. I...I don't see how she could survive something like that."

"Unbelievable," I said in awe. "We're on another planet in another galaxy and brutality like that still exists out here. How could a robot do something like that?"

"It's evil."

"No, the people that created Os-Gouvox and the Zuuminion are evil – the Eszok. Even though their zoids can think for themselves, they're still influenced by their creators.

They probably wired them to think and act just like them."

"They programmed Os-Gouvox to beat up aliens on Zuu?"

"Or worse. I don't think they programmed him just to be a bully, but Mioli's been on the run for years. To him, Mioli was Eszok Public Enemy Number One. And since she outsmarted him so many times, he probably took it personal."

"He's a homicidal jerk!"

"He killed her because she made him look bad to his creators. I guess Os-Gouvox felt we were going to do the same to him. That Gatekeeper guy told him to capture us, not hurt us. If he had the chance, we wouldn't be having this conversation. We'd be space dust."

"Well, he had his chance back on the Seership."

"No, the Gatekeeper was there. He wouldn't act out in front of his superior."

I didn't know what I was saying, but I felt it to be completely true. I could be totally wrong about Os-Gouvox's intentions. Here I am, a fresh youngling just shipped in from little planet Earth, a meaningless floating rock mass a billion miles away, and now I'm stating the corrupt agenda of a mechanical man against his ten foot tall alien boss on another world. Maybe they had some history that caused constant friction between them. Maybe Os-Gouvox hurt or killed someone that he shouldn't have and now the Gatekeeper constantly scrutinized his every move? Whatever the case was, I felt that Os-Gouvox would act of his own accord when the powers that be turned their heads.

"It doesn't matter now, Jarvis," my sister groaned. "Look at us. We're about to be dissected like marinated frogs."

Jade had a point. Things did look a little hopeless. I had hoped my newfound viku ability would provide some avenue of escape, but knowing how $E=MC^2$ didn't seem particularly helpful at this moment. My mind was a blank. I needed to know more about this environment, this world, and the creatures that lived here. I needed to know more about the Eszok, where they came from, their purpose, and the things they've done to put them in their present position as controllers of the galaxy. More importantly, I needed to know their weakness. I felt that if I knew about Zuu as much as I knew about earth, I would be more familiar with my resources and know how to use them to my advantage. But I was at a loss of knowing exactly what do to.

I must have been quiet for awhile because when Jade spoke, it snapped me out of my mental trance.

"We're going to die here, Jarvis," she said silently.

I really wanted to say something positive, something uplifting, to let her know that everything was going to be okay. When things get their worse, a light appears at the end of the tunnel. I wasn't seeing that light this time. The room developed a harsh sense of finality, like the walls and innards of this room would be the last things I would ever see. My breathing became heavy and my heart ached to break free from my chest. But like my arms and legs, it was bound to accept any fate that this room would deliver to me. My sister and I were finally at the mercy of the all-powerful Eszok.

I hung my head low, not wanting to accept what might happen to us. "It's possible, Jade," I whispered to her, "that we may not survive this one."

Jade was quiet for a few seconds then she lifted her head and turned to me.

"I know this is messed up to tell you this now," she said, her eyes slowly welling up with tears, "but thanks."

"For what?"

"You're a good brother. You make me nuts, but I guess it's because you care."

"Well, if I didn't care, you'd make a fool of yourself. And I can't have my little sister ruining my reputation, now, can I?"

"You don't need my help to do that."

Insulting each other to the very end. It was so inappropriate and oddly touching at the same time. Before I could stop it, a tear rolled down my cheek. Where did that come from? It was like a mix of emotions that didn't go together and my heart couldn't make sense of it. So it just melted. To tease each other right before our untimely demise – it was the way we communicated, so it felt right.

"Jade, if by chance, I don't make it, and you somehow get back home, make sure mom knows I love her."

At the mention of my mom, we both started tearing up. We both loved and respected our mom to the highest degree of integrity. The thought of never seeing her again, telling her 'I love you', was heartbreaking. She didn't deserve any more tragedies in her life. It was enough that her kids were kidnaped and her husband was killed in service, but at least Jade and I had a chance of returning home. And know that just didn't seem possible.

"You know I love you, right?" I said. "You're my sister."

Jade nodded sadly. "I love you, too, Jarvis."

It then occurred to me that Jade never knew about the secret my mother and I held onto for all these years. I swore I would never speak about it to anyone, not even Jade. But that didn't matter now. The secret involved her, too, so why shouldn't she know? I figured now would be the best time to know. We have no future, so we should keep no secrets.

"Jade," I said quietly. "I think there's something you should know about our family."

The moment I said those words, I wanted to take them back. I was actually trembling. What was I thinking?

"What? What do you mean 'something I should know'?"

Jade looked at me with a confused glare. For once, I wish she hadn't listened to me.

"There's a…I, uh…I mean."

I just couldn't form the words.

"Jarvis? Jarvis Johnson?"

What in the world? My ears were playing tricks on me. Had Jade just disguised her voice? She sounded older with an Asian accent. She sounded just like…

"Mrs. Cadzow!"

When Jade shouted her name, my head snapped up and I saw our high school principal creeping in through the entry doors.

"Jade Johnson! I thought I heard your voices in here!"

Mrs. Cadzow looked like she slept in her work clothes for two weeks. Her face was no longer a symbol of stern alertness but was a vision of bewilderment. She looked thoroughly lost, but she didn't seem to be without her wits. She steadily, yet cautiously, walked into the room scanning her surroundings in awe, eyes wide with wonderment.

"What happened to the school?" she said looking around and peering through the windows. "What is this place?"

"Well, it's not Tomorrowland," I moaned.

"We've been abducted by aliens," my sister blurted out.

"Aliens?" she said, mildly alarmed. "Well, I shouldn't be surprised. I heard stories when I was in the military. They're pretty much a nuisance - flying around and making those ridiculous crop circles."

"I assure you, this is no crop circle."

"Mrs. Cadzow, there's a thousand different aliens out here," Jade said. "We're just another type of species they want to experiment on."

"Yeah, you need to get us out of here before one of them comes back!"

Mrs. Cadzow looked back at the entry doors and then at my sister and me in a very unusual manner and said something I did not expect.

"Why would I want to do that?"

Both Jade and I perked up our heads and glanced at each other. Did she...? What did...? Did...I hear her correctly?

I paused for a moment. "What did you say?

"I said, 'why would I want to do that?' " she repeated, this time with clarity and a hint of irritation. "Why would I help you escape when I went through so much trouble in bringing you here?"

There was a stillness in the air that could not be explained. It was like a light, barely audible buzz of white noise hit my ears and made me super light-headed for a split second. The shock of what she said made my mouth dry, my heart pound, and my head seemingly float away from my body. She couldn't possibly be in her right mind.

"What?!"

"I believe you heard me the second time, Jarvis Johnson."

"I heard you, but I don't believe what I'm hearing."

"Then maybe you can only believe in what you can see."

What happened next was ten times uglier than my worst nightmare. There was no way I could have predicted the transformation that Mrs. Cadzow performed. She stood directly in front of us and raised her eyes and head upwards toward the ceiling. Her head continued to roll all the way back and elongate out of her blouse. As her neck stretched upwards, the skin spread outwards and a distorted face blossomed out from her collar. While her new vile face filled in and faded to a greyish hue, her arms cracked and split themselves sideways so that now she had 4 limbs instead of two. She grew about two more feet thanks to her sickly pale legs that clicked backwards in the wrong direction at the knee. And just to top it all off, she was completely nude. Her normal, no-nonsense, principal attire tore apart as her true form revealed itself. Her body was sinewy, puke-colored, and was riddled with little protrusions on her trunk and neck like she had some type of disease. Out of all the aliens I'd seen on Zuu, it was fair to say that she was the most disgusting one to look at.

"Better?"

Jade and I both screamed.

"Now can you believe what I was saying?"

Her voice had developed several layers of octaves, like she had three voice boxes that spoke as one. I could literally feel her voice waves ruffle my clothing.

"No! No way! It's not...NO WAY!" I said, my body actually shaking with anger and fear. "You're one of them? You're an alien?!"

The creature that was once Mrs. Cadzow made a low chuckle. Given that her mouth had now turned sideways, it looked like her face was clapping.

"Jarvis, do you not realize that you're an alien, too? On this planet, as well as any other besides you're own, you're considered the outsider. Other species may think you're more unusual than they are."

"Looking at you, I'd doubt that."

"Believe me, Jarvis, humans are by far the most unusual and absolutely the most rarest species we have encountered. You are definitely unique."

I remember Os-Gouvox mentioning that earlier on the Seership when he brought us to our habitat. After all the outrageous creatures we've seen on this planet, humans seemed mundane and ordinary. But I assumed it was because *I* was human, born as a human, raised as a human, and associated with humans my whole life. If I were thoroughly familiar with a type of living being my whole life, would it look unusual? I've even begun to feel comfortable with Nuvu's presence by my side (wherever he was now) and regarded him as a friend. He was a protector, a guardian. At first glance, a passerby would consider him as a magical pet that talked back, but he was much more than that. He sometimes seemed to know us better than we knew ourselves.

"What are you? Are you an Eszok, too?" I asked Cadzow, even though it was apparent that she was different from the other Eszok we've seen back in our habitat.

Cadzow's leaf-shaped eyes squinted and her leathery face pinched at the corners of her face and created what I believed to be a smirk. She wandered to a hovering desk that was covered with metal pads, screens of light, and small push buttons. She seemed to be analyzing something as she spoke to Jade and I.

"I think it may be obvious that I am not of the Eszok. I am Chizu, a race of beings who lived on a once dying planet in a desolate quadrant of space. The Eszok found our dying world over 100 years ago and promised to save our world if we helped to empower their people. With limited resources to support our planet, we honored their request and I, along with several other scientists, were admitted into their community."

"100 years ago? That's not possible."

"Actually, your species lives for a relatively short time. Normal life spans on other planets are much higher."

"Doesn't matter. The Eszok invaded worlds and kidnaped their inhabitants. That's all Zuu is – a collection of innocent aliens imprisoned and tortured for the Eszok's amusement."

Cadzow looked genuinely offended.

"Tortured? Absolutely not! The Eszok go to great lengths to ensure every species is comfortable and secure on Zuu. They need them to be as healthy as possible in their natural settings."

"They *need* them? Why?"

"The Eszok are a race of highly intellectual beings that have made significant technological advances that surpass even the cleverest of alien life forms. However, even with their superior mental capacities, they still feel that they are incomplete. Out of all the aliens they've studied, they have come to a startling realization: that they do not have a viku themselves. Therefore, they are in search of attaining one."

"But I thought every species in the universe had their own viku?"

"All except the Eszok. Why this is so, I cannot say. All I know is that the Eszok hunger for one. They have made it their lifelong mission to create an ability they can call their own. And to do that, they need to study every alien in the known universe."

That still didn't sound good for the universe.

"When you say 'study', you mean experiment on, dissect, poke, prod, mutilate…"

"Deep research will always yield several casualties in the long run. Great accomplishments require great sacrifices. Zuu wouldn't be here today if the Eszok weren't able to gather the amount of technical knowledge they've accrued from countless worlds. The ability to design their spacecrafts, the habitats on Zuu, even their homeship, the Ezokian Hesh – it was all possible by acquiring the knowledge and skills of other species. The Koz were very helpful in those regards."

"Somehow I don't think it was a fair trade or if there was any trade at all. Mioli said hundred of aliens were killed or experimented on because of the Eszok's ambitions. The Eszok killed her people. The galaxy is being raped by your masters and you don't even care."

"On the contrary, I do care," Cadzow said, expressing her freakish sideways smirk once again. "I took care of the six of you, didn't I?"

A shiver of anger rippled through my body. How could she say that? The majority of our group has met dire ends. It was just myself and my sister left. I glanced over at my sister who seemed to be overwhelmed with what was happening. She hung her head low listening to us, not even bothering to respond. I figured Cadzow's transformation was exceptionally upsetting for her since we kind of considered her as our last chance to get out of here. But now we saw that Cadzow was helping our captors and not the captives. She was not the principal of our school but an alien scientist that infiltrated our learning establishment. She was not a source of hope, but an accomplice to our enemy. What was more upsetting was what she clearly illustrated – that Jade and I were completely on our own.

"How can you say that?" I said, my blood boiling inside of me. "We're literally strung up by our necks and you're telling me you cared for us? What kind of nonsense is that?"

"Over the past ten years, I've watched over all of you. Not just your badly funded school but over your whole planet. That's how it's done."

"How what's done?"

"The Chizu are stationed on different planets all throughout known space. That's how we learn all about different alien species. We study your genealogy, your histories, your habits, your desires, everything that makes your species its own entity. We catalog our findings and turn them over to the Eszok. Assimilating into any race or culture without a single trace of our real identity is what the Chizu are masters at. It is our viku." Cadzow made a disturbing giggle. "Knowing how to siphon out their vikus into little jars is a perk."

"And that's what you plan to do with my sister and I, isn't it?"

I felt small and defenseless once again. The Chizu and

the Eszok have worked together for decades and their efforts had obviously yielded satisfying results. What chance did two teenagers have against an all-powerful, viku-hungry, planet-domineering race of aliens? Not much I'm afraid. Cadzow slowly nodded her huge head and approached us.

"I'm afraid so," she replied. I detected a hint of sincere regret in her voice. "What's troubling is that we don't exactly know how you will respond to the viku extraction. I've enacted several scenarios, but the best results are received through actual test subjects."

She turned to us with that creepy, ugly smile.

"So, congratulations! You are the first of your species."

Cadzow made a move to another one of her hovering control panels.

"Wait!" I shouted, not only to stall her to come up with a plan to escape, but also because I was genuinely curious. "You never told me what makes humans so unusual. What makes us so unique?"

Unexpectedly, Cadzow stopped in her tracks as if I had asked her something new and inappropriate. She turned and gazed out one of the huge bay windows, her mind seeming to search for the correct answer.

"I really don't know."

For real? That was her answer? I don't know?

"You're kidding? You know how to suck out the ability of a hundred different species and you don't know what makes humans so unique? Why do you make that claim if you don't know?"

"It's not exactly about what we don't know, it's about what we do know. After years of studying all the species of the known universe, we've concluded that every planet manifests a specific virtue among their inhabitants. It is a mental link to their physical viku. We have narrowed these virtues down to six common behaviors: temperance, objectivity, valor, benevolence, transcendence, and wisdom. Their actions, thoughts, and mannerisms are true demonstrations of these qualities. However, your species is the only one that displays each of these qualities. Your people are capable of creating such wonderful ideas and movements, but have also encouraged the destruction of your own kind. It's bewildering to watch your people suffer under their own imperfections when they already have the knowledge to overcome it. You prevent yourselves from ascension, yet you flourish and expand. What's also interesting is that your species hasn't even unlocked their own viku yet. That in itself makes you unpredictable, unusual, unique."

Personally, I thought it sounded kind of sad. Hearing Cadzow speak about the human race like an abnormal case study made it proof that we were our own worst enemy. She compared earthlings to every species the Eszok knew about and found our struggle to survive as one people fascinating. I wanted to slap her, but doing so would be futile as well as ridiculous. She was five times larger than me. Plus, it wasn't her fault that we humans were such nutcases. Running around like schizophrenic ants, building and destroying the one world that both sustained and enslaved us. My mom would always focus on all the good in the world and my dad would always remind me of what's wrong with it. Sadly, and somewhat ironically, that wrongness is what took him away from us. Now, my mom was left alone to fend for herself and constantly remind herself that there was still good left in the world. How she managed to pull through and function normally with two kids and two jobs, I will never know. It just seemed like whenever there was some stability in her life, she was knocked down again.

Honestly, I could relate to that. In school, I would surpass an English test with flying colors but fail miserably at a math quiz. At church, I'd be uplifted by a sermon about loving your neighbor and be immediately disappointed by the scathing gossip that would ensure after the service. There would be an event in a popular city to celebrate health and fitness and then have it bombed by monstrous teenagers with a terrorist objective. People vacationing in the South Seas would never return home because their lives would be taken in a devastating tsunami. A handsome young man with loving parents and a promising future would massacre innocent people because girls didn't want to have sex with him. It's as if our lives were meant to experience glorious highs and shattering lows just to see how we can handle a constant onslaught of tragedy, disappointment, and anguish. And then we die. What do we do then with the lesson learned, whatever the hell that lesson was? Judging from

Cadzow's perspective I can kind of understand of where she was coming from. Human survival was a unique phenomenon. It's only fascinating when you're not human.

Nevertheless, Cadzow's perverted obsession with our struggle for survival is most likely what kept us alive on Zuu all this time. It would've been easy for Os-Gouvox or any of his steel soldiers to blow us away on sight, especially since we gave them such a jolly time chasing us down. Obviously, it was the Gatekeeper's strict and specific instructions to handle us with care that allowed us the honor to speak to Cadzow face-to-...face?

"The Gatekeeper and Os-Gouvox know how critical your lives are to the Eszok," Cadzow said. My mouth fell open. It was like she just read my mind. I must have been thinking too loud again. "Although they failed at securing all six specimens for study, I think you two will suffice. Your viku may be the catalyst to a long-awaited breakthrough."

Cadzow loped back behind her floating console and tapped the crystalline surface a few times before a holographic interface flashed to life in front of her distorted countenance. She briskly tapped floating computerized buttons in the air and the apparatus that kept my sister and I hanging in mid-air began to make an ominous humming sound that I knew would signal our impending demise.

"I must prepare the extractor in time for the Eszok Hi'are's inspection. I believe the Hi'are would be overjoyed to meet you."

I was irritated at how Cadzow could be so intelligent and

so cold at the same time. She made it sound like we were going to meet the Eszok Hi'are for a Christmas dinner.

"What's a Hi'are, anyway?" I said, still trying to formulate an escape plan. My newly found viku wasn't crafty enough to reveal a way out of my futuristic handcuffs yet, so I kept talking. "Is that kind of like the Eszok king or something?"

"The Eszok Hi'are is the oldest living member of their species. The insight he brings to his race is unmatched and cannot be questioned. To challenge the Eszok Hi'are in a debate would most likely lead to your death, by him directly or through his supporters. He is not powerful in strength, but he is intelligent, calculating, and decisive. He is highly revered by the Eszok but is extremely elusive – always on the move."

I had a glimmer of hope to beseech the Eszok Hi'are's compassion and hopefully release us back to our world, but he sounded like a bigger jerk than Cadzow. To hear Cadzow talk about him, he didn't seem like the friendly, let-the-prisoner-go type.

The extractor machine began to make some weird vibrating sounds again. We were running out of time and Cadzow seemed to be losing interest in lecturing us on Zuu History 101. I had to do something now. I was just about to force myself to have a temper tantrum and make a scene when the door to the lab swung open and a new figure walked in. I had assumed that this new visitor would be the Eszok Hi'are and that our last moments breathing air would finally come to an end. But it wasn't the

Eszok Hi'are and even Cadzow expressed a surprised expression when the Gatekeeper stomped into the room.

He wasn't happy.

Chapter 14
A NOT-SO-RUDE AWAKENING

"What are *you* doing here," Cadzow hissed. I mean, she literally hissed sounding like an angry cobra with a bad cold. It must be something that the Chizu do when they're suddenly agitated. "The Hi'are could not have boarded the ship so quickly. He should still be at the compound."

"He is," the Gatekeeper said in an unfriendly tone. "Set and ready to dismiss both of us if these specimens aren't ready for viku extraction when he arrives."

"The Eszok Hi'are has nothing to worry about, I know how to do my job efficiently," Cadzow went back to briskly tapping commands on her holo-screen. "You would do well to follow my example."

The Gatekeeper rolled his sinister eyes at her, approached Jade and I, and appraised us like he was admiring an old painting.

"You got what you needed, didn't you? A couple of guinea pigs for your disgusting experiments? Don't expect me to feel regret for not satisfying your every whim."

"I needed all six subjects to complete the behavioral link," Cadzow spat out. "Without all six virtues, this whole experiment could fail. However, the viku strain seems to be unusually strong in the male. He may suffice for the others. I don't know. It's an unnecessary risk I have to take."

The Gatekeeper eyed me suspiciously and sniffed.

"How unfortunate for you." He was speaking to Cadzow but I wondered if he was actually speaking to me. "I would also remind you that the first thing the Hi'are will be concerned about is how he will transport his new visitors to the Eszokian Hesh."

Cadzow briefly paused in what she was doing and gave the Gatekeeper the slightest note of acknowledgement with a dash of annoyance.

"I know that," she muttered under her rumbling voices.

"Then you would do well to follow my example and be thoroughly prepared for your master. I did my part by searching the galaxy for these beasts and bringing them here. The least you can do is present them to the Hi'are in appropriate fashion. Assist Os-Gouvox in preparing the shuttle for departure. I will keep watch on these creatures."

"But the extraction must be..."

Cadzow started to disagree but a simple, piercing glare from the Gatekeeper quickly shut her up. It was apparent that these two never saw eye-to-eye, but it was also clear who was in charge here. Cadzow turned to leave.

"Understood," she huffed. She stopped at the door and gaped at Jade and I. "I hope you both understand how rare you are. You're the most vital key in activating a viku for the Eszok."

Cadzow left the room and the door slid shut behind her. Needless to say, that last line put my mind in a wondrous stupor. *You're the most vital key in activating a viku for the Eszok.* What in the world did that mean? It was hard to wrap my head around the fact that a whole planet was used merely as a storage facility for hundreds, if not thousands, of alien life forms from around the galaxy. But to say that we're the most *vital key* put my mind in a dither. We were different, true, but what was so great about our power? So far, I was the only one that possessed some kind of weird ability and I barely knew what to do with it. Was their something else that Cadzow wasn't telling us? We were six unassuming teenagers on a pretty planet minding our own business when a flying, silver cheerio ripped us away from our home and threw us clear across the universe because another alien race felt inadequate with their impotent viku. There was something extremely important in our DNA that made them make that long journey and it bothered me that I couldn't figure out what it was. I *had* to know what it was. If it was so vital and powerful, then maybe it was something I could use against them? Maybe I could fight them myself with this ability and save my sister and myself from a fatal viku extraction? I could feel my mind coming undone as I urged it to move its newly formed muscles and make something happen. My mind throbbed and burned and rattled and pumped and spun and popped.

And that was when I felt it.

A sensation that was both frightening and liberating all at once overwhelmed my senses. It was similar to being fully submerged in a pool of hot tar then suddenly discovering you've been absorbed into a mist of cool, energizing crystals. My mind had been figuratively split open and a rush of revelations surged through me. I could remember the motions of Cadzow's bovine-inspired eyes and track where her eyes went as she typed commands on her holo-screen. I didn't realize how closely I was monitoring her movements, but when I tried to recall what she had done, I found that I could remember every movement her eyes and fingers had made in chronological order. It was unbelievably simple! Of course, the technology she used was nothing even remotely comparable to what you would find on earth, but I understood how to use and control its interface. And to think, I still didn't know what a cache was.

What was more startling about my awakening was that everything seemed paper-thin. I couldn't necessarily see through objects with my bare eyes, but I could easily determine what something was made of, where it came from, how it was made, what it's used for, who made it, and who touched it. Everything in Cadzow's lab had a history to it or an origin and all I had to do was look at it and read its insides like I was reading an instruction manual for a child's toy. My eyes skittered around the room testing this new, mind-boggling extension of my viku abilities, quickly analyzing and placing the purpose of each contraption, machine, and doohickey that was in the room. It was an amazing feeling to have gained so much knowledge about so many new things so quickly. I was feeding off it. The more input I received, the hungrier I became. Nothing was a mystery. I couldn't say I knew everything, but I could just look into something and discover its essence. And just as I finished scanning the room, my eyes fell upon the Gatekeeper and my heart leapt for joy.

"Nuvu?!"

The Gatekeeper frowned and cocked his head sideways.

"How did you know?" he said. His body immediately shrank in size, twisted in on itself, grew thick reddish-brown fur, and transformed into the familiar feline-simian alien I've grown to love.

"What the...?" Jade gasped. "Nuvu! Jarvis, how did you know?"

"I don't know. I just...knew."

Truth was, I couldn't explain it or want to spend time explaining it. We didn't have much time before the Eszok Hi'are arrived and I felt that if he had an elite guard as his entourage with him we'd never have a chance to escape. It was now or never.

"I'll explain to you later but we need to get out of here before Cadzow comes back. Nuvu, go behind the console where Cadzow was standing. I think I can guide you through of the controls."

Nuvu bounded behind the console and tapped a few buttons. A holo-screen appeared in front of his face and he stared at the electronic interface for a brief moment. Before I could even recall what movements Cadzow had made earlier, Nuvu's nimble paws swept across the screen in a cognitive fashion. He wasn't guessing about what buttons to push, he already knew what commands to initiate.

"It's ok," he said sadly. "Me do this before."

The black disc below my feet stopped surging electricity and rose to catch my feet. The same occurred with Jade's disc as our constricted hands lowered themselves in front of us. Our glowing handcuffs shut off and simply disappeared. Even though there was nothing actually touching my wrists, they felt like they had been caught in a vise and were warm from my being hung up like slaughtered meat. Both Jade and I absentmindedly massaged our wrists as we observed Nuvu from a distance. I had hoped our little friend would be forthcoming and explain to us how he had the knowledge to control the technology of an intergalactic mad scientist. Was he Cadzow's assistant? Had we been betrayed again by yet another person we had grown to trust and rely on? Nuvu had been our hero on a number of different occasions but was he just saving us for a more dire ending? What was his motivation for protecting us anyway? He claimed that he found us when we first showed up at our habitat as if he had been expecting us. What was this little guy's role on this planet?

"Nuvu," I said softly, "we haven't known you very long. You have saved our lives more than once and for that we are totally grateful. But how did you know how to work Cadzow's controls? I don't want to point fingers, but… are you part of the Zuuminion, too?"

Nuvu looked ashamed. I was afraid he was going to say yes and Cadzow would come bursting in with the Eszok Hi'are, explaining to us how easily human trust could be swayed. But he didn't. He simply traced his finger in a circular motion on his chest. After completing the circle, he looked at me like he was reluctantly spilling a secret.

"Not Zuuminion," he whispered. "Isagetti."

I remember Mioli mentioning that word before but she didn't bother going into detail about it.

"Isagetti?" I said. "What is that? What does that mean?"

Nuvu looked at me with a countenance of sadness that was hinted with a spark of pride.

"Saviors."

I felt like I was turning the page to a whole new chapter into Nuvu's personality. He revealed that he was part of a group that considered themselves as saviors and, for some reason, Nuvu seemed hesitant to tell me. Before I could even delve deeper into the subject, a spine-tingling caterwaul echoed through the hallways just outside the door. It didn't take a genius to realize that it was Cadzow expressing her outrage that she had been deceived. How she found out, I'll never know, but she actually screamed, "Deceivers!"

"That's our cue, gentlemen," said Jade shuffling toward the door. "Time to go."

"Go where?" I said. "We're on a floating ship. We can't just...wait a second."

I decided to try out this viku thing yet again. If I could instantly decipher the inner workings of Cadzow's lab controls, why not analyze the workings of what it's connected to, namely, the entire ship? I wasn't sure if it would work but I had to try if we wanted to escape successfully. I really didn't know how to prepare myself on how to read the make-up of a whole alien spacecraft, so I winged it. Excuse the bad pun. I just did what I felt might work so I kneeled down on the floor and put both hands flat on its surface. Jade confirmed my suspicions that I must have looked like a fool.

"Jarvis, what are you doing? We don't have time for this. We need to go! Now!"

"I think I can see the rest of the ship this way. I'm trying to connect to it, be a part of it, see it from the inside out."

"Seriously?"

"Yes, seriously."

"Jarvis, I don't like this. You're scaring me. What's happening to you? Mom, told us to be a better human. You're human, nothing more."

But from my perspective, I didn't think Jade knew exactly what she was talking about. For me, being human *was* something more. I sill couldn't understand why my sister wasn't developing a viku as strong as mine. Maybe she just wasn't open to the idea of expanding her abilities and subconsciously hindered her own mind from developing further. Whatever the reason, she would be blown away by what I was suddenly experiencing. The moment I laid my palms on the floor, it was like a blueprint of the entire ship was superimposed on its surface. I could see through the ship in my mind's eye, each room and chamber totally exposed to me like I was looking at a model. My head felt a rush of exhilarating energy as minor details and floor plans filed into my memory. I could see hundreds of rooms and what they were used for. There was a gigantic room that seemed to be a main control center full of thin zoids and floating holo-screens. I remember it from the vision I had when I played with my brain yesterday. I could also see the real Gatekeeper and Cadzow quickly making their way towards us a few corridors away. But what was more important was that near the back of this massive, floating barge was a huge docking bay that held an assortment of flying vessels that could easily hold Nuvu, Jade, and myself. I just hoped that Nuvu knew how to control one of them and get us to the surface in one piece.

"Jade," I said to her, still in a complete daze at what my viku was capable of doing, "you have no idea what I can do right now."

My sister looked at me incredulously. It was obvious that she was afraid of what she couldn't understand. She didn't want me to change and become something else. Her idea of humanity was what we had been taught to believe what humans were: frail creatures trapped in frail bodies with no way to truly use their minds to their full potential. But now that I've broken through that barrier, she backed away yet again, barely recognizing her own brother.

"What do you mean, Jarvis? What can you do?"

There was fear in her voice. I didn't want there to be. I

wanted her to know that this discovery was a good thing, that I could use it to help us get home.

"I can get us off this planet," I said. The conviction in my voice sent a tangible wave of energy through my body. Jade shivered and took a few steps away from me.

"Jarvis, your eyes."

"What about them? What's wrong?"

"They're glowing!"

It's weird how I responded to that. I couldn't remember if I didn't care or if I didn't realize they were glowing because I didn't believe that the nature of my sight had changed at all. The only thing I was concerned about was getting all of us off that ship. The thought of finally escaping from this world energized me. Not only because it was my ultimate goal, but because I knew it was possible. All I had to do was to get us to the docking bay and onto one of those escape pods. Once we were in the escape pod, we could figure out our next move. But, for now, our mission was to evade our pursuers and it wasn't going to be easy if Jade was afraid of everything.

"Forget about my eyes, Jade," I said to her. "It's okay. It's still me. I have the power to get us back home now."

"I don't trust you," she said fearfully. "I don't know who or what you are anymore."

"Jade, come on, let's go…"

"NO! Mom said to be a better human, no matter what, and that's not you. You're not human anymore. You're not human!"

Jade took off through the entry doors and ran out into the hallway, easily, the most stupidest thing she could do since our pursuers were coming from that same direction. When I followed her out into the corridor, no one else was there except my frightened little sister running away from me.

"Jade! No, get back here!" I shouted. She paid me no attention whatsoever. It was just a matter of seconds before she ran smack into Cadzow, the Gatekeeper, and his robotic Zuuminion guards, and then I might never see her again. Nuvu and I ran after her, my viku tracking her movements on the ship, terrified that she would be captured any second. The corridors had high, curved ceilings and were a cool, steely aquamarine color. Blades of light stabbed through the air from lofty windows above and there were egg-shaped doors on either side. I could mentally see that each room harbored one of Cadzow's intrusive devices that could rip a creature's viku out from their body. Some of them were prototypes that did not function properly and I could sense the many deaths that unfortunate Zuu inhabitants had endured. It was heartbreaking. I was grateful that I had the ability to prevent my sister and myself from suffering those same tortures.

After rounding a second corner, my stomach lurched. Nuvu and I had caught up with Jade, but only because she was held up by her neck by the world's most disgusting alien.

"Cadzow!" I screamed. "Let her go!"

"That's not likely going to happen," she sneered. Jade's

legs flailed back and forth as she held onto Cadzow's arm that was strangling her throat. She dangled pitifully two feet above the floor and she looked thoroughly terrified. The fright that overwhelmed her was a part of me. It was like her emotions were inside of me begging for help.

Cadzow's small guard consisted of two silvery blue Zuuminion zoids. They had humanoid figures with no heads and V-shaped torsos that resembled torpedos from a WWII submarine. They both held a device that looked like a miniature glowing pitchfork in their right hand where the prong in the center was longer than the others. It vibrated a bright, neon orange color and electricity danced along its edge.

I suddenly noticed that the Gatekeeper was not present which caught me by surprise. I could have sworn I felt his presence with Cadzow's entourage. Maybe I was mistaken, but I definitely felt his aura on the ship. I just couldn't pinpoint it. But it didn't matter because Jade was my only concern now.

"Jarvis!" she gurgled, tears draining from her eyes. She could barely speak through Cadzow's grip. It wasn't right to see my sister harmed this way. I couldn't allow it. The anger that welled up inside of me felt unusually thick, authentic, and almost physically solid.

"I said LET HER GO!!!"

My voice sounded deep and otherworldly. It was unreal. I had trouble believing that it was me who had spoken. My head experienced an odd surge of discomfort as the light in the room flashed a ghostly white. Cadzow flew backwards and slammed into the wall behind her. Jade dropped to the floor, unharmed, and started massaging her neck as the two zoids appeared confused at the fall of their leader. Cadzow's huge body was twisted and bruised but she slowly came to and shook off what little injury I may have inflicted on her.

What had I done to her? I was practically a mile away from her and I literally knocked her off her feet with just a thought. It didn't seem humanly possible, but I did it anyway. I could feel that I did. Those weird, newly formed muscles in my head that were throbbing frantically against my skull told me that I had done it. There was no doubt about it now: I was becoming the human that I always should have been.

This time, I knew my eyes were glowing because everything I saw was five times brighter, more intense in color, and clearly detailed. I felt like I was burning with electricity all through my veins, but it didn't hurt at all. It was euphoric, almost magical. My body seemingly elevated to another plane of existence and I knew I would never be the same again.

"Your viku is definitely one to be reckoned with," Cadzow breathed as she picked herself up. She leered at me and for the briefest moment, I assumed that she might actually want to eat me. "But you're no different than what we've dealt with before. You can be subdued just like any other species. Hashick!"

I wasn't able to translate that last word she shouted and I quickly discovered that I didn't need to. It was a command to urge her minions into action. They lunged at me simultaneously and extended their mini electrical pitchforks directly toward my gut, completely ignoring Jade who lied on the floor in between them. She backed up into a corner, but kept her eyes on Cadzow who still seemed unable to recapture her bearings. The two Zuuminion guards raced toward me but I held my ground. I wanted to destroy them. That same thick sensation of anger began to rise inside of me again, but I never got a chance to release its force upon my attackers. A figure that seemed to be made out of the wind itself flew past me and dove straight into battle with the two guards before me.

The wraith-like figure was Mioli. Somehow, she had survived her unlawful beat down and was now kicking butt big daddy style. She looked ragged and beaten, her native clothing was ripped and torn in certain areas that revealed that she was in a lethal scuffle, but the energy that she fought the guards with proved how much of a fighter she truly was. In her grip was a long, metallic staff similar to Os-Gouvox's and she flipped it, tossed it, swung it, and jabbed it in countless quick variations blocking every move the guards made against her. The mini electrical pitchforks that the guards used sparked white dust whenever it came in contact with anything. The lighted blades burst in a million sparks in the air then quickly dissipated as they danced a hypnotic battle that was incredible to watch. It was like watching a movie. Then Mioli snapped me out of my gaze by turning to me in mid-battle and shouted at me, "Now would be a good time to fight, Jarvis!"

I completely agreed with her. I'm not very fond of violence, but this would be a good time to rumble. So what kept my feet glued to the floor? I wasn't afraid of the guards or Cadzow, so what made me freeze on the spot when I was called into action?

Lack of knowledge.

What prevents someone from acting on their impulse is either fear or not knowing what to do. Fortunately, none of those reasons applied to me anymore. I had the ability to analyze, remember, and mimic every move Mioli just made right in front of me in perfect precision. Her staff was the only thing missing. But did I actually need a staff? I was creative enough to find another answer.

The same thought I used to knock Cadzow off her feet would be strong enough to take something away from one of the Zuuminion guards. As Mioli parried with both zoids, I concentrated on the zoid closest to me. It was disconcerting to realize that there was no soul or consciousness within these large figures that moved and reacted like a living being. They were remarkably life-like in movement but there was nothing inside their hardware that made them sentient creatures. They were just moving vessels that could be manipulated by just a menial impulse of my brain. With a small effort equivalent to the snap of my finger, I used my mind to pry off one of the zoid's bulbous, armored arms. Its arm ripped off its frame and flew towards my feet.

The zoid grabbed for its appendage a second too late,

missed, and proceeded to charge me once it saw that I had something that belonged to it. I lifted the detached arm, brought it back over my right shoulder like a baseball bat, and swung it with full force across its chest. The robotic figure absorbed the impact and stumbled backward, but in no way did I slow it down. It lunged for me again and I struck its working arm with even greater force and sparks flew. Still, it wasn't enough.

Before I could get in another swing, the zoid reared back and kicked me to the floor, snatching its arm from my grip at the same time. While I recovered from my unholy impact with the floor, the zoid reattached its arm by means of snaking wires that stretched out of its arm socket and around the shoulder joint of the dislocated appendage. It fully connected its lost body member to its figure and tried it out a few times to make sure it was functional again. It then had the audacity to wriggle its fingers at me as if to say, *I got my arm back, so now whatcha gonna do?* Lying on the floor with a fierce glow in my eyes, I held up the little electrical pitchfork it had used as its weapon. The zoid, devoid of sentient emotions, still seemed surprised.

"You lost your toy," I told it, practically taunting it as I came to my feet. I swung it in front of me like a fly swatter and I felt its prongs vibrate musically within my grip. It felt beautiful, as if it was a long lost extension of my arm that had been returned to my body. I swung it back and forth a few more times to make sure its presence in my grip was comfortable. It was - it was totally secure.

The zoid lunged at me, and with a speed that surprised even myself, I blocked its attack with my weapon in the wink of an eye. Sparks exploded from its arm as it made a disturbing squeal, and in an ironic twist, its other arm now lay on the floor, smoldering on the edges where my mini pitchfork made contact. A dangerous grin crept upon my face.

"Jarvis!"

Mioli's voice shattered my concentration on my brand-new plaything. I turned and saw that she had already defeated the second zoid guard and was now embroiled in an intense rumble with Cadzow. I thought my eyes had deceived me because Cadzow now appeared to have several more elongated arms. At a closer glance, I quickly realized that Nuvu had joined in and took the form of a squid-like creature and was now wrapped around her neck attempting to strangle her.

"You can mimic everything I do," Mioli shouted. "Use the moves I did on that zoid!"

The memory of Mioli's fighting style came back to me in an instant. I remembered the way she held her staff and the angles and footwork she used to bring down her opponent. I thought I was at a disadvantage because I had a drastically different weapon, but oddly enough, it felt so perfectly right in my hand, that I hardly worried about it. This little piece of alien weaponry was mine to control and it was time to test it out.

The zoid and I began a brisk, treacherous game of swipe and jab, each of us struggling to gain the upper hand. Mioli's swift movements were fresh in my mind. I could recall every strike, blow, and block she performed moments before with such startling ease, that it kind of scared me. Here I was, an 18 year-old kid that despised physical violence was (again) being thrown into deep hand-to-hand combat with a robotic barbarian brandishing a formidable armament and a bad attitude. This wasn't me. I was someone else. I still couldn't figure out if that was such a good thing. I felt dangerous and unhinged, sensing that I was capable of adopting more combative skills with the slightest effort. Maybe Jade was right about being frightened of...

Jade!

Where was she? In mid-battle with the zoid, my thoughts came back to her. I glimpsed to where she was crouched on the floor a few minutes ago and found that she had disappeared. I reached out with my mind to sense where she was and found her presence on the other side of the ship. WHAT THE...?! How on earth did she get there?! What was even more disturbing was that I could feel another presence right next to her. The presence of its abnormal height and shape told me that it was the Gatekeeper. He had captured her. And he was running straight to the escape pods.

Chapter 15
AN UNLUCKY ESCAPE

I could barely recall exactly how I had defeated the zoid. When I had realized Jade was missing, I think I went into a mini version of a panic attack. If I had no idea of where she had wandered off to, it's most likely I would have had a full-blown meltdown. However, I knew where she was on the ship, but I didn't know how in the world she got there so quickly or if she was okay. So I kept myself from going ballistic by taking comfort in the fact that she was alive and well. What made me lose it was that the Gatekeeper somehow managed to snatch my little sister right out from under my nose. He made his move while I was distracted by this steel-plated bully and it pissed me off.

A flare of anger sparked inside of me and I remembered a sweeping motion that Mioli made with her staff only this time, I combined it with a downward motion aiming at the zoid's torso. My new weapon sliced through the air and came in contact with its solid frame, separating its form into two pieces. The chunks of zoid fell to the floor, creating loud, metallic thunks that echoed in the corridor. I stood silently for a moment, dumbfounded at what I had just done. Me, Jarvis Johnson, social nobody of Langhorne High, just felled a seven-foot tall robotic monster. Compared to my little tiff with Derek, this was spectacularly epic. I would never, in a million years, imagine myself doing what I had just done. Who had I become?

I would have to answer that question later as the struggle between Cadzow, Nuvu, and Mioli came to a head. My battle with the zoid ended just as Cadzow gripped Nuvu's tentacles in an odd fashion with two of her fingers. She had four arms so she fought both Nuvu and Mioli at the same time without difficulty. She twisted and pressed two of her fingers into one of Nuvu's tentacles and his body immediately went slack and he dropped to the floor. As Cadzow blocked and struck Mioli's staff with her bare arms, Nuvu transformed back into his original form, too dazed to move.

Mioli made a hollow, shrill sound and did a flip straight up into the air. On her way back down, she wrapped her legs around Cadzow's neck and did a sideways twist bringing the alien's towering body down in a flash. When they crashed onto the hard surface, I distinctly heard a nauseating crack which must've been the sound of Cadzow's neck succumbing from the sudden fall. She grappled at her neck and convulsed violently like a mantis getting electrocuted. Mioli stood over her, emotionless, her staff pointed at Cadzow's face, daring her to make another offensive move. She appeared as if she was going to kill her.

"The Eszok...Eszok...will not," Cadzow uttered as she writhed painfully. It was obvious that Mioli had destroyed an important part of her anatomy. Black, inky liquid ran from her disgusting maw, she tried pitifully to stand up, her breathing became strained and shallow, but Mioli glared at her without the slightest hint of pity. Cadzow looked at Mioli with what seemed to be an expression of shock, as if she was surprised that this benevolent individual had the ability to defeat her. She tried to speak again, but then, Mioli made a move that even surprised me.

Mioli twisted her staff with both hands and a deadly array of glowing spikes suddenly shot out at the opposing end. Cadzow froze, the threatening, hot blades reflected in her horrified eyeballs.

"The...the Eszok...will not..." she continued to stammer. Mioli did not allow her to finish her sentence. My stomach lurched as Mioli disturbingly jabbed her staff directly into Cadzow's face. The squish of steel and flesh invaded my ears nearly causing my gag reflex to activate.

"The Eszok will not survive."

Mioli's frigid words were followed by a vigorous series of more stabs and blows to Cadzow's lifeless form. Black liquid splattered on her mask and clothing as the rage she held within her whole life seemed to be channeled into her weapon and upon her victim. It wasn't right. What Cadzow and the Eszok did was unforgivable. What Mioli was doing was unrighteous. What happened to the peaceful alien that taught me to quiet my mind and connect to the universe?

"Mioli!" I shouted. She refused to stop. I rushed over to restrain her. "Mioli, stop! That's enough!"

Mioli saw me coming and knocked me aside before I could reach her. If she didn't have a high-tech mask on, I would assume she would have a crazed, fiery look in her eyes. However, her threatening stance was enough to make me back off.

"It is never enough!" she screamed at me. She was breathing heavily after her turbulent tantrum and I was more than cautious to say another word to her. All I could do was stare at her in alarm. We stood there for a few moments as we listened to her attempt to restore her oxygen levels. It was a relief when we heard Nuvu's groans as he regained consciousness.

"Jade," he said in a weak voice, "he took Jade. The Gatekeeper took..."

I ran to help Nuvu back onto his feet. I kneeled down, put my arm around his back, and helped him sit up. He seemed okay. Besides a few bruises and cuts, Nuvu appeared fine and in one piece.

"Cadzow used an akshu on him," said Mioli. She approached Nuvu and began to stroke a portion of Nuvu's furry neck right under his wide jaw. A pleasurable expression washed upon his face.

"What's an akshu?" I asked.

"It's a calculated obstruction of specific pressure points on the body. Cadzow has done so many studies on different species that no matter what form Nuvu took, she would've known how to disable him."

"Pressure points?"

"Yes. By directing pressure or force on a specific point on the body, you can disable or render your opponent unconscious."

That was pretty amazing stuff. Cadzow had barely put two

fingers on Nuvu and he was down for the count. I wondered if I could try that on the zoids but I kind of figured that that maneuver would only work on life forms that had muscles and flowing vitals. Mioli did a flick of her wrist while stroking Nuvu's throat and I heard a muffled snap. Nuvu hopped to his feet, wide-eyed and spunky once again, as if Cadzow had never subdued him at all.

"Better?"

Nuvu nodded enthusiastically.

"Spiffy!"

His little cuteness was imperishable. Nothing could keep this little guy down. Moreover, this introduction to akshu intrigued me. I made a mental note to urge Mioli to teach me everything she knew about this technique. Cadzow used it to conquer her opponent, Mioli used it to reverse its effects, and, best of all, it was a non-violent tactic. I had to learn more about it, but now was not the time.

"We gotta move," I told the others. "The Gatekeeper has Jade and he's way too close to the escape pods."

I paused for a moment and mentally scanned the design of the ship. Again, I noticed that it was easier to see the makings of the ship if my flesh was against its surface. I laid my bare hand along the wall and the entire blueprint of the alien vessel flashed in my mind again. Almost immediately, a route to the escape pods was fixed firmly into my brain.

"Follow me!"

The unusual thing about having the ability to see the full

construction of an alien vessel in your mind was that I understood how everything worked. This huge island in the sky was used as a transport carrier to pick up other species on Zuu. By no means was it big enough to carry every captive on the planet. It was only used as a convenience for the Eszok to travel from habitat to habitat, pick up and detain a good number of different alien species, and experiment on them right on the ship. The technology used to create this ship seemed to be a conglomerate of different cultures of different planets. It was mainly Eszok, of course, but it had the remnants of Chizu and Koz influence throughout its overall design. But there was something else about Eszok technology that I could not put my finger on. There was something oddly disturbing about how everything was put together and constructed. Then, as Mioli, Nuvu, and myself ran through the ship, its oddness was clarified – the ship itself was a zoid.

That was one of the many things that bothered me about zoids. I couldn't sense their presence because they were not sentient, or inherently aware of their own existence or possessed their own thought. The fact that they didn't have a soul might have something to do with it, too. Zoids were automatons that were programmed to behave like a real person. They weren't alive, but it sure seemed like they were. Therefore, this ship seemed like it was alive, too.

As we barreled through several levels and corridors to get to the escape pod dispatching area, we encountered an arsenal of combative light fixtures that shot electrical bolts at us, doors that peeled away from the structure of the ship and picked a fight with us, and even flooring panels that rose before us and attempted to block our way. It was futile though. Mioli was a natural fighter. Not one of the obstacles slowed her down. Although I led the way, Mioli defended me whenever we ran smack into another distraction. Nuvu was equally awesome as he effortlessly transformed into a menagerie of outrageous alien creatures that quickly overpowered every attack. I, on the other hand, merely repeated what Mioli had done to take down our attackers. There was no argument that I was just as good as Mioli when it came to defensive sparring because I was just a literal copy of what she could do. She jabbed and stabbed with her staff, I jabbed and stabbed with my mini electrical pitchforks. My weapons were different but the moves were the same.

I began to notice that my body was tiring out and my muscles were weakening. My body could barely keep up with the commands my mind was giving it. Even so, I pressed on, ignoring my throbbing arms and legs. I was struck several times in my chest, something had made a deep cut in my thigh and above the right side of my brow, and my hands were starting to burn from holding my three-pronged lightning rods. As much as I despised brute force, I couldn't deny the euphoric feeling of cutting down my enemies so easily. It was emancipating and empowering. Whether or not excessive savagery was the right emotion for a human being to experience didn't matter at this point. It felt magnificent and I wanted more.

The moment we reached the dispatch bay for the escape pods, I was hit with a combination of emotions. Jade's aura could be felt merely yards away from me and I could tell something was wrong. The strength of her emotional signal was noticeably diminished. It wasn't weak, it was just altered and had a different vibration, but its signature was definitely hers.

We entered into a cavernous space that had an open ceiling almost thirty feet high. Light and warm air swarmed around us wildly as we traversed a wide walkway that spanned over empty space. I looked over the edge and saw the planet's rocky surface almost several hundred feet below. On either side of the walkway were docked about thirty to forty head-shaped escape pods. They weren't shaped like human heads, but more like Eszok heads. They were sloped downward in the front and had eye slits for driver windows. Their creepiness was so substantial that if the ship were actually in trouble, I'd bypass the escape pods and go down with the ship. It felt like the whole Eszok race was glaring down at us anxious to release their full wrath at any moment.

Suddenly, one of the pods lit up, steam shot out from one of the thrusters, and I immediately panicked. About seven pods down on the left side of the walkway, the pod came to life and its figurative eye slits opened wide. Mioli, Nuvu, and I rushed toward the pod and saw the Gatekeeper sitting at the controls. No doubt about it, I could totally sense Jade inside. It was weird though. Normally, I could sense what she was feeling. However, she was currently experiencing no emotion at all. No fear, no anxiety, no pain, nothing. She was both there and not there at the same time, as if the space she occupied in the universe had become a mini vacuum clothed with her soul. My heart ached at the thought of what this intergalactic game warden had done to her. *Jade*, I thought, *what's happened to you?*

When we came within 15 feet of the pod, a wicked, shattering force came out of nowhere, striking my mind and body with such brutal force that I thought I was going to die. Every muscle in my body tightened and stung and I collapsed in mid-run onto the hard floor. The few seconds I lied motionless on the floor my eyes blurred and watered. But as my vision returned, a figure loomed in between two of the escape pods on the opposing side of the Gatekeeper's ride. It crept out of the shadows slowly as steam and smoke swirled around its shiny red and metallic skeletal body. The figure had his staff pointed at me in a threatening manner, poised to skewer an unsuspecting salmon in the river. My vision cleared and my heart raced. It was Os-Gouvox.

For the first time since we encountered Os-Gouvox, his presence had a signature force. Unlike the other zoids that gave off no emotional or cognitive essence, my viku had developed enough that I could pick up something tangible from this particular zoid. There was barely a signal from his presence, but I could now detect and identify it, like a horsefly buzzing around in my head. He didn't have a soul. He was soulless, but aware of his own existence and that created a void in the universe that was hard to ignore.

Os-Gouvox cautiously stepped closer to my weakened body. The electromagnetic blast from his staff knocked the wind out of me and threw a few of my internal organs into a virtual milkshake. However, I still had enough energy to move my head and track Os-Gouvox's movements as he stalked around me.

"A Trauv from the planet Gubov can survive a full day once you sever its head from its body. Duvonians breathe oxygen but can live up to 142 hours deprived of it before they expire. A Mmynx can plummet 500 feet before a single bone in its body can break. So, tell me, human, what kind of test will it take to end you?"

"A math test," I replied. Unfortunately, I forgot that this guy had no sense of humor.

"I tire of having to lower my standards to detain you. Now that you killed a senior scientist, you've basically given me permission to terminate you. I thank you."

I glanced around and noticed that Mioli was just beginning to come out of her daze after Os-Gouvox's blast. She lied face down on the floor behind me just inches away from the edge of the walkway. Nuvu was nowhere to be seen. However, I sensed that he was nearby, watching from out of sight, waiting for just the right moment to pounce. I had to keep Os-Gouvox distracted.

"Why are you so intent on destroying a human? Is killing every living thing part of your programming?"

"It appears your viku still hasn't reached its peak performance. You're as dim as the northern sun. Your death is nothing but valuable data for the Eszok. Every move and decision you make to avoid your demise is recorded in my memory and is reviewed by the Eszok. I am their eyes, I am their voice – a mediator between their highness and lower life forms such as you."

"Well, this lower life form is about to kick your butt. Make sure your masters are watching."

I was tired of hearing this blockhead ramble on about his wonderful position in being the Eszok's mouthpiece and henchman. My body still felt sore and weak and I badly needed the energy to get up and take this guy down. That was when Mioli's akshu technique popped into my head. I racked my brain to recall the exact movement she made with her fingers and wrist when she revived Nuvu. As Os-Gouvox continued to circle me, figuring out my weakness, I moved my hand up to my jawline and felt around for what I thought might be the right muscles. Within seconds, I found something that seemed out of place. A bulge that felt unusually tighter than the surrounding muscles and tendons. I took a chance and perfectly mimicked the move that Mioli did on Nuvu and instantly sedated the muscle. It was like an energy drink was suddenly pumped into my veins. Pain in every part of my body disappeared and I felt like I could run two marathons back to back. My body shuddered at the shocking rush of energy, but Os-Gouvox seemed to ignore it. He probably thought I was shuddering in fear.

What a fool, I thought.

"It should be agonizingly simple to bring you down. What is your vital center? A quick blow to the head? A bolt of lightning down your back? What is it? What is your weakness?"

"Actually," I said, "it's FRIED CHICKEN!"

Nuvu understood his cue. Before Os-Gouvox could react, a shower of laser beams rained down upon him from somewhere above. I scattered out of the way, quick as a flash, while Os-Gouvox dodged and ducked from Nuvu's surprise attack, fending off every beam that came his way. I ran to pick up my mini pitchforks and noticed that Mioli had jumped to her feet and was heading toward our common enemy.

"Get Jade out of the pod," she said as she started to spar with Os-Gouvox. "I'll stop...AARGH!!"

Mioli was clearly no match for this highly trained, elite class zoid. She barely got three moves in when Os-Gouvox made an unrealistically fast dodge, duck, and swipe and knocked her right off her feet. He then shoved his staff under her back and pushed her off the walkway, sending her body helplessly through the sky like old trash.

"MIOLI!"

"Good riddance," sneered Os-Gouvox.

I ran to the edge and saw her body getting smaller and smaller, her death only a few hundred feet below her.

"Nuvu, catch her!"

Nuvu soared over my head and transformed again into the great, blue flying creature that saved me from the Rovers earlier. He dove straight for her but she seemed so far away already. There was no way he could reach her in time.

"Let's make it a little more challenging for your friend, shall we?" Os-Gouvox said, just before he pointed his staff at a massive conduit thirty feet above our heads. A white bolt shot out of his staff and struck the conduit, causing an explosion that rocked the walkway. I held onto the handrail as a series of ear-splitting, electrical fireworks exploded above our heads. Then, without warning, all forty of the escape pods dropped out of the dispatch bay. Forceful gusts of wind suddenly pushed and pulled at me from all directions and I had to grab the handrail to keep myself from getting sucked out into the atmosphere. I could barely glance over the edge to see the giant escape pod skulls falling all around Mioli's plummeting body. Somewhere in the all that falling mess was "flying" Nuvu, intent on catching her before she met her doom.

"NO!"

I turned toward Os-Gouvox and my heart did a little leap of joy. There was still one escape pod left in the dispatch bay and it belonged to the Gatekeeper and Jade. I could still feel their presence inside the pod. The only problem was that the pod was already in flight and on its way out of the dispatch bay.

"JADE! NO! STOP! STOP!!"

I began to run toward it, so panicked and desperate that I had no idea what to do once I reached it. All I knew was that I needed to stop it. I couldn't let it get away. My sister was in there. My own flesh and blood and the one human connection I would have on this whole planet. She was my home and family. She trusted me. I needed to get her out of there. Her life depended on her brother's power and I was the only one available to stop the pod from flying God knows where on this freaky, crazy planet. I had to stop it.

I felt like a helpless child chasing after his lost balloon. My mind was so frantic that I couldn't even concentrate on how to use my viku powers to stop the pod from escaping. Sadly, I didn't have to. Os-Gouvox cut me off, swinging his staff at me once again. We quickly became enmeshed in another battle of physical skill and ingenuity, each of us refusing to relent to the other. It was obvious that Os-Gouvox was a superior fighter. But I had learned from watching Mioli, the other zoids, and even Os-Gouvox himself on how to control my weapons and keep my opponent on the defensive. The down side to that was that I could only recall moves that I've seen before. I couldn't do anything new or make a swing that would surprise my enemy – which is exactly what Os-Gouvox did.

Whether I was distracted by the Gatekeeper's pod leaving the dispatch bay or being too confident in holding my own against a killing machine, Os-Gouvox faked a swing, reversed his stab, and pulled one of my pitchforks right out of my hand with his staff. He swung his staff against my face and knocked me to the ground causing my other weapon to fly out of my hand and across the walkway. My head was spinning so wildly that I thought I was going to throw up. I was completely exhausted and completely out of moves and ideas. Os-Gouvox must have automatically catalogued every offensive and defensive move I could muster. Now, I lied pitifully on my stomach with a bloody gash on my cheek and attempted to crawl away into a little corner of shame as the Gatekeeper flew off with my defenseless little sister. My enemy continued to antagonize me as I struggled with the urge to just give up the fight.

"Don't stop now, human. I was just beginning to enjoy our little dance. You learned a bit more than I expected in such a short time."

Os-Gouvox slammed his staff on my back and sparks flew while my back shot pain through my entire body. I screamed out painfully and lied still on my stomach. In the distance, I could see the Gatekeeper's pod slowly drifting further and further away. Jade was in there. I promised Jade that we would leave this planet alive, but that wasn't going to happen now. I had failed us. Jade, at least, might have a chance of surviving, but Os-Gouvox was going to kill me.

I was going to die, here and now.

"The same goes with me as well," my murderer continued. "I learned something very quickly in these few delicate moments together."

I could almost hear him grinning. Really? A zoid with no facial muscles, grinning wickedly?

"I've discovered your weakness. It's your connection to other humans, isn't it?"

"Just shut up and kill me," I strained to say.

"That female in the Xeeths. She tried to retrieve that egg for the male stung by the Mort Kuup. That bull-headed male threw a stone at my masters to protect the rest of your pathetic souls when you arrived. The pale female in black even failed to protect you when you and your sibling were on the Seership. These foolish notions that you can actually protect each other is your weakness - your fatal flaw."

"There is nothing weak about wanting to protect your friends and family."

"It is ineffectual, human. You still lost your clan, even your sister."

"Guess again, Frankenbot. She's still alive. She got away."

I gazed at the Gatekeeper's escape pod, which was now a great distance away from the ship. At that moment, I briefly considered that it really was an escape pod, an escape from Os-Gouvox's murderous instincts.

"Actually," Os-Gouvox said callously, "she did not."

What's that supposed to mean? The next second, Os-Gouvox gave me an answer. He picked up his staff and pointed the business end of it at the escaping pod. I figured that there was no way the bolts from his staff could reach an object that far away.

I was dead wrong.

A sphere of light and energy discharged from the tip of his staff and smoldered over with a web of electrical bolts. The weapon hummed loudly then released an awful sound, sending an ultra voltaic beam of energy directly at the Gatekeeper's escape pod. The pod expanded outwards in all directions, releasing huge plumes of fire and smoke instantly. Debris draped the sky as trails of white smoke streamed through the atmosphere. I don't even remember hearing the pod explode, I just remember my body going completely numb.

I wanted to deny what I had just seen. I wanted to believe that what just happened did not happen. It felt as if my mind was playing a cruel trick on me and was manifesting one of my worst fears. The pod, and its occupants, had been destroyed. No, this was a dream. It had to be. This was just a sick and disturbing nightmare heightened in reality by my stupid viku abilities. There's no way I could've let this happen. I found that I couldn't move. I couldn't even breathe. The shock of losing another family member embraced my shoulders, my neck, my mind, my body, and finally, my heart. It was a thick, vile shadow that swallowed my entire existence and began to suffocate my heart. My chest seemed to collapse in on itself as the air in my lungs vanished. I tried to inhale to catch my breath, but instead, an unearthly, inhuman wail fell out of my mouth. The scream echoed throughout the dispatch bay. My eyes felt like they were melting as liquid filled my sight and heavily streaked my face.

My body felt broken and weak but I didn't care. I grabbed the handrail and bawled uncontrollably, pulling myself up to my feet, unable to mentally accept Jade's death.

It was horrific, not only the sight of the soaring debris of the escape pod, but also the gloom that came over me. It was physically unnatural. As I stood there on the walkway grasping the handrail, shaking from an overabundance of intense sadness and loss, I became ultimately vulnerable. Any emotion that boiled in my gut would've been distorted and enhanced without my control – and that's precisely what happened.

An unholy manifestation of madness developed inside of me. I've never felt anything remotely similar to this sensation in my entire life. It scared me because I thought my insides were literally on fire, as if Os-Gouvox had fired his staff at me when I had my back turned. But as I turned to face him, he was astutely aware that something was not right which was definitely a gross understatement.

He lowered his staff and slowly took one step backward while my body commenced a disconnection from the physical world. Every cell in my body changed into an inextinguishable form of energy that I could not describe. A magenta and yellow-colored light emanated from my body and I felt my feet leave the floor. My head was on the verge of exploding, an astounding pain enveloped my soul, and I relinquished control of my limbs.

I had become wrath incarnate.

Os-Gouvox shuffled a few steps back then held his ground

and aimed his staff at me.

"You are nothing but another species making a feeble attempt to survive," he announced arrogantly.

"Right," I boomed loudly with a voice that clearly wasn't mine. "You keep telling yourself that."

I snapped my hand backwards and Os-Gouvox's staff was ripped from his grip. The staff slowed as it approached me and hung in mid-air. It dismantled itself into several pieces, floated around me, and then attached itself to my arms, legs, chest, and a part of my face. It had become a part of me. I had no idea how I was doing this. I didn't even feel like I was in control. All I remember was having one significant thought – *Os-Gouvox killed my sister.*

I raised my hands toward him and his heavy robotic form floated up from the floor. Although I was several feet away from him, I could feel his cold steel frame against my fingertips, vibrating and struggling to break free from my grip. He couldn't move. I was holding an invisible voodoo doll of Os-Gouvox in my hands. I wanted him to die. He had to pay for taking my sister's life, for taking all of the innocent lives that once were held captive on the Zuu planet.

Os-Gouvox killed my sister.

The thought alone consumed my mind and became the catalyst for every action I made afterward. Os-Gouvox was helpless in my psychic clutch. I bent him over backwards in an effort to break his spine in two. His computerized voice bellowed through the air, but I ignored it. How could a zoid experience any kind of pain? He was not sentient or made of flesh like the captives on Zuu so it was not possible for him to experience the abhorrent sensation of pain. Therefore, he must be faking it. He was attempting to play on my sympathies so I would desist my attack and allow him a chance to counterattack and overtake me. I refused to give him such an opportunity.

While he arched backwards in mid-air in front of me, his right arm detached from his body. He screamed.

Os-Gouvox killed my sister.

His other arm twisted away from his body. He yelled again.

Os-Gouvox killed my sister.

His right leg was dreadfully wrung off his body. A moment later, his left leg was jerked off and thrown overboard into the sky below. His body made strange blips and bleeps, lights flickered in his chest and eye sockets, sparks rained down from his mutilated joints, and wires hung sadly from his broken torso. Still filled with the uncompassionate directive he was programmed with, he stared straight at me with what I identified to be genuine hatred. He didn't need facial muscles for me to detect it in his voice.

"Destroying me is pointless," he said to me, his voice chip sputtering and crackling. "Another Sarok will replace me and finish you. The Eszok now have everything they need to control you."

"Except the ability to destroy me."

I imagined injecting both of my hands into the middle

of his chest and pulling him apart. My thoughts became a reality as Os-Gouvox's battered torso reared back and ripped open. His metallic rib cage split in two while the last sounds his programmed voice made were startlingly similar to human anguish. His suffering was cut short for both sides of his torso crashed onto the floor in front of me. His spine and skull stayed in tact.

Os-Gouvox killed my sister.

His skull rocked slightly back and forth as the thought continued to permeate every pore of my burning skin. Suddenly, his head jerked up at me. In a split second, I caused his head to crumble flat and left a significant crater of broken metal on the floor.

Os-Gouvox killed my sister.

The wrath inside of me began to subside and my thought took on a different decree.

I killed Os-Gouvox.

Chapter 16
UNIVERSAL REDEMPTION

For some odd reason, the fact that I defeated my enemy was just not satisfying. It should have been enough that I departed from my original, pessimistic character, learned how to bear a weapon, held my ground in physical battle against robotic machines, knew how to read the architectural structures of alien vessels just by touching them, and destroyed my sister's murderer. But it wasn't enough. I wanted to destroy the cause of her murder. All I did was crush one of the tools that brought suffering to countless alien species and my human clan. Right now, I had the power to overcome anything and everyone, including the Eszok. And if I had the power to bring an oppressive tyranny of alien rule to its knees, why shouldn't I just do so? Os-Gouvox was just a warm-up to the real thing.

There was no reason to restrain myself. I had nothing to lose. Everyone was gone. Derek, Cindy, Alex, Marlene, and now Jade had all fallen in their journey to survival. I no longer could sense the presence of Mioli or Nuvu either. Whether it was because my viku plunged my soul into an alternate form of existence and blocked their signal, I wouldn't know. It didn't matter. I was alone now. I was a burning figure of wrathful human energy on a warpath hungry for justice no matter what the cost.

I looked at my form and did not recognize a single inch of it as my own body. My skin was barely visible under a glowing veil of orange light that surrounded my body. On top of my skin were pieces of Os-Gouvox's staff that had somehow fused themselves to my form. I didn't understand why, but as I thought about it, I could feel something surging through me. A foreign energy that was notably inorganic seemed to flow from where the pieces touched my skin and energized every beat of my heart. It gave me extra power to endure what was happening to me. My subconscious told me to fight it, but how could I when it felt so fantastic? I let my guard down and drank in the rush of fire. I consumed a wave of volatile energy. After doing so, I felt inexplicably glorious.

I could have sworn that every one of my limbs detached from my body and dissolved into the atmosphere. The world around me became a part of my skin and I swallowed it whole as it devoured me. I closed my eyes and found that I could still see! I didn't even need my eyes to experience sight because I could see everything including myself. It was similar to having a dream where you watch yourself doing things but you also remember doing them yourself. I was the equivalent to an out-of-body experience.

The structures around me in the dispatch bay seemed unwelcoming to my unearthly inhabitance. The walkway I was on shook violently and broke apart but remained suspended in mid-air. Big, lop-sided chunks of steel floated beneath my feet and around my head. I didn't realize how destructive I had become. My senses were in a world of unmatched ecstasy while the world outside of my senses was in a catastrophic storm. I saw the giant alien vessel tearing itself apart all around me as I stood rigidly in a peaceful daze, oblivious to the fact that my psychic powers were causing mass destruction. Debris as large as 4-story buildings circled my body, crashing over and under me, colliding with each other, breaking into a billion pieces and floating around my body. I was the center of my own universe and the rubble from the Eszok's ship had become my own private galaxy. It's destruction fed my power. After watching all this through my mind's eye, I knew I was capable of more. Much more. My viku seemed to empower itself and usurp every function of my brain. Another rush was just about to consume me when a soft voice unexpectedly stung in my ears.

"Jarvis, stop."

The voice was gentle, modest, and non-accusatory. It didn't sound notably male or female but rather a mix of the two. It was so meek and soft that I was surprised to be able to hear both words so clearly over the deafening roar of the mayhem that surrounded me. I had no idea where it could have come from. I didn't sense one sentient being within my immediate area and there was no way someone could just sneak up on me. The words came out of nowhere. They pricked my mind, causing the building rush of fire to completely subside. The auditory invasion stalled my senses and I slowly opened my eyes.

Life appeared frozen in time, pristine, flawless. The universe was split open before me and I could tell immediately that I was only viewing a mere fraction of a fraction of what actually existed in our time and space. Light, mist, planets, stars, wormholes, ghostly forms, people, aliens, creatures, animals, galaxies, molecules, atoms, dark matter, life – everything was suddenly exposed to me. It was unimaginably beautiful, so why was I so utterly petrified? This is what humans wanted, wasn't it? To know everything? To have nothing hidden from them and be able to answer every question in life correctly without a single doubt of its validity? Well, here it was in all of its glorious splendor and I couldn't even gaze upon it with my own eyes... because *I* was still imperfect.

What I had viewed was perfection. It was obvious to me that the known universe was a well-designed piece of work – the way it functioned, how one phenomenon would assist another phenomenon to create a phenomenal outcome, and yet, it appeared to do it all of its own accord. It was revealed to me, at that moment, that it was not meant for me to understand it or at least, my soul wasn't ready to understand it. The reason being was that my aura felt a physical discomfort that could not be put into words. I was a spiritually naked invader in the house of perfection. The actual presence of pain in my body triggered fear for my life, and the fact that I wanted to live told me I was imperfect. I didn't deserve to see what I was seeing unless I knew that I could survive its revelation. I shouldn't have had the fear of losing my life. I was not ready. The voice made that clear. I had to stop. I closed my eyes and an emptiness absorbed my body. I was falling.

I couldn't determine how many days I've been stranded on Zuu. The cycles of day and night were unclear here. There would be a period of strong daylight for several hours, then an equally long period of twilight that was similar to dusk. After twilight, a second sun would rise that was much cooler and weaker than the first, then both suns would shine jointly for a good 8 hours, and then both would set, bringing a warm glow of unknown constellations against the inky night sky. Would that cycle be counted as one day? I wouldn't know. I didn't know how the celestial cycles were determined here. So I truly didn't know how long I was unconscious.

I thought I might have blacked out for several days because what I experienced took a serious toll on my body. When I opened my eyes, the sky was full of black smoke and ash. It seemed the universe was on fire, but I quickly realized that I was lying flat on my back staring straight into the heavens. I tried to move and I thought I must have gained a thousand pounds instantly. I could barely move my head and my hands and arms hardly wiggled. My legs wouldn't even receive the signal from my brain to move. Any kind of motion was virtually impossible. So I just lied there, alone, staring up at the burning sky wondering what happened exactly.

The crackling of fire surrounded me as heat enveloped my body, so I must be in hell. I died. I must have died and gone to hell. Two problems with that: I don't believe in hell and from what I've heard, clouds and planets wouldn't be visible from hell. So I dismissed that idea and just assumed that I was paralyzed on the ground somewhere on Zuu. So what was on fire? The ship. Specifically, the debris from the Eszokian vessel that I destroyed. Remnants of the gigantic ship must have been scattered all around me. It's a small miracle that I'm even able to think coherently at all. But how did I manage to destroy a whole ship in the first place? My viku. My viku was to blame. I allowed it to take over my mind and soul and since I was unprepared for its full manifestation, it fell completely out of my control. Yes, it was magnificent and wonderful, but it came with a bitter cost. I lost a part of myself when I tried to embrace it.

Jade was dead. Os-Gouvox killed her. I wanted revenge. So I killed Os-Gouvox. There was something ultimately wrong with that order of thinking. I felt it. I remember vividly Mioli's rage against Cadzow and now it was overshadowed by my own ferocious behavior. My natural power was not given to me so I could reap vengeance. It's like giving a person a hammer so he can beat people over the head with it. That's not what it's used for. Its purpose is beneficial, not harmful. This unique ability was given to humans for a specific purpose. I didn't know what it was yet, but I did feel that I had misused it. And now I had to deal with the consequences.

I began to hear voices from far away. My viku had sensed two life forms immediately. It was Mioli and Nuvu. My senses had increased greatly because I could feel their auras against mine as if they were right next to me. There was also a third sentient life form that hovered within my radius. It was a new, unfamiliar form that I could not identify. I attempted to focus on its presence, but as soon as I did, it disappeared. It didn't run away or move to another spot. It just vanished as if it wasn't there at all. Even with my expanded viku abilities, I had no idea of what or who it was. My alien comrades came closer. I assumed that they could see me by now.

"Jarvis! Aavooooo!"

Nuvu spotted me first. He released a call that reminded me of a bloodhound impersonating a tropical birdcall. He was crouched on top of a hill several hundred yards away to my right. Painfully, I turned my head to get a better view of him. He had returned to his original form and was scampering down the hill to get to me. At a more careful inspection, I saw that he wasn't on a hill at all, but on a massive, hulking piece of Eszok ship debris. It towered over myself and the surrounding area. I looked around slowly and was shocked at how much the landscape looked like a burning junkyard. Plumes of gray smoke dotted the raggedy environment that was overcrowded with crumbled, giant pieces of Eszokian aircraft. I was amazed that I had survived the fall, but I fully believed that my survival had something to do with the provider of the voice that told me to stop.

My mind wandered for a few moments about that voice. Could it have been Jade speaking to me from beyond? She had just ceased living and I was entering another level of existence.

Maybe she found a way to connect to me? Or could it have been Mioli? Earlier, we had the ability to communicate with just our minds and not even move our mouths. Was she trying to communicate to me from the planet's surface? Maybe I was creating more destruction than I had realized and she sought me out mentally to stop whatever it was that I was doing? Or was it someone completely new? I never had a chance to even sense their approach. It was as if they just appeared out of nowhere.

Although I reached a much higher level of intellect since I arrived on Zuu, I was still baffled by all of this. I felt more confused and lost than when I was plopped into our "earth" habitat. Where do I go now?

Nuvu rushed over to me, kicking metallic rubble out of his way. Mioli was closely behind him. Her mask had a significant crack spreading from the lower side of her mouth up to her right eye socket. The miniature web of cracks hinted at the possibility that her mask would come apart. I would be lying if I said that I hoped her mask would stay in tact because I was constantly curious about what she looked like. However, she could not breathe the atmosphere on Zuu and would perish if her mask broke. I wouldn't want her to risk her life just to satisfy my curiosity. Nuvu had several cuts on his arm and a nasty gash on his chest, but he looked perfectly peachy.

"Great Spirits! You're alive!" Mioli said aloud. It was somewhat peculiar to see Mioli worried about me. She was always so stoic and regal. It was refreshing to see her break character for once. "I lost all connection with you. I assumed you had fallen."

"Well…I sort of did."

My voice was barely a whisper. Hoarse and swollen, my throat ached with every spoken word. I noticed that even breathing made my chest hurt and I still couldn't move my legs.

"Jarvis had great fall," Nuvu said excitedly. " I watch you fall. You look like setting sun."

Nuvu was being poetic. Whether it was just meant to cheer me up or not, I had no idea. It just sounded weird.

"I was on fire," I moaned. "Wasn't I?"

"You were swallowed in light," Mioli said. "I…I could barely see you. What happened?"

"I don't know."

I lied to them. I knew. At least, I believed I knew what happened. I just didn't want to tell them.

"Are you hurt?" Mioli asked. "Your eyes are flooding with blood."

Of all my body parts that were throbbing with unbridled agony, I felt nothing wrong with my eyes or my head. They felt clear and opened and new, as if I had never used them properly before. They seemed like shiny and new appliances that were begging to be put into action. But, still, I was able to reach up to wipe my cheek and my fingers came away from my face soaked with bright, red blood. I didn't even flinch.

"Actually," I said calmly, "my eyes are completely fine."

Mioli cocked her head curiously.

"Are you able to move? Can you make yourself get up?"

Oddly, at that particular moment, the question was unbelievably absurd.

Of course, I can get up, I thought.

Just seconds ago, my body felt broken and distressed, but I had power now to heal myself and the realization of that quickly made all the pain in my body recede into nothing. A cool wave of ice spread throughout my body. I lied completely still as I told the bones in my body to repair themselves, the tendons and ripped muscles to reattach themselves, for my heart to stop pumping blood to open wounds, and for receptors in certain areas of my healed body to reactivate and function normally. I told my body to repair itself and it did, pain-free.

This was a miracle. And then my mind told me, *No, Jarvis, this is not a miracle*. The human body heals itself all the time. Your cells die off and replicate constantly without your notice every single second, every single day of your life. When you break your arm and injure yourself, your body is fully capable of healing itself over time. All I did was tell it to hurry up and heal itself now. I was powerful enough to expedite its process with just a thought. Although I was covered with dirt and minor scratches, I felt right as rain. I stood up, I mean, literally stood up from a lying position without even bending my knees. It looked like I had fainted in reverse.

"Yes, Mioli," I said quietly. "I can make myself get up."

Mioli and Nuvu had an awed expression on their faces. Well, Nuvu did anyway. I wanted to explain to them what had happened on the ship, what happened to Os-Gouvox, and what had happened to me.

"What happened to Jade?" Mioli must have sensed my thoughts again. That was the next thing that was going to come out of my mouth.

"Jade died."

Silence ensued. The fiery destruction around us crackled and snapped illustrating how devastated one can feel on the inside. I was full of a new, incredible power, but I couldn't help but feel unconditionally hollow. I was just an empty shell of a person. I started walking away from my two confidants and headed in the direction of the Gatekeeper's last position. Why, I wasn't sure.

"Jade, your sister," Mioli whispered sadly. "Are you certain she is...no more?"

"Os-Gouvox fired on her and the Gatekeeper's pod. It exploded in mid-air. I...I...don't sense her presence anymore."

"Jade," Nuvu started to tear up. "Sorry. So sorry."

"Nuvu, don't... please, I don't...," and I broke down. I didn't prepare myself for the rush of tears that followed. I must have crumbled and sobbed for a good five minutes. They say that there are five stages of grief when you lose a loved one. Even though my mental capacities had increased, I was not immune to my human sensibilities. My emotions had elevated from what they used to be. This feeling of grief was debilitating. It seemed like all the color had been drained from reality and my head twisted in on itself. I held my head and cried for my little sister. I cried for my mom who would never know that she lost another family member to a horrible person. And I cried for myself, because just like last time, it was all my fault.

My mother and I never talk about what happened to me when I was a little kid. We went through years of counseling to get my mind right, but when you experience something as horrifying as I did, you can never be the same again. When people think back to their childhood, they would normally remember things that made them laugh or smile, how exhilarating it felt to ride your big wheel down the hill, when you met your first good friend, or when you had the chicken pox. My memories included weekly visits to an old man in a royal blue suit that was unnecessarily friendly to me and reeked of cheap cologne. I remember sitting in a big leather chair, focusing on the ugly designs of a tacky shag carpet while he constantly asked me to remember things. I couldn't remember exactly what he asked me, I just remember crying a lot and the dreaded feeling I would get when my mother drove anywhere near his office park. He always had mint chocolates in his lobby and I'd load up on the way out. But the joy of eating those chocolates was eclipsed by the anger, dread, grief, and sadness that reigned over me when I was in his office. I hated that place and everything I had to discuss in there. I think it helped me out in some ways better than others, but I always look back and think that my life and the outlook I had about other people would be drastically different if I had never experienced what I went through. And now, I'm experiencing another traumatic event with an immediate family member. I would never admit it out loud, but hell, I'm just going to say it. It's just not fair.

It's not fair to have your loved ones taken away from you at such a young age. It's not fair to live a life that's laden with death and heartache. I'm only 18 and my life is supposed to be full of promise and potential. Why am I constantly reminded of how horribly miserable it is? I'm sick and tired of the need to find solace in my life. What's the point of finding it when it can just be taken away from you? In that sense, I felt I was not strong enough to control my own power. Truth was, I really didn't know what to do with it. I just wanted to make the pain stop. Stop the anger, stop the guilt, stop the killing. I directed all of that at Os-Gouvox. It was now apparent that I made a dire mistake.

Mioli mentioned earlier that a zoid cannot be killed, but destroyed. Killing, by definition, means to take away someone's life. Therefore, to kill someone means they have to be a living soul. Os-Gouvox was a zoid, a robotic being that imitated life. Mioli believed that he did not have a soul, so he couldn't be killed, just destroyed or deactivated. Something inside of me told me that that was not the case. His fatality did something to my aura that physically affected me, telling me that I took a life. I felt nothing when I tore apart the other zoids, but when I ended Os-Gouvox's existence, my mind switched into fury mode and all bets were off.

I let emotional rage take over and my viku seemed to be at odds with the universe.

Yes, the universe itself told me that what I did was wrong. That must have been the voice. Even Mioli acknowledged that the universe was a soul. The voice told me to stop. The universe told me to stop. I exploited my abilities and now I had to redeem myself.

The profundity of what I had done came over me like a wet, heavy shadow. I don't remember where Mioli and Nuvu were when all these thoughts were bombarding my senses. I must have been huddled in the ship wreckage for a long time, severely pensive, unable to distinguish what my next move or word should be. How do you redeem your existence with the universe? Saying I was sorry was grossly inadequate. I didn't know what to say years ago when I felt it was my fault for the death of a family member. I sure didn't know what to say now. Who do I say it to? My sister? The universe? Myself? There was no old man in a royal blue suit to talk to here. I had to figure this out on my own. Twilight had arrived when I finally decided to give my respects to my sister first.

Jade's soul needed to be laid to rest. The way her life was taken must have been a frightening experience for her. I'm still not totally sure or confidant in my beliefs about what happens to you after you die, but I still know that proper respect must be given to the body after a person passes away. I don't need the universe to tell me that. That's just a given. A gracious gesture to the sanctity of life is always appreciated.

I continued to stumble in the direction of the Gatekeeper's escape pod, wading through fields of endless ship remains while Mioli and Nuvu followed several yards behind me. They didn't speak a word. They just watched me from a distance, probably just curious about where I was going or what I had planned to do. Honestly, I didn't know myself. I had seen the escape pod explode with my own eyes. It burst apart in a cloud of fire and smoke. If anything was left of my sister, would I really want to see it? I pushed the thought of seeing her mutilated remains out of my mind and promised myself that once I sensed the location of her body, I would not look upon it. I would ask Mioli to incinerate the body the cleanest and most respectable way the universe would allow. I did not want the last images of my little sister to be associated with gore and horror.

After several minutes of scouring the ravaged landscape, I crested a small ridge that rose over a miniature valley. Within this valley, were several of the Eszokian skull-shaped escape pods strewn about in various degrees of total ruin. It looked like a morbid death field with giant alien heads looming over their dismal realm. Somewhere in all that desolation was my sister's body. I froze. My feet refused to move. I could not go any further. The idea that I might even catch a glimpse of her lifeless body petrified me. But I had reached my destination and I had to do something.

What was both startling and confusing was how my viku motivated me to do things before I could even think about holding back. I needed to learn how to control my thought processes because ideas began to jump into my mind a lot faster than they used to. It was a lot to take in at one time. Although I stood on the ridge concentrating on the information that flooded my mind, a specific idea revealed itself as the best and easiest way to find Jade's body – eliminate everything else.

A scintillating vibration encapsulated my spine and I spread my palms out in front of me. I reached out to mentally grasp every piece of ship wreckage that my eyes came in contact with. I raised my palms higher, almost at shoulder height, and the strain that overwhelmed them made my arms shake involuntarily. It was as if the energy that flowed through my muscles was forcing me to lift the world with my fingertips. Surprisingly, I was! Not the whole world, but the entire landscape around me, including myself. My body drifted up into the sky as every single piece of aircraft wreckage rose into the lavender clouds with me. The large selection of skull-shaped escape pods all faced me and their eye sockets actually seemed to be glowing with an odd spiritual energy. I spread my fingers out wide and forced my consciousness to seek out Jade's body. Whatever was not associated to my sister's form, I asked the universe to take it back. In other words, I requested that the universe take every ruined object and particle, claim it as its own, but leave my sister's body. Thankfully, the universe accepted my request.

As I mentally weeded out the floating remains of the Eszokian ship, the searched pieces would smolder with bright light and disappear. I can just imagine what it must have looked like to Mioli and Nuvu. My rigid body with my hands splayed out, completely surrounded by hovering wreckage that gradually dissolved from existence. I didn't have to have an out-of-body experience to know how surreal I must have looked. Energy and light radiated from my skin and my eyes became miniature suns as I scanned thousands of pieces of detritus. I didn't sense Jade's form anywhere. The ship pieces kept disappearing and I still received no sign or presence of her body. Eventually, a few thousand pieces remained, then a few hundred, and then only a dozen. The last few remnants of the Eszokian vessel were diffused into the dry, tingling atmosphere and I looked around at the land below me and saw that not one piece of the destroyed ship remained on the ground. The landscape had been completely expunged of any sign of ruination. I felt a rush of excitement through my entire being as my viku suddenly made me realize something.

"She's not here. She's still alive."

It was irrefutable. Her body was nowhere in the area. Not a single shred of clothing. Not a single molecule. I couldn't sense a single thing that possessed Jade's signature, nor the Gatekeeper's. It didn't make sense because I saw with my own eyes the escape pod explode into a billion pieces. But neither one of them were here, and what justified the fact was that my viku had suddenly locked in on a faint, soft, active signal. It was the same signal I sensed when it was trapped in the Gatekeeper's escape pod. It swirled and jumbled in a little tiny ball far, far away, but it was definitely Jade, and I was definitely positive that she was alive. I was sure of it. It still seemed to be a minimized or stunted version of her energy, but it was enough to ensure hope that I would find her again.

When I returned to solid ground, both Mioli and Nuvu backed away from me. I wasn't surprised. If I saw a person with white flames lightly drifting from his skin and eyeballs I would keep my distance, too.

"Jarvis?" Mioli asked hesitantly. "What's happening to you?"

"I'm becoming what I was meant to be," I told her. "I'm becoming...totally human."

There was no other way to explain it. This form I was accepting was my *true* form. I felt more comfortable in my soul than I had ever felt before. In no way did I feel perfect or almighty or any less of a person. I felt thoroughly informed and totally capable of almost anything I could ever hope to accomplish. This was what it meant to be human – to be entirely human. These so-called "powers" should not be seen as extraordinary, they are just manifestations of what I know I can do. It's just that my mind is now strong enough to carry out my thoughts to another level of reality. I now had no physical boundaries and no mental limitations. I could literally do whatever I wanted to do.

On the other hand, the consequences of my choices were now ultimately exposed to me. I could no longer claim ignorance because I now realized, with an even greater intensity, how my actions can affect the balance of the universe. Sounds epic, but I couldn't deny that I now had the responsibility of being a better human. My mother's words may have just been a note of encouragement at the time, but now it was my driving force. I was granted the ability to see the universe clearly and discovered how I had the power to change it. Most people would have been able to understand that possibility after reading a self-help book or watching a movie or enduring numerous counseling sessions. Me? I had to be kidnaped from my home world to understand who I truly was. Weird thing was, I still didn't know. I just knew what I wasn't, and that was an isolated loner with no future. I was never alone. As a human, I could never exist alone because my viku required human connection. My survival depended on it. After I sensed the existence of Jade's energy, the others gradually revealed themselves to me.

Marlene's signal was the first to pop up. She was underwater somewhere, silent, yet alive. I already knew where Alex was located and I was particularly interested in returning to him because his energy signature was the strongest. When we left him, he was in a calm state of a coma, but I could sense that his mind was having a virtual party of activity. Cindy's signal was weak and appeared to be quite some distance away. I worried about her welfare the most. The one signal that I was working on was that of Derek's. As much as I disliked the guy, I did not wish him ill will. Sadly, his signal was buried deep within the earth and I couldn't tell if he was dead or alive. It was rather intangible, but it was there, nonetheless.

My knees hit the ground and I was shaken out of my otherworldly trance. Nuvu helped me rise to my feet again while Mioli stared at me. I wanted her to help me. I wanted her to tell me everything I had to do to get my sister and my companions back. But even as I thought these things, I knew she wouldn't be able to solve it all. I assumed that she heard my thoughts again because I saw her gently shaking her head.

"Don't ask me what I can't do, Jarvis," she said to me. "You know I don't have your power. You are capable of the unknown."

"I realize that," I nodded. My head felt unusually heavy. "But I'm not exactly sure of what that is."

"Then find out who you've become. The universe will reveal things to you if you let it."

I understood what Mioli was telling me to do. She was telling me to do what she taught me to do back at the Kembeqri forest. What did she call it? Ushan? I needed to plug in again. I had a feeling that it would be different this time around. I had unlocked several levels of my mental library that were incredibly raw and full of psychic power. There's no telling what the universe would do to me once I reached out with my mind and figuratively held its hand. Would it invite me in like an old friend and allow me to drink heavily from its refreshing well of knowledge? Or would it rebuke my arrival and demand retribution after disturbing its balance because I used my viku to annihilate Os-Gouvox? Would it give me assistance in finding my friends, my home, or even myself? Would it even consider that I was worth helping?

I had these abilities and unmatched knowledge, but even I didn't know the answer to that one. I had to find out. I couldn't continue further without proper direction.

"I'm going to need some time."

The words just hung in the air for a moment. No one moved or responded. It felt like an eternity. I had hoped Mioli and Nuvu would understand. I wasn't asking them to take a hike. I just needed a mental recharge. Nuvu finally made a slow, subtle move at my feet. He looked up at me with those giant, turquoise eyes and told me everything with just one look. He shut his eyes and hugged me around my legs. He felt so soft and hospitable. I knew I wouldn't see him or feel his presence again for a long time. I kneeled down and hugged him back.

"You are my guardian and my friend," I whispered to him. "Thank you for keeping me alive."

Nuvu's eyes glistened. I could sense that he wanted to tell me something. The words wanted to come out, but he was holding back and I wondered why. He could tell me anything and I would understand. Surely, he would know that. He stared at me and gave a warm, sad smile then turned away.

"We are very close to the Faumese habitat," Mioli said as I stood up. I turned to face her. "They are a welcoming species. You will find us there when you return."

An uneasy sensation hit my gut. Why did she say it like that?

"Where am I going?"

"I cannot say," Mioli said. "You may go everywhere and

nowhere all at once. It's different for everyone. You are human so your experience will be…unique."

Mioli gazed at me for a moment then turned away and headed east toward an enclosure that loomed miles away on the horizon. She walked slowly, studiously, in no rush at all and I wondered if I would ever see her again. She read my thoughts so easily but she was still somewhat of a mystery to me. There was a wall between us that I knew I could get through. From her side, it must be like a one-way mirror. She could see me, but I couldn't see her - at least not completely. Not yet. Maybe things would be clearer after I deliberate with the cosmos. I didn't know for sure, but there was always hope. The others needed me. I wanted to be ready – for anything.

It took me several minutes to find a spot that was quiet, intimate, and safe. I found an alcove in the middle of a group of tall, swirling boulders. They seemed to be frozen in motion as they stretched up from the soft soil toward the largest sun. They appeared to be reaching for enlightenment.

I would do the same.

The sand was powdery and firm beneath my feet as I made a seat in between the stones. I positioned my legs one over the other and then did the same with my arms, just like Mioli taught me. I was surprised how comfortable and how natural this position felt. I could sit in this position for days.

My head drifted back slightly as I straightened my spine, staring intently at the midday stars.

It was peaceful.

Absolutely, inconceivably peaceful.

I closed my eyes.

My mind opened.

ACKNOWLEDGMENTS

I can't count the number of times I felt like giving up and not finishing this book. I stopped writing for awhile, started writing again, gave up again, wrote like a madman for a month, then stopped, read my manuscript over, hated every page, and then started over again. From beginning to end, this book took me about six years to complete, surely not the normal time length for an author to complete a novel. But when you have a thought or an idea that eats at you every day of your life and you're constantly wondering and thinking about a story that you feel should be told, you should not ignore it. You need to tell it. So, here it is - a book that I thought would never get done. Although I had emotional struggles believing I could do this (and those struggles continue to plague me to this day) I did have a strong support system to push me to finish what I started.

To Mom and Dad, Horace and Stella, who have always supported my every whim, every venture, every word, and every drawing I have ever done my whole life. With your constant enthusiasm for my creative talents, I have always found it inside of my heart to keep dreaming and make you proud of whatever wonderful worlds I can create. I still remember when you surprised me with a cake when I was accepted to the Laguna College of Art & Design. I knew you were happy for me, but that day will always be a heartwarming, vivid example of how much you wanted your son to succeed. Thank you for everything! I love you both very much! To my sister, Shannon, who is pretty much my second

Mom. I seriously don't know where I would be without your guidance and support. Besides owing you a lot of money, I owe you my success if any comes my way. Your social connections have helped me more than you know and you inspire me to be a better person on a daily basis. Tough love is normally met with resentment, but I need it to get me off my butt to do what I was meant to do. Thank you for cracking that whip! Your love is reciprocated greatly through everyone you know and I hope you know how much we all appreciate everything you do. I thank you and love you each day I'm alive.

To Kimberly Ratificar, Deanna Nissin, Richard Gutierrez, and Efren Gonzalez, you guys are pretty much my window to the outside world. Without you, I would be a sosh like Jarvis – lonely and too proud to admit it. You guys have kept my spirits up and helped me to forget about my negative qualities, reminding me that I'm a person who is worthwhile to spend time with and whose dreams are not completely out of reach. Thank you for being my friend, for rejoicing over my ideas, and ensuring life is better with true companions who love you. Thank you. And wherever you are, Tuesday Warren, that includes you, too. My parents and I miss you and hope you and Sunday are doing well.

To the first professional who read my manuscript, Cheryl Morris, whose enthusiasm and criticism has helped shape Zuu to become a better story than it originally was. Thank you for your advice and I'm looking forward to sending you the sequel VERY SOON! To Fabian (Wilson) Saravia, a ridiculously talented illustrator who had the ability to read my mind and flesh out the characters in glorious detail. Thank you for helping me in bringing these characters to life.

I also want to thank anyone and everyone who I've ever worked with or went to school with and have expressed any kind of interest in hearing my story. This was a long, grueling process and it's nowhere near to being finished. This is only the first book and I assure you that somehow, some way, Jarvis and his companions will return to earth. But it's not going to be easy. Their journey will be full of self-discovery, upsets, surprises, twists, and turns – much like my own journey in completing this book and the ones to follow. So I want to thank everyone who loves to read and who wishes to continue on an adventure into the unknown worlds of our universe. I promise you, if you can be a little patient, you will not be disappointed.

COMING SOON

ZUU II
THE EXODUS

Visit www.ZuuNovel.com for updates.

GATEKEEPER

DS-SOLVOX

Made in the USA
San Bernardino, CA
17 November 2018